JUSTICE FOR ALL

ALEX J. FISCHER

For my Family and Friends

1

———

Jim laid a hand on his familiar orange car. "Is it done? I need to be sure the systems I had you install work." He looked at his mechanic with a masked face.

Amelia frowned. The faint sound of rock and roll played in the mechanic's office. "I'm a little worried why you needed some of these upgrades, if I'm honest. I shudder to even call the one system an upgrade. It's more of a contingency - for what, I don't know."

"Does it work?"

"You have no clue how hard it was for me to install the explosives under the tutelage of your expert. Why the hell did you need to ensure the car could explode? As far as if it works? Your expert said it would. Obviously I'm not too keen on testing it."

"I can't tell you why I might need that. I hope he didn't piss you off too much."

"He was knowledgeable, sure," Amelia said with a shrug. "He just had no people skills. You'd think you'd have more when you're in a wheelchair."

"He didn't used to be in one. He got that defending my

mother from an assassin. Let him act a bit of an ass. I apologize for him."

"Damn," Amelia whistled. "Yes, the nitrous boosters are working fine. I tested those. I had to be careful with the routing of its exhaust. We had to plant the explosives under the hood, so let's hope you don't get anyone looking there or you'll field some interesting questions. Are you planning a suicide or something? I don't want to be responsible for the death of Masked Justice here."

"I'm not planning on killing myself, no." Jim leaned against the car and crossed his arms. "I am preparing for the possibility it may be needed to accomplish my mission though."

"You do this before every mission?"

"No," Jim kicked off the car and walked over to the shorter mechanic girl. "This is the biggest mission I've ever undertaken. The bastard sent an assassin to kill my father and mother. We barely thwarted the attempt on my mother. Then they came after me. I don't mind telling you the name of my target as thanks for your hard work, in addition to the cash, if you promise to tell no one."

"You would?"

"Sure. I've already accepted the possibility of my death chasing this to its end. His name is Charles Baskins. You know him?"

"Only people who ignore politics don't know him," Amelia said, covering her mouth. "He sent those assassins after you and your family?"

"Yes."

"Why?"

"He wanted me dead, and he hired a sadistic mother-fucker to do it by the name of Hans. You remember the bombings that occurred a month ago? That was his handiwork."

"That was him you and that guy you were chasing?"

"No. That was Specter. Charles had his wife killed and framed him for it. He had Specter's kid kidnapped and held his life over his head unless he did their bidding. I stopped him."

"This Baskins guy sounds like a real asshole," Amelia said. "He's trying to abolish vigilantism, you know."

"Believe me, Amelia, I'm aware of what he's doing. I have my sources. What about the windows?"

"I upgraded them to the best on the market. They'll still falter if enough lead gets flung into them, but they'll last the longest of any glass. You have my personal guarantee there. Your armor had to be removed and replaced with new plating. That took the longest and cost a pretty penny."

"I owe you thanks."

"You don't owe me a damned thing."

"True. I paid already." Jim allowed himself the luxury of a quick chuckle.

"That's not what I meant. I realize we haven't spoken much since you employed my services, but you better believe that I've been following your adventures. Recently I've found this delightful blogger and reporter that's been obsessed with you. She goes by the name of Angie Summers."

"Yes, I remember her alright. I got her out of Specter's last stand. He had the warehouse wired to blow with explosives. We had to play a game of cat and mouse while she was tied to a chair, as I recall."

"Her stories are true? I thought she may be bullshitting."

"No. She tells the truth. Though she doesn't know I'm

doing this. Did you know Baskins attended my father's funeral and had the gall to talk to my mother?"

"The one he tried to have killed?" Amelia's nostrils flared. "The nerve of that pompous hot air bag."

"I don't know why I'm telling you this." Jim opened the nearby passenger door and sat down. "Maybe I feel you deserve to know. You've done so much to help me, and you get no credit."

"I'm just happy to help my hero do what he does best. You've not only saved my life, but you've saved my livelihood. People love this shop, and I'm almost up to my eyeballs in business, all thanks to you. It's a shame you're not single, though, or I'd have been able to show my appreciation fully."

"Sorry." Jim looked up at the young twenty something girl. "You're probably lucky True Justice didn't hear that. She gets kind of possessive sometimes."

"Your girlfriend is a vigilante too?"

"Kind of - not really," Jim said. "She did it once and never again. She's one of us though. I've also known her since I was a small child."

"I never really had a chance."

"Afraid not."

"I have one more big question, and I'll be satisfied."

"Shoot."

"Why do you suspect you'll need the explosives for this job?"

Jim looked long and hard at the concrete in the mechanic's shop. He finally gazed upward at Amelia with a look of determination. "Charles Baskins didn't just betray me and try to kill my family and friends. He was my childhood friend as well. He is a member of the Pedophile Hunting Republic who cast me out."

"Why though?"

"I saved a young girl whose parents sold her into slavery. They thought I was grooming her or some such stupidity. You may know her by the name of Blind Justice, best friend of Silent Justice."

"I thought the PHR was a rumor."

"Nonsense. Since then, I've been compelled to join the Vigilante Justice Coalition. Anyway, Charles was my first contact in the PHR. He was my best friend, but he was also my partner. He taught me how to use this." He reached down and patted the sheathed blade hanging on his hip.

"What about the second blade?"

"The expert who oversaw the installation of the explosives trained me. He was another assassin of the VJC."

"He taught you how to fight and you're worried he might be better than you, so you want an option where Charles dies, regardless."

"That's about the size of it." Jim returned his gaze back to the floor. "I'm also having a specially made vest made of the same stuff. It'll be connected to my pulse. Should I die, it'll explode, killing him."

"Why go to such lengths, though? If you die, all your work you do will go to waste."

"Someone is depending on me to get this job done. It's not just revenge." Jim stood up with a grunt and moved over to Amelia. "My partner is sitting in jail as we speak. I have reached a deal to free him."

"If Baskins dies, Jason Walton gets out."

"You're quick."

"Then Jason Walton is connected with you."

"You didn't hear that from me, and I'd better not find you told anyone," Jim said in a stern tone.

"I'd never," Amelia quickly tried to assure him. "He must

mean a lot to you if you're willing to sacrifice yourself for his freedom."

"You ever had someone worship the ground you walk on before, Amelia?" Jim rested a hand on her shoulder. "It's a heavy burden. He is willing to die in prison for me. I need to be willing to die to free him. It's only right."

"I'm betting True Justice isn't liking this. I know I damned sure wouldn't if my boyfriend was contemplating killing himself."

"If the explosives went off, I would have already been dead. My heart had already stopped. It's not suicide if I was already dead. It's a safety precaution anyway."

"If they can't identify your body, your friends and family will never be found out. That's cold, efficient, and damned ruthless. Are you that prepared for death?"

Jim locked eyes with her. "Yes."

"That look," Amelia shivered. "God damn. How can you be so stoic?"

"I accepted my fate years ago. I knew my death was always a possibility. If it can free my partner and kill my former best friend who betrayed me in one fell stroke, so be it."

"For what it's worth, I hope you don't have to use them."

"Me too," Jim said.

"Come on." Amelia moved past Jim and sat down in the driver's seat that had the door already opened. "Look here," she said. She pointed to a new button. It was a huge red button beside the radio. "This is your little bomb button. You press it three times in rapid succession, and it explodes. That's to keep it from accidentally being pressed. It also has a remote option." She reached over to the glove compartment and opened it. She reached inside and found a small box, which she handed over to Jim. "Inside that is the remote control for it. It's the same rules. Three quick presses of the big red button and boom. Try not to use it, huh? I've put too much work into your baby."

"No promises." Jim handed it back for her to stow away and climbed outside.

Amelia exited the car and looked up at Jim with wide eyes. He saw tears emerging from her eyes. She lunged forward and wrapped him in a hug. "Please don't kill yourself out there."

Jim looked around, making sure nobody saw her outburst. He slowly raised his arms and returned the embrace. "Come on. I'm not skilled at emotional moments like this."

"You can't simply tell a girl you're contemplating this kind of thing and not expect this. You know you're important to me. What did you expect? Without you, my life would be over. I'd be some sex slave, and my business would have gone tits up. What am I supposed to do when my hero says he may sacrifice himself?"

"Uh," Jim awkwardly patted Amelia's back, "there, there."

"What in blazes is taking you so long?" The front door of the mechanic's shop burst open.

Jim saw Brett wheeling in with a mask covering his face after slamming the garage door shut behind him.

"Oh, I see what's happening here. I didn't know you two were having an affair. I'll keep this from your girlfriend, shall I? She'd kill you."

Jim pushed Amelia off him quickly. "You know damned well that's not what's happening."

"It sure looked like you two were cozy. Did she brief you on how your new systems work?"

"Yes," Amelia said. She peeled herself off Jim to face Brett.

"Good. Then let's get going already."

"How did you drive here?" Amelia asked.

"We had a friend drop us off," Jim said. "That's all you need to know."

"Now girlie," Brett said. "If you're through saying goodbye to your little hero, we'll be going. Speaking of which, choose a better damned object for your hero worship. This idiot isn't worth it."

"You always are such a supportive teacher," Jim said.

"Supportive doesn't make you tougher."

"Try to keep him alive and in one piece, would you?" Amelia faced Brett with a serious expression.

"I'll try. I always do. It's not up to me. I won't be there when they fight. If you want him to survive, you'd best pray for him to win. His opponent is the best swordsman in the country. Hell, possibly the world. He beat me after all. At least Masked Justice is the only warrior to have ever wounded him."

"That's why he has that scar on his face!" Amelia snapped her fingers at the sudden realization.

"You told her who we're going after?" Brett slapped Jim hard in the back. "Damn it, man. Have you never heard of smart handling of information? She could ruin us."

"I would never," Amelia said quickly. "He saved my life. I'd sooner die than sell him out."

"It's an amateur move telling a civilian. I know I taught you better than that."

"She had a right to know why she was installing such dangerous systems and being subjected to your haughty presence."

"Haha," Brett's fake laugh underpinned his anger.

"Girlie, it'd be best if you forgot everything he told you. If you tell anyone, I'll deal with you myself. Don't think just because I'm in this chair that I'm harmless."

"It's sweet and all that you try to protect him, but there's no need."

"I'm protecting myself." Brett looked away.

"Whatever." Amelia could see through the charade. "You two be careful. I don't want to hear of another explosion, knowing my expertise had a hand in killing you."

"I'll do my best to not need it," Jim said. "Stay out of trouble, alright?"

"No promises," Amelia said with a wave goodbye.

Jim watched Amelia go back to her back office before turning to Brett. "She's a friend. I know I have her silence. You think you could let a guy make his last rounds in peace?"

"It sounds like you've accepted death already."

"You're the one who said accept death as a possibility," Jim said before a quick slap to his leg from Brett quickly cut him off. "Damn it." He rubbed the spot and glared at his mentor.

"I said to accept it as a possibility, not plan for it, you numbskull. When warriors plan to die, they find a way to make it a reality. I'm just trying to teach you that your actions have ramifications."

"Someone's sitting in jail. Trust me, I understand that."

"Let's get going already," Brett wheeled himself to the passenger side. "Help me get the chair inside, and we're off."

"Yes, sir."

Allen's detective agency that night...

"Why are you here anyway?" Allen looked at the group of vigilantes.

"Easy wheelchair access." Brett slapped the sides of the device he sat in. "That and I might have already searched through your office and made sure no listening devices were planted. You don't have a webcam connected to that computer, and I might've accessed it to double check while you were outside working."

"You broke into my office?" Allen stood up from behind his desk and slammed his palms on the desk. "Why am I even surprised? How does a man inside a wheelchair sneak anywhere?"

"Just because I'm bound to this infernal contraption does not mean I stop training. If I want, I could walk using my hands and open your door with my foot."

Allen looked over at the rest of the group, containing Skye, Jim, Ashley, and Cynthia. "He's lying, right?"

"About some things," Jim said. "This is the last time we'll be doing this, so please endure our rudeness, alright?"

"If you're sure," Allen said. "I have no other appointments tonight. It's not like I don't know what you're doing anyway."

"We're just going over details and minutiae," Brett said. "It can't be worse than the last job."

"The one that involved multiple charges of arson. Yeah, I remember that night." Allen looked down at his desk with a downcast expression. "It was the last evening I knew Jason was safe."

"The last I heard, he was fine." Skye stepped forward from the group and moved to the nearby wall to lean against it. "He said the PHR had some of their dumber brutes try to get to him."

"How'd that turn out?" Ashley asked, taking the other wall, leaving Brett, Jim, and Cynthia in front of the desk.

"He couldn't tell me much over that damned device they have since it was being recorded. I got the impression they caught some blades to their person repeatedly in brutal fashion."

"Ok, enough about prison brawls." Cynthia shook her head at the mental image. "You cannot be serious about going to DC and trying it."

"What do you propose?" Brett asked. "Leave Jason in there and hope Charles doesn't send another assassin to kill more of our family? I'd prefer knowing that mortal enemy is beneath earth, or failing that, blown to smithereens."

"What was that?" Cynthia asked.

"Nothing," Brett said.

"What about not talking to folks about unnecessary concepts, teacher?" Jim asked.

"Be quiet," Cynthia said with a punch to Jim's arm. "What did you mean by blown to smithereens? You plan to plant an explosive or something? How many innocents would die that way?"

"Lady, that security firm is a lot of things," Brett said. "Innocent isn't the adjective I'd use. Corrupt, brutal, greedy are all words I'd use, not innocent."

"They did nothing to us," Cynthia said.

"It's not like we've never had collateral damage anyway," Ashley said. "If there was a time to shrug, it'd be regarding Baskins. He won't give up. As long as he's alive, we're all in his sights."

"I will attempt to not kill anyone else besides Charles. I won't lower myself to his level and go after his parents, though I could."

"There won't be explosives, period," Cynthia said.

"Knowing you, you'd end up killing yourself accidentally. I hardly trust you with those blades and the gun."

"What a vote of confidence," Jim said.

"She's just worried, though she'll never admit it," Skye said.

"I am not."

"Yeah, you are," Ashley said.

"It's irrelevant. You're going there to shoot or slash at him, not use explosives, right?"

"Yes," Jim said. "It was a figure of speech, honey."

"What an overreaction," Brett said. "Anyway, we're heading out tomorrow morning. We have one more meeting tonight before we turn in for the night. Jim and I will go. We're just picking up some supplies."

"What kind of supplies?" Cynthia narrowed her eyes at Brett.

"Ammunition, some electronic devices I'll need, things like that." Brett didn't meet her gaze, choosing to look at Allen instead. "It should be no problem with the cash the coalition is paying us."

"At least it was in cold cash, and I didn't have to cash out crypto," Jim said. "Look, I'll return home before you know it."

"You'd better," Cynthia said. "I had a rough day at my office, and I need rest. I'd rather not be waiting up all night wondering where you are."

The phone on the detective's desk rang and was answered within a single ring. "Hello," Allen said.

"Hey there, big guy." Maggie's best seductive voice came over the phone. "Are you done with work tonight?"

"Having a small meeting here and then I'm heading back. It won't take long."

"Don't keep me waiting now. See you soon, baby." The line went dead, and Allen hung up.

"What?" he asked the bewildered looks of the group. "It was Maggie."

"You're together with her now?" Ashley asked.

"You got a problem with that?"

"No," Ashley said.

"Good. If your meeting is over, I have a date." Allen stood up and motioned toward the door behind them.

2

"You're sure this guy works this late?" Jim asked. He momentarily looked over at Brett in the passenger seat.

"He's up," Brett said. "I had this appointment with him since last week. Why? Are you nervous?"

"Who wouldn't be when they're meeting someone who crafted the explosive vest they're going to be wearing? What if he sucks and wired something wrong, and it explodes during a pivotal moment?"

"He's the best in the business, kid. Forgive his lack of manners, but there's no better craftsman I'd trust my life to."

"Or death in this case," Jim said.

"That's only if you lose and your heart stops. He's just insuring you'll get the last laugh. Isn't that priceless when you think about it?"

"I suppose so. At least Jason would get out of jail, even if I lose."

"You ever find out where you're going to store these before we leave tomorrow morning?" Brett asked. "We won't be able to keep it in the trunk outside or anything."

"I assumed you'd keep them. I can't hide anything from Cynthia if she puts her mind to it, and she'd see me walk in with the package."

"Damn it. Yeah, I can keep it with me if your woman scares you so much." Brett paused, staring out the side window away from Jim. "You know nobody else will want to go when they hear our stipulations."

Jim stared ahead with dead eyes. "That they'll be forced to wear one? I imagine so. I will not mention it in front of Cynthia, only Skye and Ashley. They deserve to know the risks if they decide to accompany us. Discovering even one of our dead bodies turns everyone's life upside down."

"You think they'll accept that rule?"

"Knowing them," Jim said, "no, I think they'll try to chase us. They don't give up easily as you've found out. They're idealistic fools like I once was."

"Once?" Brett's attention snapped back to Jim. "You still are a fool."

"Not an idealistic one. When I started this crusade, sure. I wanted all pedophiles dead. I admit that. Now? I look at what I'm doing, and I'm wondering the age old question."

"Why am I doing this?"

"No. How long until I'm dead? I've hopped away from exploding buildings, been in life and death duels, and I stop to think. How am I still alive and how long will my luck hold? I'm not getting any younger."

"Thinking of getting out of the game after this job is done?"

"Maybe. Cynthia would love that."

"We both know you'll never leave those fools. The first time one of them fell into trouble and Masked Justice would rush off like a damned idiot."

"You're probably right," Jim said with a smile. "I should

stop thinking of such things. I could die tomorrow, and it'll prove to be a waste of time."

"Don't doubt yourself," Brett said. "The strive to survive is the strongest feeling man can feel. Men have made miracles happen on the battlefield for centuries, all rooted from one simple statement. 'I'm not dying here,' they said. That's the attitude you need. This is just insurance. Hang a right here."

"Sounds weird to me. Not wanting to die is one thing. Buying these vests that will leave me unable to be revived is another. It seems wrong."

"Is it any more correct to have you die and then watch Jason spend the rest of his life inside prison?" Brett asked.

"It just doesn't feel right."

"You know why we both have to."

"For everyone I know. Yeah, I understand." Jim slowed down as they neared a red light.

"It's just up here. Pull into the nearby parking lot and we'll exit to walk the rest of the way. I'm surprised you're alright with this, if I'm honest."

"Cynthia may not like it and may forbid it. I don't like it either," Jim said while pulling the vehicle into the sparse lot. "I just realize it's needed." He parked the car and turned the engine off.

The pair got out of the car. Jim helped Brett get his chair ready and then pushed him along toward their destination.

"You know you don't have to push me."

"What would people think if they saw me letting someone wheel themselves while I just walk along? Don't worry about it."

"I didn't realize you let society's norms and values affect you so much. See the building over there?" Brett pointed toward a small one floor structure that had its lights open.

Its open sign had flipped to closed, however. "That's the place. Just enter there. He said it'd have the closed sign up. Just go inside."

"That's not suspicious," Jim said with sarcasm tinged in his voice.

"The guy doesn't want the public coming in while he's working on sensitive projects like this one," Brett said as they approached the glass door with the sign hanging on it.

Jim tried to open the door, only to find it locked. "Did he say he'd lock the door?"

"No, hold on." Brett managed to dig out a phone from his pants pocket and brought it to his ear. He quickly dialed a number. "Frank? We're here, but the door's locked. Okay then." He hung up. "He said to head around the back. It's unlocked."

"Fair enough." Jim wheeled Brett around the building until they found said door. "How much is all of this, anyway?"

"You really want to know?"

"Try me. It couldn't be more than the vehicle alterations we had done."

"Each vest is approximately twenty thousand dollars. We're making four in case the girls want to risk it. You do the math."

"How much is the Coalition paying us?"

"More than enough. They pay and care for their own. Don't piss them off like you did your last employers. Take it from me."

"I don't quite trust them either, but at least they're helping me out," Jim said.

"A wise position to take. Trust should be earned, but keep in mind that they've done much to earn it. Keeping Jason safe is paramount among them, along with the boatload of cash they've dumped in our laps. Not to mention the interference they're giving you."

"Maybe you're right." Jim and Brett finally reached the door. He tried opening this one to find it unlocked. He pushed Brett inside into a bright tile clad hallway.

A nearby door opened from one of the four doors they could see. A middle-aged owner with a bushy brown beard and a balding head poked his head out. He emerged into the hallway and waved them over. "There he is!" he yelled. "It's been too long."

Jim pushed Brett over toward the man.

"It has been too long, Frank." Brett said as they approached.

"What the hell happened to you?" Frank asked as they entered the now open door into what appeared like a tailor's workshop, judging by the needles, thread, and assorted tools. The ominous stack of explosives in the corner broke that illusion quickly. "Why are you in that contraption?"

"I got hamstrung by Hans."

"That psycho? Why did you tangle with that dangerous lunatic? I know you're damned good, but he's one of the best in the world."

"Was one of the best, past tense emphasized thanks to my pupil. Why, you ask?" Brett looked up at Jim and then returned his attention to Frank. "I was defending someone that I promised to, and I wasn't going to run."

"You protecting someone?" Frank's eyes were wide. "Is the sky falling?" He looked over to Jim. "Who's the kid, anyway?"

"You're looking at my pupil. He's the one who's going to take on our biggest job we've been planning for years."

"Him?" Frank stepped up to Jim and inspected him from head to toe. "He doesn't look like much."

"He beat Hans handily, suffering only a minor stab wound in melee combat, in a snowfield, while Hans had explosives planted nearby. Do not underestimate him."

"This guy did?" Frank finished his inspection. "Who are you anyway, kid?"

Jim looked down at Brett. "Can this guy keep a secret?"

"You don't know who you're talking to, do you?" Frank let out a hearty laugh. "Kid, I'm one of the founding members of the coalition. Your secret's safe with me."

"Treat him as you would me," Brett said.

"They call me Masked Justice."

"You're him, huh?" Frank asked. "I always imagined you'd be taller, if I'm honest. It's probably for the best though. Being taller gives people more targets in a sword fight. To have beaten Hans means you must be agile, skilled, and have nerves of steel. He's no pushover."

"You can say that again. There were times in that duel that I thought I would die, if I'm honest."

"You nearly did die many times in that duel," Brett said. "I had to listen to every meeting of swords, if you'll recall. How many times did he try that roll maneuver I warned you about?"

"More than once."

"That cursed technique is rumored to be impossible to block," Frank said. "How are you not inside a wheelchair along with your boss?"

"I had to get inventive quickly."

"Inventive?" Frank asked with a raised eyebrow.

"I'm curious too," Brett said. "He got me with that technique twice. I couldn't see it. How did you dodge it?"

"The first time I noticed I could retreat and hop to safety. The second instance, I had to get creative."

"Care for a demonstration?" Frank asked.

"Sure, I guess I can humor you." Jim backed away from the gentlemen and checked above him to ensure the ceiling was high enough for the technique he had planned. Being satisfied with the height, he continued. "He rolled straight toward me, and I knew I couldn't dodge back or to the side far enough, so I took the only advantage I had." He held out his right hand as if he had a blade in it and did a perfect front flip, holding his hands out above his head, mimicking the move where he drug his blades across Hans's back. He landed and did his best impression of an Olympic gymnast, holding his hands above his head. "How was that?"

"You trained this guy?" Frank asked.

"Why do you sound so dubious?" Brett asked.

"You'd never try that daredevil maneuver inside a life-or-death fight. I'm surprised is all. Anyway," Frank cleared his throat, "we've wasted enough time. Let's get to business. I have the vests you ordered, though I'm a little concerned with why you needed them."

"Worst-case scenario," Brett said. "The kid's not invincible and, as we know, Baskins needs to die. This is our best chance, so we're capitalizing."

"Why did you need so many though?" Frank asked, leading the pair over toward the nearby work bench. It was littered with spools of thread, suspicious bars of things Jim couldn't recognize, and four stacked vests. "Two I could understand, but four?"

"For if our cohorts decide they want to accompany us," Brett said. "We don't think they'll want to wear them, so they'll stay here; but extra explosives can never be a bad thing."

"I take it you want the special treatment for at least one of these?"

"That's right. We want Masked Justice's vest to be wired to his vitals. Mine, I can do with a suicide switch if needed."

"That's a tricky business, calibrating it to his vitals. That'll take time. Is that alright?" Frank asked.

"I've got time," Jim said, "but I'm more concerned with how this all works. I'm not comfortable around explosives since I have a history with them, and they're never on my side."

"So I've heard," Frank said. "Well, medical technology has advanced in the past two decades, but this monitoring technology is in its baby stages. It's stable, don't worry, but you need to pay strict attention to what I say about how to arm and disarm it."

"I'm all ears."

"Let's say this one is yours." Frank picked up the top vest and held it up. "You'd put it on." He handed it over to Jim, who put it on. He opened a drawer in the workbench and pulled out a prepackaged medical device. "See this?" he asked. "You're familiar with something like this?"

"I am," Brett said.

"What is that?" Jim asked.

"It's what I need to implant inside you. Now don't get all anxious. It's not surgery. Consider it more akin to an outpatient procedure. I've implanted dozens of these into our operatives. Anesthesia's unnecessary. Anyway, this monitors your vitals. Once we sync this with the vest via the proprietary software we designed, it's ready. Once your vitals flatline for five seconds straight, it signals the vest to explode, killing anyone in the nearby vicinity. No human can outrun the blast radius, so just get near the bastard and he's dead."

"What's the effective radius?" Brett asked.

"I crammed these vests to the brim with explosives," Frank pointed to the bars sitting on the table that Jim didn't recognize. "Each of those bars is the equivalent of one hundred sticks of TNT. I put over twenty bars woven into each vest. If he's in the same two-hundred-meter vicinity, he's going to die. It doesn't matter how many walls are between you and him. It'll bring down almost any building on top of him to boot."

"I must say," Brett wheeled even closer to the work desk and inspected Frank's work, "these are masterpieces. You've come a long way since you were trying your hand at making combat vests all those years ago."

"You made those vests?" Jim asked.

"I take it you've been wearing them?" Frank asked with a smile.

"I've gotten shot point blank while wearing one, and all I suffered was a bruise and some soreness. They're amazing."

"That vest was probably from my recent years. When I started, they weren't nearly as refined. It took a while and quite a few agents' lives before I perfected the tensile strength of my vests. It's difficult to craft them so strong and not have them be stiff to wear."

"How long does it take for you to implant your monitoring chip?" Brett asked.

"No more than twenty minutes, I'd estimate. I will have to uninstall this, should you survive. They're not meant to be in the human body longer than a week. This is a short-term concept. Now remember, you do still have to arm the system before it's active. I'll give you the remote for each vest. I've marked them, so you know which is for which. Brett, you're familiar with that system."

"Sure am. I've worn these before as an agent."

"Understood," Jim said. "I hope I have that problem of getting it uninstalled."

"Me too," Frank said. "Now come with me and I'll get

you ready. Do you have a preference where I place it?" He led the pair further away from his workbench and outside the room.

"I'd imagine some spots work better than others. What's the best spot for a clean reading of my vitals?"

"Scared the thing will register you dead before your time, huh?" Frank asked. "I can't say I blame you. So long as you don't have me install it inside your hand or foot, that shouldn't pose a problem. It measures blood flow and heartbeat. So long as it has one of those two, you're not considered dead. Personally, I'd put it in your armpit."

"Why there of all places?" Brett asked.

"There is a tiny chance that if it gets slashed with a blade, it could register as he's dead. How often do you get slashed in the armpit?"

"More than you might think," Brett said. "What about his back?"

"That would work."

"If you show your back to Charles, you're dead anyway," Brett said.

Frank opened the lone door at the hallway's end. It had a raised table inside. "I must ask you to wait out here, old friend," Frank said to Brett. "You don't want to watch this anyway. Trust me."

"You know best," Brett said. "Just be careful, buddy. That's our future you're operating on in there."

"He'll be ready, don't you worry. When have I ever let you down?"

"Never," Brett said before Frank shut the door, leaving the wheelchair limited man alone inside the hallway. Brett spun himself around and wheeled his chair toward the far side of Frank's hallway, looking at the door Jim and Frank disappeared into. "We lay the groundwork now. Let's hope we never use it." He pulled out his phone again when he felt it vibrate in his pants pocket. "She's clingy," he said. He could see it was Cynthia calling. He answered it. "Yeah?"

"Are you two almost done picking up your supplies?"

"We'll be at least another twenty minutes. Why are you so anxious? We'll be back soon enough."

"I just have some news for Jim that he needs to hear is all."

"News? What news?"

"It's private and important. He needs to hear it first. He'll understand why I'm so antsy after he hears it."

"Whatever. He's getting our stuff as we speak. We'll return within the hour."

"The hour?" This answer obviously displeased Cynthia. "You said it'd take like fifteen minutes."

"I know I act like it, but I'm, in fact, not omnipotent. I make mistakes."

"You lied."

"Maybe. Just be patient. You'll have your boy toy soon enough. I'm hanging up now." He hung up before she had time to protest any further. "I don't know how he deals with her. She's a pain in the ass," he said to himself.

Back at Jim's apartment later...

"Sorry I'm late." Jim closed the apartment door behind him. "It ran a little over what Brett promised." He hung up his coat on the nearby coat rack and called out in the apartment. "Honey?"

"In here," Cynthia called. She stuck her head out of the kitchen. "Were they out of the supplies you needed?"

"No, on the contrary," Jim said. He entered the kitchen

and saw Cynthia eating a cup of yogurt with a spoon. "The employees were slow."

"Is that right? Well, it's about time you returned home. You know, I'm still not convinced of this going to Washington, DC thing."

"You know why," Jim said.

"I know why you think you do. Hell, I know you're going anyway. You always needed to save the underdog. I just don't like it."

"Is that why you needed me back in a hurry? Babe, I don't want to argue."

"Neither do I," Cynthia said. "There's a much more important reason I wanted to speak to you before you sneak off tomorrow morning."

"Technically it's this morning now."

"Don't be a wise-ass. You're too stupid for that."

"Ouch," Jim said, approaching Cynthia. He bent down and stole a kiss. "There's the girl I know and love. What's on your mind, Cyn?"

"You know I don't like that nickname."

"Too biblical sounding for you?" Jim snickered.

"Be quiet. This news is more important than mere teasing," Cynthia said. She finished the yogurt cup and tossed it across the room into the wastebasket in the corner. "Do you realize this could be the last evening I see you? I thought about that reality earlier."

"Thanks for the confidence," Jim said.

"That's not what I meant, and you know it." Cynthia abandoned the spoon on the kitchen table atop a napkin and stood. She moved to Jim. "I don't want to go to sleep tonight."

"Oh, baby." Jim opened his arms wide, allowing Cynthia to step into them. He wrapped them around her and held her close. He felt her place her face on his chest. Within a few moments, he felt a wet spot permeating his chest. "Don't cry, baby. I know how you feel."

"Do you?" Cynthia looked up, her eyes now full of tears. "I might never see you after tonight. How can you possibly tell me not to worry? You're the love of my life, damn it! What if we swapped places? What would you do?"

"I wouldn't be able to leave you alone."

"So don't ask me to forget it and just pretend. I can't live my life that way." She wrapped her arms around his back and squeezed hard, eliciting a groan from Jim. She stopped and leaned back. "What was that?"

"It's just a kink in my back is all." Jim tried to cover any signs of pain he felt with a smile down at her. "Thanks, sweetie. Maybe you should have been a chiropractor."

She squeezed again, trying to cause another squeak of pain, but received nothing. "What is that?"

"What's what?"

"That on your back. Turn around and pull up your shirt." Cynthia disengaged the hug and tried to get behind Jim, who was turning with her movement.

"Come on, would you stop it?" Jim backed up to the wall, trying to impede her progress toward seeing his back. "It's just a wound I received in training is all."

"Then you won't mind my looking at it then." She grabbed his hand and yanked him from the wall. "You know I'll just look while you're in bed. I'm seeing this either way. Now make it easier for us both already and let me see it."

"If only we had this problem more." Jim sighed.

"Huh?"

"You trying to undress me so desperately, I mean."

"If you're feeling strong enough to jerk my chain, then it must not be too bad. Still, turn around and lift it." She rested her hands on his shoulders and turned him around. "Stand still too. I'd swear you move around like a twitchy thirteen-year-old getting a physical from a female doctor."

"Does that mean we're playing doctor later?"

"Only if it'll shut you up." She lifted the shirt since he wasn't making the effort himself. She saw a small white cloth taped to Jim's back. "I don't remember this." She reached out and touched it gingerly. "What is this?"

"Like I said, nothing. It barely even hurts anymore."

"It's not bleeding," Cynthia said. She leaned in to inspect it and ran a hand softly over it. "Are you sure it doesn't hurt? Answer me honestly. I don't want you to lie to make me feel better. We can always postpone your trip for when you're at one hundred percent. I don't want you going on this journey if you're still injured. It'd affect your chance to win, and I won't let that happen."

"Honey, I swear to you." Jim turned around and his shirt fell back down. "It's nothing. Now, what had you so concerned you waited for me? I know you had something."

"You remember how I've been throwing up recently?"

"Oh no," Jim placed a hand on Cynthia's forehead. "Was I right? Do you have the flu?"

"What? No, you idiot. Listen before you start assuming." She swatted his hand away from her head, but the blush illuminating her cheeks betrayed her. "I had an idea, so I visited the store." She fidgeted in place and focused her gaze on the apartment's floor.

"Okay, and?" Jim asked.

"I got a pregnancy test. Must I spell out everything to you?" she asked, stomping her feet.

"You don't mean?"

"I am," Cynthia said. "I'm pregnant with your baby."

Jim stood there, wide eyed, absorbing the life altering information he'd just received. "Really?"

"What the fuck do you mean, really? You believe someone would joke about this?"

"No, it's just..." Jim hugged her without warning. "I wasn't expecting to hear that." He placed his hand on the back of her head and pulled her close with his other arm. "I can't believe it."

"Amazed? We both knew it was a possibility," she said. "That's why I don't want to watch you wander off to possibly die."

"Don't do that," Jim said. "Please."

"I know you will. But I just needed to tell you before you departed, so you had another reason to return alive."

"I never planned to die, babe." Jim guided her out of the kitchen and down the hallway toward his bedroom.

"There's something else you should know," she said as they stepped into Jim's bedroom.

"More?" Jim took a step backward and threw his shirt into the basket in the corner. He sat down on the mattress and beckoned Cynthia over. "What more could there be?" he asked.

"She's going to kill me if I tell you, though." Cynthia took a seat beside him and leaned into his side. "She wanted me to promise not to tell you."

"Who or what are you talking about?"

Cynthia locked eyes with Jim. "You can't allow Skye to go with you."

"Why on earth would I forbid it?"

"You don't understand, seriously?" Cynthia shook her head. "Seriously? She and Jason were together before he got arrested."

"Yeah, they were together beforehand."

"Oh, for God's sake. She's pregnant, you idiot!" she yelled.

He looked up at the ceiling. "Oh, I see now."

"Yeah. She can't risk her baby, even to free her man."

"Is that our choice?" Jim asked.

"If she doesn't want to protect it, someone must. It deserves someone to stand up for it. Why not you and me? Do you think Jason would want her risking her and his son's or daughter's life? I don't think he would."

"She's going to be pissed."

"Let her. She's going to learn what responsibility is quick. In the long run, she'll thank you." She leaned her head against his shoulder. "As a woman, trust me. She will be mad for now, but when she's holding that baby, she'll thank you. Trust me."

"I guess she'll have an angry morning then. Can you try to look out for her while I'm gone?"

"I'll try, but she has a mind of her own. If she wants to follow you, she will."

"Just try to is all I'm asking."

3
_____

Charlie heard the not-so-distant roar of a crowd as he climbed onto the bus he had used to campaign. "Another speech down. Henry, how many do we have planned this week?"

"We're flying to DC tonight," his aide Henry said. "After that, we'll have to fly out for each rally you're holding in Oklahoma."

"Plus the plane rides back. I'm going to be incredibly jet lagged." Charlie sat down with a loud exhale. "Why am I campaigning so early?"

"The polls show it helps gather support. I haven't seen this high of an approval rating in decades."

"That's right. Henry, has there been any movement from our favorite vigilante lately?"

Henry held a clipboard and examined a few pages. "There's been no sign of movement or any exploits from him, sir."

"I don't trust that one bit." Charlie gazed out the window to his side and witnessed an immense crowd of people waving at him. Charlie gave them a wide smile and a wave of his own. "He's out there, and he's planning something. I'd bet my life on that."

"Sir, perhaps he took your advice and went into hiding like you told him to."

"You don't know Jim," Charlie turned away from the throngs of his political supporters and looked at his aide. "I've never seen him like that. He was pissed. Jim's not the type to give up and let it go." He stood up from the bus seat and moved toward the back of the super-sized vehicle to a table. He sat down in front of a mess of papers.

Henry moved along with his boss. "We already have security trained to look for any signs of vigilantes, sir. Shall we increase the number of guards again? I'd caution it may be a waste of money. Nobody can sneak through the guards we already hired."

"Do not underestimate the man. I keep telling you. I trained him and I know what he's capable of. He may be foolhardy and an idiot, but he gets what he wants done and damn the consequences. That's the scary part. An assassin without fear of death that's convinced he's correct is the most terrifying nemesis in the world. Doubly so if he's proficient in blades and guns, like he is."

"Sir, we already have over four dozen men and women on the payroll. Surely we don't need more."

"We both know he's on the coalition's payroll now. That means they'll do anything they can to help him. I needn't remind you they have the oval office and both the House and Senate now. Do you realize what that means?"

"That they won't get in trouble by assisting him?"

"That, yes." Charlie snapped his finger and pointed at the nearby refrigerator near Henry. He waited as his aide got him a drink from inside and handed it over. Charlie opened it and took a drink before continuing. "It also means that they could offer more than aid. Advanced military technology is on the table too. Toys that my security could only dream of will be at Jim's fingertips. If he has backing from the authorities, the police of DC won't search for him too awfully hard. We're on our own. So yes, Henry, I want more fucking security. Is that understood, or must I hire them myself?"

"I'll make the arrangements. I assume we want them as soon as possible?"

"We don't know if he's out in that crowd as we speak," Charlie said. "Yes, hurry it up."

"Just calm down, sir."

"Calm down?" Charlie clearly did not find Henry's attempt amusing. "Have you ever had someone hunting you down that hated you with every fiber of their being? Have you ever nearly been killed? I have, and I don't intend to face it again. I paid my dues for this organization and I'm going to use all the perks to keep what I've gained. Make it happen, and have them briefed on the likely assassination attempt."

"Yes sir," Henry scribbled down the orders. "Is there anything else?"

"I want surveillance on Benning's apartment. If he's there, I wish to know when he leaves."

"We already have that, sir. He has a tv. Let me call our man who's watching that feed. We isolated it when the law went into effect. Still, he's been careful and hasn't let anything slip last I checked. Let me call him and see what's been happening." He pulled out a phone and dialed.

Charlie paced around the narrow walking space, waiting.

"Yeah," Henry said. "We need a status update on Benning."

"I heard interesting news, sir," the man's voice on the other end said. "His girlfriend is pregnant and the way the conversation was heading, I'm guessing someone else is too. They left the room so I couldn't hear the end of it."

"That is not relevant. Are they leaving and coming here anytime soon? Think hard. This is important."

"Come to think of it, she was trying to convince him not to leave somewhere tomorrow morning. I don't know where. They were purposely vague about it. She also was convinced he was hiding something on his back from her. He claimed it was just an old injury, but I don't think he was telling the truth. Call it a hunch," he said.

"Anything else?"

"Other than she didn't want him to leave, I can't remember anything."

"Got it, keep watch. I must go." Henry hung up. "Ok, there's some news."

"Out with it," Charlie said.

"Apparently his girlfriend is pregnant."

"I don't give a damn if Cynthia's pregnant. Why would I?"

"She was begging him to not go, afraid he might die. They said he was leaving tomorrow morning. There's also the matter of the wound on his back."

"Wound on his back?" Charlie's attention snapped to his aide. "What thing on his back?"

"Apparently, he had some bandage over his back that he was trying to hide from her. He claimed it was nothing, but she insisted on seeing it. That's all I got from the call, sir."

"Thing on his back," Charles lifted a hand and rubbed his chin. "I might know what it is. Was it a severe injury?"

"It didn't sound like it."

"It's either a training injury or an implant. There's no

method of knowing what kind it is. It could be anything. Damn it all," Charlie slammed the side of his fist into the nearby wall with clenched teeth. "I don't like this. There are many mysteries we're ignorant of."

"Sir, if I might say. Worrying will not make this better."

"Shut up," Charlie said. "You ever had an assassin after you? I don't think so. You have no clue."

"Are you afraid, sir?"

"You're damned right I am!" Charlie yelled, losing his temper. "The man has become a cultural icon for his obsession, and I'm now his target. Do you have the slightest inkling of what happens if I die? Our movement fails, and the coalition solidifies its stranglehold on American politics. I wasn't lying all these years when I said it'd be akin to the wild west if the Coalition wins. America will grow into a dystopian hellhole where vigilantes become the new tool of oppression for police and authorities. I tried to end that where it was, but Hans failed and stirred up a hornet's nest because of his sadism. I understood it was a risky idea, but how was I to guess this would be the job he'd fail?"

"That's probably because you had his father killed, sir. I'd be mad too if someone murdered my father."

"No shit," Charlie said, clearly exasperated with his aide. "Why do you think I insisted on bringing my gear on all these campaign runs? It wasn't for fun. I thought he might attack tonight. That's why I had the bulletproof glass in front of me for my speech."

"That's not his MO though, sir."

"MO means nothing with Brett in his ear," Charlie said. "He's a tactician, crippled as he is now. He's as dangerous as Jim is. We need to forget everything we think we know about them. Brett will use that against us. Misdirection was always his game. Show something shiny and attack from another angle. Now fetch more security instead of sitting here talking all night. When are we due back in DC?"

"Tomorrow morning early. We'll drive all night. I suggest you get some sleep, sir." He bowed his head momentarily before leaving his boss at the back of the bus.

Charlie sat down and tried to relax, but couldn't. He looked out over his adoring supporters. He spotted a few women blowing kisses among the rest. "I don't like it," he said to himself. He looked downward and saw his hand trembling. He grabbed it and kept it still. "Damn you, Benning. Damn you to hell. Why couldn't you die like your father and make my life easy? You never eased other's lives, only complicated plans by always play the hero, Jim, you idiot. You do not know the world you'll bring about if you succeed."

The crowd outside erupted in cheers as Charlie felt the bus's engine start and pull out. He waved out toward his supporters before facing forward. "If I die, this country will devolve to a point where vigilantes will roam the streets. I'm trying to keep the peace and you're so simple-minded. You'd send us back to the wild west just to satiate your need for vengeance. I can't allow that to happen."

4

"Good morning." Jim saw the pair of girls enter the parking lot. He was leaning against his car while Brett sat nearby.

"It's about time you got your lazy asses up," Brett said.

"Fuck you." Ashley let loose a massive yawn. "I had a hard time sleeping, knowing today was the day."

Skye spoke once the pair approached the men. "When are we leaving?"

Jim and Brett exchanged glances before they answered Skye.

"There are stipulations if you're coming," Brett said. "There's also one other matter we need to discuss."

"Seriously?" Ashley asked with a frown. "What now?"

"Skye, you're not coming with us for this one," Jim said.

"What?"

"You know perfectly well why."

"She told you?"

"Who told you what now?" Ashley asked. "Did I miss something?"

"You didn't tell her yet?" Jim asked.

"Cynthia was supposed to keep it a secret, girl to girl. I see that flew out the window as soon as you two were alone."

"You want to tell her, or shall I?" Brett asked.

"Tell me what already?"

"I'm pregnant. You happy now?" Skye asked. "It's not your decision if I go or not, boss. I am an adult and I make my own decisions."

"You're going to risk the life of the baby you and Jason created so recklessly?" Jim asked. "Is that what he'd want? I know it's not."

"How would you know what he wants? He doesn't want to sit in jail for the rest of his life either. The odds are better if I go."

"You're not joining because of our other stipulation," Brett said. "This applies to Ashley too. Pop the trunk, would you?"

Jim did as he was asked.

"Look at this." Brett opened the trunk. There lay the vests they'd bought the previous night from Frank. "If you go, you're required to wear one of these."

"These are just vests," Ashley said. "Why would that be a stipulation? We already wear those."

"These are not normal vests," Brett said. "These are the explosion kind."

"Whoa," Ashley said, taking a step back. "I thought you agreed you wouldn't do anything like this?"

"You believed him?" Brett asked. "This is for your loved one's sake more than anything. If you die during this, you will explode, so your identity will never be revealed. I cannot in good faith force one of these onto a pregnant woman."

"Like a suicide bomber vest?" Skye asked.

"They are far more powerful than the ones various other middle eastern groups fashion themselves." Brett reached up and barely closed the trunk. "These are made with advanced explosives. Jim here received the deluxe edition."

"What's that mean?" Skye asked.

Jim turned around and lifted his shirt.

"See that?" Brett asked. "That's an implant that monitors his heart rate and blood flow. If he dies while he has that vest on, it explodes automatically. You don't want to be anywhere near if that happens. It's a safeguard. If he loses, he still wins."

"That's a pyrrhic victory if I ever heard of one," Skye said.

"A what now?" Ashley asked.

"A victory whose cost outrivals the benefits," Skye said. "It's not worth it."

"We all understand if I fail, and I don't wear these, that Charlie would persecute all of you. I can't allow that to happen. Jason will be free by my hand regardless of our duel's outcome. If that's why you want to come along, trust me. He will die."

"I'm going," Ashley said. "Wearing the vest doesn't bother me. I've prepared to die for years. If this ends it, I'm going. You're not stopping me."

"Then get in," Brett said. "Skye, sorry, but no."

"Damn it all. Jason said the same words the last time I visited him. When I told him I was pregnant, he begged me not to leave. I know what he meant."

"Then honor his wish," Jim said. "I'll get your man home safe and sound. It's not like these two would allow anything short of perfection. Watch out for Cynthia too, huh?"

"You can't just leave me here to twiddle my thumbs and wait," Skye said.

"That's precisely what we plan to do. Look, keep working and watch the news. You'll know when he's coming home. Keep your mind busy, and you won't have much chance to worry."

"Shut the fuck up about not worrying," Skye said. "My boyfriend and future husband is sitting in jail waiting for this mission to be done, and you're telling me I can't go?"

"Is it worth risking the life of your future child?" Brett asked. "Look, this isn't a discussion. I'm not risking the kid's life. You need to grow up and become what you are, a mother. Your needs are not your paramount focus anymore. Your focus should be on that life growing inside your belly. Don't throw that away just to chase a madman drunk on power. You'll experience a long and happy life. We're going to ensure that."

"You two will grow old and raise a family. You'll thank me in twenty years, even if you hate me currently." Jim threw open the driver's door. "Come on, everybody. Get in. We're leaving now."

"You son of a bitch." Skye stepped toward Jim and slapped him hard across the face.

"You done?" Jim asked, voice cold. "We're leaving." He got inside and slammed the door shut.

"Don't forget about me," Brett said. He wheeled himself to the passenger side front seat and threw the door open. "Someone get my chair, will you?"

"I got it, old man," Ashley said after Brett got himself into the vehicle. She folded it up and threw it in the back seat beside where she'd sit.

"Ash, you're going with them?" Skye followed her roommate. "You're okay with wearing one of those?"

"If it's what I have to wear." She climbed inside but

didn't close the door yet. "You possess a future; me, not so much."

"This isn't over!" Skye vowed as Ashley slammed the door in her face and their car engine started. She watched as it backed out of the parking space and pulled out into the early morning traffic. "Fine," she said to herself quietly. "You want to play it this way? Two can play at this game." She turned and didn't enter her own car, but walked toward the apartment complex...

Moments later...

Skye knocked on the familiar door she'd visited so many times before and waited. She didn't have to wait long before a tired-looking Cynthia opened it for her.

"Yes?" Cynthia asked. "I thought you all were leaving. Why are you up here?"

"You talked with Jim, didn't you?" Skye pushed her to the side and invited herself in. "Do the words privacy mean anything to you?"

"What?" Cynthia closed her door and faced an irate Skye. "What happened now?"

"He forbade me to accompany them. You know why I imagine. After all, only one person learned I was pregnant. That was you. How did he know? I wonder. I assume you told him."

"Maybe I did. Excuse me for caring about new life."

"Cut the virtuous horse shit. I deserve every right to help get Jason out. If Jim was sitting inside jail, you'd be the first one out the door, but you kneecap me? What the fuck?"

"Okay, now let's just sit down and lower our voices." Cynthia pushed past Skye and moved into the kitchen to sit down at the table. "Come on already."

"I don't give a witches' tit about waking up anyone."

"Obviously." Cynthia rolled her eyes as she mumbled to herself. "Now sit down." She pointed toward a nearby chair. A pot of coffee sat between them. Jim's abandoned cup was still there, along with Cynthia's.

"You told him to not allow me to go. Don't deny it. We both know he's not observant enough to put it together that I'm pregnant."

"No argument here," Cynthia said.

"You're not denying it?"

"Why would I? I did it and I'm proud of it."

"Proud? Why?"

"Protecting the innocent is what we do, isn't it?" Cynthia asked like it was the most normal conversation to be having. "That's what I did. Who's more innocent than the unborn?"

"My body, my choice," Skye said, locking eyes with her.

"Let's not devolve into petty political slogans. That'll annoy one of us when the other inevitably doesn't agree. Besides, a baby owns its own body. Just because it's in yours, doesn't change that if we wish to grow pedantic. It may shock you as a lawyer, but I believe all life is sacred."

"I'm going - you realize that. I'll just be going separate from the boys."

"Ashley left with them, I take it?" Cynthia asked. "Otherwise, she'd be here complaining like you."

"She accepted the stipulation they popped on us."

"Stipulation? What's that?"

"Well, since you let my secret loose to Jim, I suppose it's only right I tell you Jim's latest secret."

"You do like sowing the seeds of discord when you're angry, don't you? What is it? What is this proof that's supposed to irritate me? I know that's what you're trying to accomplish out of some childish sense of vindictiveness."

"You seem intent on pissing me off this morning."

"Hormonal swings do that, sweetheart. It's not something you want on a battlefield. Thanks for proving my point."

"God, how does Jim deal with you?" Skye's eyes widened and immediately dashed out of the room toward the bathroom.

Cynthia had a knowing smile, if a bit smug. "Morning sickness gets you every time. Thanks for proving my point," she whispered, careful not to be heard from the current sufferer of said ailment. She heard loud retching and vomit splattering into the toilet nearby. "That's what it sounds like from this end? It's nicer than experiencing it anyway."

The toilet flushed nearby, and the door slammed, indicating Skye's arrival.

"Have a fun morning sickness session?" Cynthia asked. "Imagine if you all were fighting. How would that have played out? You know I'm right. You're just angry, and I understand. I'm angry that they left myself. I'm doing you the favor here and your future son or daughter."

"You think you're mad now?" Skye said, wiping her mouth. "Wait until you hear this."

"Here we go. What is it?"

"You saw that thing on Jim's back, I take it?"

"What about it?"

"What did he tell you it was? Did he say it was a training injury?"

"That's what he claimed. It was a lie though. I knew that from examining it. It was too small, too precise. It looked like an implant."

"That's exactly what it was. You know what it was for?"

"I have some idea," Cynthia said.

"That's to monitor his vital signs. If his heartbeat stops for longer than a few seconds, it sets off their newest toys."

"Toys, huh? Would they be the volatile kind of toys?"

"The most dangerous type," Skye said.

"I figured as much." Cynthia shook her head and took a long drink from her mug of coffee.

"You what?" Skye asked.

"Honey," Cynthia reached across the table and grabbed Skye's hand, "I already knew when Jim said he wouldn't use those kinds of toys that he would. I saw it in his eyes. It hurts knowing he lied, sure; but do you know why he did? He may be an idiot, but he's a well-meaning idiot. He did it to make sure your boyfriend doesn't rot for all time. Love or hate his methods, he's trying to make sure you two spend the rest of your lives together happy."

"You knew about this?"

"I've known him his whole life." Cynthia laughed sadly. "Of course I knew. It hurt he felt the need to lie to my face, but I understand why he did it. He didn't want me to worry. It's infuriating, but still sweet in its own way."

"You're as crazy as he is."

"Maybe I am," Cynthia said, finishing the coffee. "At the end of the day, we're no longer our old selves. We're mothers, barring some horrible tragedy. Our lives are no longer just our own. He recognized that fact and was trying to keep us safe. Love it or hate it, that was his motivation, pure and rage inducing as it may be. He loves you too and wants you and your kid safe. I disagree with his methods as you obviously do too. Do you trust him?"

"What?"

"Do you trust him?" Cynthia repeated the question. Her gaze never wavered from Skye's eyes.

Skye looked away and answered. "Yes."

"Then trust his judgement in this, as infuriating as it is. He didn't do it to take away your power or to make you feel helpless. He did it to help you and Jason's future. Like I said before, sweetie, he's an idiot. A self-righteous idiot that always is self-sacrificing for his friends and family. You don't like it right now because he's sacrificing himself for your sake and you're not used to it. I get it."

"No one's ever been willing to die for me or my family, though."

"That's where you're wrong. From the moment Jim entered your life and he spoke to you, you've had one. Ever since you joined this impromptu family, you've had that kind of support. Now I would ask you to respect his wishes and not follow him, for your son or daughter, if nothing else."

"I can't sit on my ass." Skye got up from the table again and paced in the tiled kitchen. "What am I supposed to do? Should I just sit here to hope and pray?"

"If praying's your thing, sure. Prayers wouldn't do any harm."

"I need to help," Skye said. "I'm never on the sidelines."

"Maybe you should visit the good detective. I'm sure he could conjure you something to occupy yourself. Maybe you could even do Jason's old job?"

"That wouldn't help them."

"No. It would, however, do some good for someone local. Isn't that enough? Besides, you wouldn't be in mortal danger behind a desk. You know computers well enough. I'm sure you'd be fine."

"No," Skye shook her head. She bit a piece of her fingernail off before spitting it out in a nearby garbage can. "No. I'm going to DC."

"Skye, don't," Cynthia said.

"Don't try to stop me. I'm leaving." Skye walked out of Jim's kitchen and ran out of the apartment before Cynthia could follow her.

"That damned fool." Cynthia looked longingly at the door. "Kids will be kids, right? I guess I'll call Jim and warn him. He gave me that number before he left in case I needed to reach him. This warrants it."

5

———

"Hey, I know I didn't mention it before, but we have something we need to do before we plan our primary mission," Brett said.

"What's that?" Jim asked with a momentary glance over at his mentor.

"Nothing too awful. We're meeting with the higher ups of the coalition."

"When you say higher ups," Ashley said, "who exactly do you mean? I'm not dressed for a formal meeting."

"They won't be going to give two damns about what we're wearing. We're not politicians. They only care about the combat efficacy you two have. This is an unofficial meeting, for obvious reasons. As such, we're going to a special person's house. They're already aware we're nearly there, so they should be expecting us."

"Stop being vague. Where are we going then?" Jim asked.

"Did you vote for the president last election?" Brett asked with a smile.

"You're not serious?" Jim asked.

"I'm deadly serious. The President himself wants to meet you along with other shot callers of the coalition. I'd suggest you be as nice as possible. They hold Jason's fate in their hands."

"They will hold up their end of the deal, yes?" Jim asked.

"Yes, they will."

"They'd better," Ashley said. "We're not doing this for pleasure."

"Speak for yourself," Jim said.

"Okay, not all of us," Ashley said. "I'm here to ensure you don't get yourself killed, so that vest doesn't go off."

"Slow down," Brett said. "See that gentleman standing beside the road? The one next to the long ass limousine?"

"I am not picking up hitchhikers," Jim said.

"No, dumbass. That's our contact. They'll take us to the location where we're meeting. Stop. and let's get out. He's waiting for us. Ask him if he's got somewhere to be. That's the code."

"You'd better be correct." Jim slowed and pulled to the side of said road behind the gentleman and his stopped car. "The last encounter we need is to deal with a serial killer hitchhiker." He stopped his car and exited. He stood behind his open door and leaned on it, looking at the man. "You got somewhere to be?"

"I do now." The man hurried to Jim's car's other side. He grabbed the wheelchair that Ashley handed him and got it set up while she exited the car. "Come, sir. Let's escort you to where your meeting's being held."

"Easy." Brett lowered himself into his wheelchair and let the new man push him toward his car.

"Don't worry. After your meeting, I will personally escort you all back here. We guarantee no police or tow trucks will mess with your car. It's been arranged." He let Brett move himself into the backseat before stowing the wheelchair, while the other occupants climbed into the backseat with him.

The interior of this new car was spacious, smelled fresh, and housed a mini bar ready and waiting to be used.

"Swanky limousine," Ashley said, inspecting where they found themselves.

"Only the best for our important guests." Their escort climbed into the driver's seat. "Feel free to eat or drink anything back there. They are for your use only."

"We appreciate the hospitality, Mr.?" Jim asked for their driver's name as the engine started.

"Call me Michael. My name is Michael Miller."

"Thank you, Michael," Jim said. "We're not really used to the VIP treatment, so excuse us if we make any faux pas, please."

"Given who you are, sir, I don't find that difficult to believe. Can I say something?"

"Always, Michael."

"You're my hero, sir, doing what you do."

"I'm no hero. I just serve justice where the system failed. That's all, no more, no less."

"I've read the reports, I've seen the newscasts, and I've talked to a few of the people you've rescued, sir. I chose my word carefully, with all due respect."

"Every man is entitled to their opinion." Jim looked out at the nation's capital. He watched the Washington Monument as they drove by. "I'm just a man doing what I feel is correct. Some think me an outlaw serial killer, you know."

"Not everyone draws the same conclusions from the evidence," Michael said over his shoulder. He kept his eyes glued to the road as he drove. "What about you two?"

"I take it you're vowed to silence?" Brett asked.

"Yes, sir. Under pain of death. I am not to repeat anything I hear in this car to anyone, including family."

"Good, because we'd have to kill you if you weren't," Brett said. "We take security seriously, and that's putting it mildly."

Ashley leaned forward toward the front. "He's not joking, though he is a bit of an ass. You seem like a nice guy. We don't want to hurt a fan, either."

"How much do you know?" Brett asked. He watched the bustling DC traffic grow thin as they exited the city limits.

"I know Masked Justice and a few others were coming, and I was to escort them. They did not specify if Blind, Silent, True, or Guardian would come with him. I was trying to figure out the beautiful young lady there. You strike me as Blind Justice, if I had to guess."

"What makes you think that?" Ashley had a playful smile on her face.

"Silent Justice excels in bow and arrows. Your build suggests you're more of a physical girl. Blind Justice takes after Masked in that they use a blade."

"Checking me out that much, huh?" Ashley asked. "A girl might get the wrong idea if a man's checking her body out that hard."

"Am I right?"

"You'll never know, will you? Unless our dear friend here already told you all."

"Did you?" Jim asked.

"I'm surprised you'd even ask me that after all we've been through." Brett placed a hand over his chest. "What do you think?"

"It is your job," Jim said.

"My paygrade's not high enough to whatever intel the

higher-ups have," Michael said, clearly trying to break the awkward verbal impasse.

"He's guessing - take from that what you will." Brett's genial smile was still firmly in place. "How much further is it, Mr. Miller?"

"We're only a few minutes out."

"What rank are you, Mr. Miller?" Brett asked casually. "I'm just wondering what to call you in my reports."

"Initiate. I got roped in since they needed muscle, or I'd never have made it."

"Got it," Brett said. "Initiate Miller did not know his place and deserves punishment. I advise we watch him closely."

"You're not serious?" Ashley visibly balked at the words.

"Fine. Maybe I'll overlook the misconduct if it helps us focus on this meeting. Smile, nod, and be agreeable for everyone's sake."

"I can be diplomatic," Jim said.

"We're here." Michael pulled the car through a large, open gate. They were beyond the capital now, outside a secluded, monstrous mansion. They pulled into the wide half mile of the driveway. A large mansion lay ahead, with different vehicles clearly visible in front of it. Visibly armed men met them just inside the gate. He rolled down the window. "Miller reporting with the guests of honor."

"Understood," the leader of the group of armed personnel said. "Go ahead."

Michael stepped on the gas, and they drove down the oversized driveway. They reached the end and parked. "This is where we part ways, lady and gentlemen. I wish you good luck with whatever you're involved in."

"We don't need luck," Brett said. "Now help me outside, Initiate."

The group exited the car and were quickly approached by yet another group of armed personnel. The woman in front reached out a palm toward the group. "Mandatory weapon confiscation. Anything you'd like to declare now?"

"I have a pistol in my belt line," Jim reached his hands out to his side slowly, "and a knife in my right pants pocket."

"There are no weapons on me," Brett said.

"I have a pistol here." Ashley mirrored Jim's movements, making no sudden moves.

Three of the security rushed toward the group. They removed the weapons from them and ran a baton over them. It didn't beep, so the leader nodded. "You're good now. We will give these back to you when you leave. I'll escort you to the meeting room if you'd follow me."

The group fell in lockstep behind the security leader. She led them inside the large mansion and through the home, coming to a stop in front of a large set of double doors with an intricate pattern of the American flag carved into it. She grabbed the knob. "Here we are," she said.

Muffled speaking could be heard inside, but it proved impossible to gather what they were saying.

She opened the door to reveal an enormous table lined with chairs holding numerous faces they'd seen on television. Secret service men stood along the wall, and many snapped their attention to the newly open door.

"Ah, welcome," House leader Pennywise stood up from his chair near the end of the table. He reached up and stroked his white bearded chin. "Please come in and take a seat. We've been waiting to meet you."

"I hope you all haven't been waiting too long." Jim stepped inside the intimidating room, and he led the trio toward the three seats that were unoccupied. "I'd hate to force such important folks to wait on our behalf."

"Nonsense. I'm Alfred Pennywise. It's a pleasure to finally meet you in person."

Jim and the other two took their seats, with Jim in the middle seat. Ashley sat to Jim's right and Brett to Jim's left. "The pleasure is ours," Jim said, trying not to look amazed by the names surrounding him. "I never thought I'd get the chance to meet such powerful officials."

"You flatter us," Pennywise said, taking his seat again. "Mr. Benning," he gestured toward the man sitting at the table's end who had never removed his intense gaze from Jim and Ashley, "I'd like to introduce President Perry Sherman."

"It's an honor, Mr. President."

"Not as much as it is mine," President Sherman said. He wore an immaculate suit, tie, and styled hair. Every strand of his hair was immaculate, and his clothes had no visible wrinkles. "I've been wanting to meet the infamous Masked Justice ever since the first television hit piece on you. You've been through quite the transformation in the public eye as of recently, haven't you?"

"Yes, sir. No thanks to Charles Baskins."

"Yes," Pennywise said. "The man is insufferable."

"That's putting it mildly. He had my father killed recently."

This revelation caused muttering at the table. President Sherman held up a lone hand, quieting the table. "You have proof of this?"

"Mr. President," Brett spoke up, "we know it was a Republic hitman. He sent Hans after us. We do not know his last name, but I assure you, he also tried to have his mother taken out. That is why I'm inside a wheelchair sitting before you and not standing."

"Why did he wish to kill you so badly, though?" Sherman asked.

"I can only guess it's because you sent your operative here to accompany me. He said he'd been sent to kill Baskins before. Since Baskins had betrayed and tried to kill me years back, it only makes sense that Baskins grew paranoid. Wouldn't you if your betrayed best friend was a known accomplice of a former assassin of yours?"

"It was not our intention to draw attention to you and yours," Pennywise quickly said.

"I understand that. Now let's move forward to why we're here today instead of rehashing a painful past, please."

"Quite so," Sherman said.

"A partner of mine is being held in jail."

"Brett told us of that," Pennywise said. "The only method by which we can free him is if the president pardons him."

"I am fully prepared to do so once Baskins is dead. I would do it now but, forgive me Mr. Benning for being blunt, I don't have the required support to undertake such an overt action. See, for the all the faults of our opponents, they've built your former friend up to be a core component of their party. He's lionized their base. Right now, it's almost an even split in the country for support for us versus the PHR's lackeys across the aisle backed by the Republic. They'd try to have me impeached and investigated if I pardoned him right now."

"It will be different if he were to disappear?" Ashley asked.

"If something unfortunate were to happen to Mr. Baskins," Sherman said, "then it would be different. It's a dangerous game they're playing. If Baskins were to die, they'd lose their public face. Their party's cohesion would dissolve. Without the young firebrand, the rest of their party consists of the same establishment faces. He's the one giving their party hope for a change in this country. That's it. They stand on a knife's edge right now."

"We would seize American politics for at least the next fifty years," Pennywise said. "We've been taking a more controlled approach. Our members comparatively are more popular individually."

"They've essentially put all their eggs in the Baskins' basket though," Ashley said.

"Precisely," Sherman said. "If their front man falls, their entire movement goes with them. They've built narrow, where we've built wide. One loss won't affect us nearly so much as them. The counter point is that they can rally more support with their Baskins. So, you see our dilemma here. As long as your former friend is alive, my hands are tied - unless you want to wait until the end of my term. Then I can pardon whoever the hell I want."

"We'd rather not wait if it's all the same, Mr. President," Jim said. "I believe I understand the situation. May I ask another question, if I may be bold?"

"Please do," Sherman said. "I've had the entire morning cleared for this meeting, and I intend on filling you in completely."

"How far does the Republic plan to venture with this police initiative they're pushing? I mean, they're already spying on Americans in their homes using their own webcams and computers. The last I heard, they wanted police to have wide authority to fire on criminals."

"They've taken quite the radical stance, it's true," Sherman said. "Mr. Pennywise, perhaps you'd be best to explain this. It is your domain, after all."

"Thank you, sir," Pennywise cleared his throat. "They

don't tell me what they're planning, but I have sources that cross the aisle to tell me their plans. Take this with a grain of salt. Rumors are that they're wanting to create a nationwide gun registry. That leaves a bad taste to us. Registries always precede a gun grab if we're being frank. He's doing this under the guise of stopping vigilantism."

"This is unacceptable," Sherman said. "While we don't condone all vigilantism, we cannot toss out the baby with the bath water. Guns keep many innocents safe when they otherwise would be victims. We cannot allow further rights to be violated for their supposed safety. That is our public stance and our private one."

"That's not all," Pennywise said. "He wants to authorize a nationwide hunt for vigilantes. In fact, they want to turn it into a holiday of sorts."

"A holiday?" Jim asked.

"Yes, they've approached me with a bill that's ridiculous, if I'm honest. They want to make June 15th a holiday labeled 'The Hunt'. This would allow brave citizens to volunteer at their local police department, and they would go hunting for vigilantes. It's utterly insane if you ask me. It's legalized mob justice." His voice turned from the formal one to a sarcastic one. "Mankind never commits atrocities in huge mobs when that happens, right?"

"You see our dilemma," Sherman said. "We're the last ones holding the barbarians at the gate, figuratively speaking. The Coalition is trying to preserve the American spirit as best we can. We just think we should use those brave enough to fight."

"You don't mean just us, do you?" Jim asked.

"Don't get the wrong impression, Mr. Benning," Sherman said. "We're not condoning vigilantism on a broad scale or anything. Our ultimate goal is to establish a new branch of law enforcement where people with your skills and drive would aid the police officially. Imagine the wanted posters of the wild west. Bounty hunters would get dead or alive orders."

"Legalized vigilantism," Jim said. "I assume there would be guidelines and safety precautions?"

"Obviously," Sherman said. "We simply wish to utilize the skill set of warriors like you for the greater good, not to be hunted like dogs and waste that potential. They would be subject to the same rules as everyone else. If they're found to be killing someone that didn't have a bounty, they'd be expelled and arrested themselves."

"Alright," Jim said. "I didn't need convincing, but this is the correct course of action. Do we know where Baskins is?"

Sherman raised a hand and snapped his fingers. A nearby secret service agent stepped out from the wall and placed a manilla envelope in front of Jim. "Here," was all he said.

Jim opened the envelope to a stack of papers and photos taken of his former best friend. "You mind if we keep this for research?"

"Please do," Sherman said. "It was made especially for you. The last we heard, he was out campaigning. We believe he'll be in and out of DC for the next week. He's quite the early bird for campaigning. If you ask me, he's doing some questionable things for fundraising, but that's old hat in our profession, sir."

"Right." Jim scratched his head as he looked through the various pages. He saw Brett leaning over to look, so he placed the pages between them, so it was easier for him to see. "This should help. Thank you."

"Oh no, sir," Sherman said. "You're doing us the favor.

Now we have some bad news. It's not all sunshine and rainbows here."

"When is it ever?" Jim asked.

"Quite so. Mr. Baskins has grown quite paranoid lately. I assume that's your doing. The rumor is that you're the only one who has ever harmed him."

"I slashed his face pretty good. That's right," Jim said. "Has he been playing that scar up for pity points like I imagine?"

"You've no idea," Pennywise said. "The man brings it up anytime he wants to push his agenda. 'Oh, poor me, a ruthless vigilante almost killed me. We have to stop them all by any means necessary.' He's like a broken record."

"It's smart, but he overplays it," Sherman said.

"He's a complete jackass, but he always understood how to make himself the center of attention." Jim pushed the envelope fully to Brett so he could focus on the conversation at hand. "This won't be easy."

"All we ask is that you don't involve any other member of congress or civilians. Meaning, please don't hit him at one of his rallies. His followers may worship him, but they don't deserve to be hurt simply because of disagreements."

"Agreed," Jim said. "It's always been my code that innocents aren't hurt. That's why I only take certain jobs."

"We also offer one of our own personnel as help if you'd like," Sherman said.

"I wouldn't imagine the government would want any involvement in this. I figured I'd be disavowed or something."

"This isn't from the government, dear boy," Sherman said with a wink. "This would be from the Coalition. You aren't forced to take him, but we thought we'd give you the option of another skilled operator like yourself. He'd follow your every order, and he's ready to die for the cause. We made sure of his training ourselves."

"Operative you say?" Brett pried his eyes from the intel and looked at President Sherman.

"I thought that'd catch your attention. Yes, this is the biggest hit in the history of this country, even more so than President Lincoln's unfortunate theater trip or JFK's horrific incident. We wanted to offer you any assistance possible. They would also be able to obtain any weapon or tool to assist you. I recommend you accept this offer."

Jim and Brett exchanged momentary glances before turning to the President. "So long as he knows how to follow orders," Jim said. "I wouldn't mind personnel who understand the lay of the land and how to secure needed supplies."

"Perfect," Sherman smiled. He pointed toward one of the secret service members near the door they entered. "Fetch him, won't you?"

The agent nodded and wordlessly exited the room.

"You already know him, I believe," Sherman said. "He goes by the name Michael Miller."

"The driver?" Ashley asked.

"He is far from just a driver, Ms. Brooks," Sherman said. "He's trained with a blade, a pistol, and long-range rifles if you want to use that advantage. I doubt Mr. Baskins would expect that from you."

"True," Jim said. "I never was skilled at long-range shooting."

The double doors opened to reveal the agent and Michael entering the room.

"Mr. Miller, thank you for joining us on such short notice." Sherman waved him into the room. "Come inside. Meet your new team."

Brett gave him a glare, making the young man visibly nervous. He gave a deep bow but otherwise said nothing.

"Please forgive his lack of manners," Pennywise said. "He's trained to kill, not make small talk, apparently."

"Good," Brett said. "That's what we need."

"As I was saying earlier," Sherman said. "Mr. Baskins has grown paranoid lately. He's increased his security, and he has put out an open contract on you, Mr. Benning. They know you're hunting him. They probably know you're inside DC now. That's why this meeting has such heavy security. Don't be surprised if you're forced to deal with them before you can get near Mr. Baskins."

"It's never easy Mr. President," Jim said. "I anticipated he'd sent more of his men after me. He never liked getting his own hands dirty."

"He'd be sending the best they have left at you," Pennywise said. "You killed Hans, one of their top assassins, but he was one of many. I urge you to take the utmost caution, sir."

"Anything else before this meeting is adjourned?" Perry Sherman asked.

"Is there a time-limit?" Jim asked.

"No," Sherman said. "There is no immediate need. So long as it's before the elections, we're good. The sooner you complete it, the sooner I announce Mr. Walton's pardon." He cleared his throat. "This aspect is obvious, but this secret conversation never officially occurred. Nobody is going to hear of this. Is that clear?"

"Yes sir, Mr. President," Jim said.

"Understood, sir," Ashley said.

"I'm sworn to silence," Brett said.

"I live to follow orders," Michael saluted the commander-in-chief.

"Good," Sherman said. "Now I wish you all luck." He

pushed his seat out and got up from the table. "If you'll excuse me, I'd like to get a round of golf in before I return to work."

"Have fun, Mr. President," Brett reached out and grabbed Jim's arm, making sure he stayed seated. "Hold on," he said, loud enough for his partners to hear. He watched as President Sherman was escorted from the meeting room with most of the twitchy, frowning guards. His gaze shifted to Mr. Pennywise. "I hope all goes well, sir."

"Godspeed." Mr. Pennywise was approached by the remaining two guards inside the room. One had his jacket and helped the politician into it. "Watch your ass. Mr. Baskins may be a horse's ass, but he's not a man to be messed with lightly."

"We thank you for your concern, sir," Jim said.

With that, Mr. Pennywise and his guards exited the room.

"I suppose you all would like me to show you to where you're staying the night?" Michael asked. He rubbed his hands together. "It's not here, just in case you got the wrong idea. I have no idea who's house this is."

"Focus, Initiate," Brett barked, jolting the young man still. "We were planning on finding our own place to stay."

"You could," Michael said. "We've got a place picked out for you that's private, but if you prefer, I can forget it."

"We'd require scanning the place before we agree," Brett said. "Show me where it is."

Michael pulled his phone from his pants pocket and quickly opened a map. He came over and handed it to Brett. "Here, sir. This location's where I was ordered to recommend. We've scouted the place out, secured it, and approved its location. It's nowhere problematic should anything bad happen."

"Meaning it's quiet," Ashley said.

"I do like a smart girl," Michael said, daring a wink toward Ashley.

"I'm not going to like you, am I, Mr. Miller?" Brett asked.

"Nobody will mind if there's gunfire. It's about a hundred meters from an all-night gun range. No one will report gunfire. Now explosions? That's another story."

"Maybe there is hope for you," Brett said, handing back Mr. Miller's phone. "Take us there now. We need to inspect it and get setup before we do anything."

"Right away. Follow me and we'll be there soon…"

Half an hour later, deep in a forest…

Michael finally brought the car leading theirs to a stop. A small house was nestled deep into the surrounding trees. A small, thin road led back to a main road. It had a second story and a balcony visible on its second floor.

Everyone exited their respective cars before reaching back in. Ashley and Jim had wands in their hands at the ready.

"It's been checked before," Michael said as he approached.

"Then you shouldn't mind us checking again," Ashley said. "Nothing wrong with caution if we're going to make this our base. Why don't you show us around?"

"I could show you all the armory we had set up prior to your arrival," Michael said. "We've also got top of the line computers inside for you."

"Show us the armory first," Brett said, now in his wheelchair. He saw the ramp leading up to the porch. "You all even made it wheelchair accessible. How nice of you,"

"We had a crew here last week." Michael led the group

to the home. He pulled out a key from his pocket and unlocked the door. He let them inside first, then followed them in. "The armory is upstairs if you want to visit it first. I think you'll be impressed."

The foyer had a staircase on the right, along with multiple open archways. It had a mobile seat attached to a metal support to help transport Brett up and down the stairs. To the left was a dining room. To their right was a living quarter. In front of them, in the next room, was the tiled kitchen.

"That wouldn't be the first instance I've heard those smooth, promising words," Ashley said. She let Michael pass them and followed him up the nearby stairs in the foyer.

The hallway upstairs was hardwood floored. Michael flipped a light switch, illuminating the wide hallway. He led them right to the end of the hall before he opened the door. "Feast your eyes on this," he said, opening the door and motioning inside.

Jim was the first to enter the gargantuan armory. His eyes went wide at what he saw.

Along the wall to his left, there were multiple full dummies encased in full glass containers. The bright lights above highlighted the clothing to anyone in the room. They had different color, specially tailored hoodies and masks over their mannequin faces. To his right were the weapons. Multiple tables had every firearm he'd ever heard of, ranging from handguns to assault rifles. Beside that sat the ammunition for said weapons. On the wall behind the firearms there was an openable glass case. It housed swords lining the entire wall of all shapes, sizes, and weights.

Brett was the next to enter behind his pupil and looked

to his left. "What in the hell?" He wheeled himself fully into the room.

"This is a hell of a collection." Ashley pushed Jim forward, making room for herself.

"What are these outfits?" Brett asked. "I don't remember these being standard in regular safe-houses."

"You mean these?" Michael walked over to the human sized glass cases. "Everybody knows Masked Justice and his cohorts wear hoodies and a mask covering the nose and mouth. We decided you all could use an upgrade. They're made of bullet and blade resistant specially woven with top-of-the-line polymers. It won't stop a blade, but it'll turn a mortal wound into a manageable cut. It'll also surprise the hell out of any opponent. His blade is likely to drag slower than he anticipates."

"At least you got a red one." Ashley walked up to said ensemble.

"You got my black and white too," Jim said. "I like it."

"We weren't positive if we needed the purple set," Michael said, pointing to the last one in the room. "I told them to put it in here anyway, just in case Silent Justice came along." He noticed the group now wondering over to the tables of weapons laid out.

"It doesn't matter what you need." He came up behind the group. "If you need something, we've got you covered."

"Where are the bow and arrows?" Jim asked.

Michael pointed toward the door. A dedicated table covered half of the wall. It contained numerous bows and quivers chocked full of arrows, just waiting to be taken. "Like I said, anything you need, we have it. I guarantee it." He pointed toward the only remaining wall, across from the entrance. "On the final wall, we have the gadgets and such that could prove useful. You should know what's available."

"That's essential," Brett said. "I hope for your sake that it's got everything it normally does."

"As requested," Michael said. "There are no windows in this room. It's for those who value their privacy. For anyone wondering, grenades are with the gadgets."

"Grenades?" Ashley was visibly shocked.

"You know how to use one? We wanted to plan for any eventuality. Who knows when explosives will be handy?"

"I'm familiar with their operation," Brett said. "These two aren't. You said explosions would draw attention here?"

"People here are accustomed to hearing gunshots, not explosions. I wouldn't risk it. If nothing else, I'm proficient in their use as well, should you ever need one thrown." Michael bowed to the group. "I look forward to working with you all."

"Alright. Well, take us to the planning room next, Mr. Miller," Brett said. "We need to familiarize ourselves with every room before we leave. That applies to both of you two."

"I do enjoy a good house tour," Ashley said.

Michael led them out of the armory room and across the hallway into the door opposite them. "We placed these rooms next to each other for ease of access and convenience. This way you can plan your next move and then get armed right away. It's perfect if there's ever a time you need to hurry."

"I like that design." Jim followed Michael into the next room. He brushed past Michael toward the oversized desk. Four desktops sat next to each other on a huge table covering the entire wall. "Why are there four?"

"That's so I can link those. It'll make presenting floor plans, planning out your moves, and reviewing research easier. While you don't want them linked, I undo it and each computer is on its own again. That's ideal for internet access. You don't want them all discoverable. They're all wireless, but for when it's a group activity, you take them offline. While they're LAN linked, someone is in charge and can guide the others through the plan."

"This will be my domain while we're here," Brett wheeled himself closer. "I'm familiar with the process."

"You're lucky I oversaw the stocking of this place. The original guy only wanted one desktop. I knew you wanted more."

"I am loathe to say it, but you were right."

"Here's a more pressing question." Ashley moved back to the custom-made clothing they were to wear. "How did you know our sizes?"

Michael joined her at her side. "We were provided that information, miss. I'd assumed you all had provided that information. I wasn't involved in the tailoring process. That was from someone else."

"It was from Frank," Brett said. "Jim and I met him before we left Denver. They're the best of the best. As for how they crafted them, I found the sizes on your clothes' tags while you were outside, little Missy. Now, don't get your panties in a bunch. You should thank me."

"I should show you the rest of the property," Michael said. "We have bedrooms for each of you, tailor made. I think you'll be pleasantly surprised."

"I'd love to see that." Ashley moved closer to Michael.

"You two go ahead," Jim said. "I'd like to inspect the different weapons you had in the armory first."

"I need to get my station ready here," Brett said, turning on the nearest computer. "You two go without me, too."

"If you'll join me..." Michael asked, gesturing toward the door.

"I'd love to," Ashley said.

The young pair of adults abandoned the two older adults and ambled into the upstairs hallway.

"We had rooms picked out for each of you," Michael said. "It was my idea to customize each room. I figured nothing shows support like that little personal touch." He stopped a few doors down the hallway. "Please, this is the one we had picked out for Blind Justice. Or do we need the Silent Justice bedroom?"

"Still want the answer to that, huh? This one's fine for me," she said with a giggle.

"I knew I was right." Michael said, walking into the bedroom. Another full-sized mannequin sat inside a glass case near the door. It had the same red hoodie and mask ensemble adorning it. A king-sized bed dominated the room along with a walk-in closet and its own personal bathroom. "I hope you'll find it to your liking, miss."

"This is downright luxurious compared to my meager apartment."

"When you work with the coalition, you receive the best equipment, accommodations, treatment, and the best personnel."

"You're humble, huh?" Ashley asked with a bemused tone. "Don't get too carried away, cowboy. Don't get the wrong idea. I may like you, but I'm a lady."

"I would never disagree there. Sorry. I've always been told I'm a shameless flirt. I don't even realize I'm doing it most of the time."

"That's dangerous. Who knows how many young innocent women you've corrupted with your silver tongue?"

"Women have said many things about my mischievous tongue, but silver is not usually among them."

"Easy there," Ashley said.

"Sorry." Michael looked down at the ground.

"You take things too seriously." Ashley noticed his downcast expression. "Just take it easy on the innuendo around me. Alright?"

"I understand. It won't happen again. Most of the girls I try that line out with find it amusing."

"I'm not your average girl, Mr. Miller. You'll learn that soon, assuming you survive long enough. We're partners now. I always learn about my brothers and sisters in arms. You will be no different. Now I've been wondering something, Mr. Miller. Can I ask a personal question?"

"I don't mind."

She sat on the bed while Michael stood across from her. "Why did you join the coalition, anyway? You seem like a nice guy. Why get involved in this?"

"You really want my sob story? Everyone in our line of work has their reasons."

"Ain't that the truth?" Ashley fell back and let her shoulder-length brown hair fall in any direction. "If you don't want to tell me, that's alright. Let's change the subject then."

"It's fine. You're expected to trust me with your life. Wanting to learn a bit about me is expected. My father was a construction worker. My mother died during childbirth, so he raised me by himself. When I was age fifteen, I experienced the most eventful day of my young life. I'll never forget it. I returned home to find the police at my house. They informed me that some impatient scumbag decided they didn't want to slow down in the construction zone and barreled through. He was fleeing police and crashed through said construction zone - not completely - and he escaped law enforcement at the cost of my father's life. My father happened to be in his way and got ran over during his escape." Michael's face was stiff and showed no emotion as he recalled the events.

"Damn," Ashley said, sitting up. "I'm sorry."

"Don't be. So I wanted my own form of justice. I found the asshole. I took care of him so he'd never create another orphan again. As you may imagine, I was found out." He rolled up his right shirt sleeve to reveal a tattoo of a large intricate C. "I got this in jail. As it turns out, I gained the attention of the coalition with that move. My murder charge got thrown out on a technicality, and I was recruited. Does that change your opinion of me now that you know I'm a murderer?"

"Do you understand who I hang with?" Ashley asked with a laugh. "That explains a lot. Sorry to make you dredge up memories like that. Do you know my life story? Your organization seems the type to look it up."

"All our intelligence on you is from Brett. I do not know your past, nor was I going to ask. I figure you'll tell me when you're ready. There's no rush."

"I appreciate that."

The door behind them swung open to reveal Jim. "Holy shit," he said, ogling the giant room. "I take it this is her bedroom."

"Yes sir," Michael quickly turned around. "Shall I show you to yours?"

"That'd be acceptable. Let me borrow him just for a minute," Jim said with a wink at Ashley.

She glared at him after Michael turned his back to her. "Sure." She watched the two leave the room and fell backward. She blew a strand of hair out of her face as she stared up at the tall ceiling.

6

A ngie stood beside her car. She held a camera in her
   right hand, pointed at the mass of humanity in front
of her. Many of the signs held slogans showing they were
not in favor of vigilantism. Some of those signs had words of
support for Charles Baskins. "As you can see, everyone, the
anti-vigilante march is occurring right now."

She looked to her left, swinging the camera with it. A
familiar-looking bus pulled up beside the stage they had
prepared at the base of the demonstration outside the
capitol building. "It looks like the guest of honor has
arrived." She looked at the laptop she had on top of her car
without moving the camera. It was open to the livestream
she hosted. She looked at the chat flying by. Viewers from
both sides of the political aisle watched her stream, judging
by the arguments being lobbed at each other. She ignored
them and turned back to the protest.

"No more vigilantes!" the crowd chanted repeatedly.
They raised their signs with every chorus of the short and
simple slogan.

"There must be over five thousand protestors." Angie

had parked on the very outskirts of the organized protest. She placed the camera on a tripod, providing it stability but occasionally turned it to gain a better view of the area. She zoomed in on the bus. "That must be House Representative Baskins now." She took the camera off the tripod and moved closer to the action.

Charles exited the bus and was met with a wave of cheers. He waved to the crowd before his guards escorted him up to the podium on the stage they'd prepared.

"Remember, folks," the person who was on the microphone before he arrived said. "Let's keep it peaceful. Let's hear it for our best hope of ending the vigilantism that has plagued our nation for years now. Welcome, Representative Baskins!" He moved to the side of the podium and let the freshly arrived Charlie take his place. He shook hands with him and backed away a few feet.

Charlie cleared his throat. "Thank you for showing up and showing the rest of my cohorts just how much America supports this movement we've created. We will create a world where we don't worry about people taking the law into their own hands and accidentally killing our children. These vigilantes are unbalanced and a danger to our precious society. It's not a crime to point that fact out, no matter what the coalition says."

"For the politically unaware," Angie spoke from behind the camera. "The old political parties have fallen by the wayside. Mr. Baskins represents the Traditional Representatives, while the other party is simply called the Coalition. I know if I didn't explain it, somebody who's been living under a rock would flood the chat with the question. I've seen it too many times."

"If we can grow this movement, we won't even need the presidential approval. We're not that many seats from accomplishing it. Get your friends." Charlie pointed out to the crowd. "Drag them to the polls, and inform them how important voting is. Our safety is paramount. We trust the police, not crazy people who like to roleplay as a hero."

Another round of applause and screams met his words. Many young women were in the front row, in front of the security forces keeping the crowd at bay.

A gunshot rang out. Angie's camerawork captured a man beside Charlie fall to the ground on the stage. Charlie ducked and rolled. She followed him and the guards fleeing off the stage and into the bus. Once Charlie entered the bus, they immediately shut the door and peeled out, leaving the chaotic crowd of civilians to their own devices.

Meanwhile, the security close to the incident had tackled the gunman to the pavement below. She ran closer, trying to secure an angle. Her chat in the long-forgotten laptop scrolled by. Many of the messages were in all caps telling her to run.

She approached within twenty feet. The crowd that once made her job difficult dispersed. People retreated as far as their feet could carry them. The only souls left were the security force, the perp, the mainstream cameras who had kept their distance, and Angie herself. She saw the gunman and the security struggling.

Another of the security stood above, pointing his weapon downward at the would-be assassin and yelled. "Put it down or I shoot!"

The guard on top lost his grip on the gunman's weapon arm and the gun barrel moved to shoot.

A shot rang out, and Angie had caught the act in perfect clarity for her viewers. One of the security turned and saw Angie filming. He rushed over and reached a hand out toward the camera lens, blocking the view. "Ma'am, we need you to leave the area immediately."

"Alright." Angie lowered the camera at the command. She backed up, showing her compliance. "Was anyone else hurt?"

"Besides the victim and assassin? No."

Angie continued backing up and turned around, heading toward her vehicle. She got back to it and saw the laptop she'd left alone. "Sorry, chat. I guess that's the entire stream. The march is over." She ended the stream and filed away all her things before she climbed into the car.

Angie started the engine and pulled out and away from the incident. Within a couple of minutes, her cellphone rang in her pocket. She answered it. "Yeah? Who is this?"

"What a brusque way to greet a friend," Jim's voice said. "Are you alright after that?"

"Huh? How did you know about that?"

"Maybe I just wanted to support my friend and watch her livestream. Is that so wrong? I was worried. I hope you don't mind, but I screen captured the stream for later."

"Knock yourself out. Is that why you're calling - to see if I'm alright?"

"You have a sheet of paper nearby?"

"Why?"

"We need to meet and discuss what's going to happen soon. I think you'd be interested in knowing the news ahead of time. There's just one condition." Hushed voices whispered on the other end of the line, but she couldn't understand their words.

Angie pulled over to the side of the road and grabbed the nearby notepad and pen she'd placed on her dashboard previously. "What's that?"

"You would be sworn to secrecy under penalty of death. I

do mean death. For the safety of both of us, you cannot report on anything I tell you until it happens. You will not speak to or tell anyone about our meeting. You deserve to hear what'll happen, so you're not inside the line of danger again like that march. Speaking of which, you should have done what your chat said and ran."

"I agree with those terms. Besides, approaching allowed me to capture the event in perfect detail. Don't worry."

"You're lucky that maniac didn't shoot you. Be at this address." Jim rattled off the location of where they were staying. "Do not head to the front door. Head around the house and knock on its rear entrance. We'll talk outside. I cannot allow you inside, but trust me, it'll be worth the annoyance. You'll not wish to miss this news." The line went dead as Angie finished writing the location of her next stop. "Being buddies with a vigilante must breach ethical or legal problems, but who gives a damn? He'll have a good story." She checked over her shoulder before she pulled back into traffic and was off to her destination.

At the base of operations outside...

Angie saw the telltale orange sports car along with another she didn't recognize. "This is definitely the place." She got out of her car and brought along her notepad and pen. She circled around the large structure and climbed the stairs, then knocked on the rear entrance and backed away. Before long the door swung open to reveal Jim with a mask over his mouth and nose like the first instance when she met him. "Nice mask."

"Come," Jim closed the door behind him and dragged her away from their house into the gargantuan backyard. Trees surrounded them on every visible side. Jim stopped in the middle of the clearing and turned to Angie. "You're probably wondering why I'm even here, aren't you?"

"The thought crossed my mind," Angie said. "You live in Denver. Why the hell are you in DC of all places?"

"Do you remember what happened to you in Denver?"

"At the warehouse? I'll never forget that night. Why? Is a maniac set loose here?"

"That's not quite what I meant. I meant, do you remember how I was caught up in something bigger than myself? It's the same here. I cannot outright tell you why I'm here, for security reasons. My team didn't even want me to call you, but I convinced them you'd help while pursuing your own goals."

"What do you want me to do?"

"Were you planning on getting an interview with Charles Baskins before you headed home?"

"Baskins? The politician who was nearly assassinated tonight? I wasn't planning on it. His security would throw me out on my ass if I tried to."

"I saw that incident, and something doesn't smell right. That's the other thing I'd like you to help with. You got clear footage of the attacker's face. We're looking up who he is. That's something you will be able to publish, depending on who it is. I suspect Mr. Baskins was never in any real danger."

"The attacker was shot in the face," Angie said, not believing Jim's theory. "I doubt he volunteered for a performance that would be his last."

"You underestimate Mr. Baskins. I know how he operates. False flag operations would be a simple matter for him. I bet you anything the man was simply doing this job so his family would be taken care of. Think about it. A nationwide protest was on every news network condemning vigilantes.

Don't you find it a little odd that someone brought a gun and shot at their proverbial messiah? It doesn't smell right. It reads like what Baskins' publicist would write. You're interested in the truth? I am as well. It could prove useful."

"What exactly would you wish me to do?"

"Simply try to secure an interview with Baskins at this address tomorrow morning at ten am." Jim reached into his pocket and pulled out a folded piece of paper. He handed it to her. "Don't ask why. Who knows? Maybe you'll even get lucky."

"I thought he was leaving tonight for the campaign trail."

"His security would just assume you're a dogged reporter. They won't think twice."

"You want a distraction. What are you planning?"

"Nothing," Jim said, looking to the side. "Will you do it or not?"

Angie bit her lip, weighing the choices. "You won't tell me why you're doing this. You want into Baskins' place. I can only imagine why. If you're right, then he's sacrificing pawns to protect himself. That's reason enough for me to mess with him a little. Nobody would bat an eye at a reporter, even an independent one trying to secure an interview with one of the hottest commodities in American culture. Sure, I'll do it. Just don't make me an accessory to anything too wicked. Alright? I'm sure I'll be on camera while I'm there."

"Just be natural. You'll do fine. You're simply going to be turned away at their gate. We both understand reality."

"Probably, especially after tonight. Some in my chat thought it might've been you in the crowd earlier, you know."

"We both know that's not my style. This whole thing stinks, Ms. Summers. I want you to help us dig to the bottom of this. I know we can trust your discretion, and I am loath to put you in danger. That's why this is all I'm asking of you."

"I appreciate the notion, but this is a dangerous job if you report right." Angie's voice grew softer. "I saw that your mother was alright. I'm glad that assassin thing didn't play out like I worried it would."

"Yeah. I still have to finish that whole business. You're visiting the one behind it tomorrow morning."

"Huh? Wait a minute. You mean...?" She could hardly get the question out.

"I said too much. Forgive me, but you're just easy to talk to. You remind me of my girlfriend in a lot of ways. You're headstrong, intelligent, brave, and compassionate. I shouldn't have involved you."

"I appreciate the compliments, but I make my own decisions, sir. Besides, hearing Masked Justice say you remind him of his girlfriend is a compliment I'll take to my grave with a smile."

"Needless to say, if you're ever questioned about us, you don't know me."

"Like you said, I'm not stupid. Don't worry so much about me. You focus on whatever it is you're planning."

"I appreciate the good press you've been giving me, though I'm worried you're drawing attention from people who hate me. That's something you're familiar with too, I suppose."

"When you report on people's dirty dealings, you tend to piss off said powerful folks. Sure, I've got some online beefs with other content creators about you and your little gang, but that's small potatoes. I've not been visited by any law enforcement, if that's what you're implying."

"I was more concerned about more official people

coming and questioning you. Has anyone in suits came to question you?"

"After the warehouse, yes. I simply told them what happened, minus the getting in your car part."

"Try to keep your head down, alright?" Jim placed both hands on her shoulders. "I don't want you getting hurt doing this for me. I'd never forgive myself if anything happened to you on account of me."

"The sentiment is appreciated, but I can take care of myself, Mr. Justice. How long of a distraction do you require tomorrow morning?"

"As long as you can manage. Don't push your luck. Those security boys will have a short temper after tonight. They won't hesitate to push you around."

"It'll all be on camera. They won't be able to do anything too bad. Besides, I'll be livestreaming the attempt. Their hands will be tied."

"Don't count on that contingency, but that's smart." Jim removed his hands from her shoulders. "Now are you alright?"

"What?"

"It's not every day that someone sees multiple folks die in front of them. You're likely shaken after that experience."

"It's not the first time I've filmed people die, Mr. Justice. It won't be the last, I'm sure. Now, can't you at least give me a hint why you're here?"

"I already did," Jim said with a hint of amusement in his voice.

"Oh." Her eyes lit up. "I see. Shit, you're not serious?"

"To kill the snake, you must cut its head off, Ms. Summers. The time for half measures is over. I've found the root of the problem, I assure you."

"For your sake, I hope you're right. If I'm right, the consequences of what you're doing are far beyond anything you've accomplished before."

"I'm aware of that, but I must do it. Someone important to me is counting on me, and I won't disappoint them. For better or worse, I'm locked into this fate. Now return to your lodgings. Drink some tea, and sleep. You'll need your rest for tomorrow. Come, I'll escort you to your vehicle."

"What a gentleman." She walked alongside Jim back toward her car. "All I'm doing is asking and pestering his gate keeper?"

"That's all. Just do what comes natural for you. Don't do anything weird, or it'll draw attention to you."

"Why the mask?" Angie looked over at Jim. "I already know what you look like."

"Call it a security measure. My cohorts believe in redundancy when it comes to safety."

"They don't trust me."

"They don't know you like I do. Still, we're under enough stress, so I decided to oblige them." They were now in front of the house, nearing the vehicles parked out front. "Don't worry about us. Just focus on getting your stories. I guarantee you'll have some big ones soon."

"That statement itself is a hint," she said. She stopped by her car and turned to Jim. Getting on her tiptoes, she kissed him on the cheek. "Be careful with whatever you're doing tomorrow. Promise me you will be."

"I always am. Now drive safe." He reached out and opened the driver's door for her. He watched her get in the car and slam the door shut. She rolled the window down and looked at him. "It's always a whirlwind ride when you're involved. You know that?"

"There's never a boring moment. I'll see you tomorrow."

"See you then."

"No, you won't," Jim said with a hint of amusement. He watched her turn the engine on and wave to him before she took off down the gravel trail leading away from the estate. He turned and headed to the base when the front door opened.

There Michael stood. He came out and met Jim halfway. "What was that about? Who was that?"

"Aren't you curious? She was an old friend that's going to help us tomorrow."

"With what?"

"You'll see. Come on, let's go. We need a strategy meeting before we all head to bed tonight." Jim slapped Michael on the shoulder as both men moved back to the house. "Trust me, Mr. Miller. I have a plan."

"Do they work often?"

"Kind of."

7

―――――

"**I**s our star actor ready to play her role?" Brett asked once everyone gathered in the computer room.

"She is," Jim said.

"What are you talking about?" Ashley asked. "I'd appreciate knowing the plan."

"You two will have a little date tomorrow morning," Brett said.

"Excuse me?" Ashley asked. "I didn't come here to date."

"Relax, kid," Brett said. "With the supposed failed assassination earlier, Baskins will have increased security. We can't just sneak in and kill him as we'd prefer it. This will require some alacrity and intelligence. So that's what we'll implement."

"What are you getting at?" Michael asked. "You want intel on his house layout or something? We can find that online, even if he used a private contractor."

"No wonder I couldn't find it," Brett said. "You're going to help me find that plan right now. Take a seat and get working while I explain what we're doing tomorrow morning," he said.

Michael did as he was told. "If I remember correctly, he hired the Collins company to build that fortress. Paid them a boatload to get it done in a hurry, too. I'm on it."

"Now it's essential we know the layout that Mr. Miller is providing soon," Brett said. "We also will need to know guard patrol routes, the times they patrol, and everything between. Jim is going to sneak in there tomorrow morning and plant cameras everywhere he can manage."

"Are you nuts?" Ashley asked. "In broad daylight?"

"Most breaking and entering incidents occur in the morning, not night - fun fact," Michael said as he worked. "There's a reason for that."

"Few expect thieves in the early morning," Jim said. "Now I'm not going inside without cover. That's where Ms. Summers and you come in. You're going to distract the guards while I'm inside. Ms. Summers will take the front entrance. You two will take the rear."

"Distract them how?" Ashley asked. "It's not like throwing a Molotov in there will help anything."

"No, lunkhead," Brett said. "You two are going to go hiking near his home. You'll take a camera and act the happy couple, grabbing some photos which will help us find out the best method of entry. Jim, where do you plan to make your infiltration?"

"I'll tell you that once Mr. Miller there has the plans."

"Noted," Brett said. "Ashley, you two will approach close enough that his guards feel the need to send someone outside to admonish you. They'll probably threaten to call the police, and that's fine. Play ball with them, but try to keep them occupied as long as you can. With any luck, if you're annoying, they'll send even more personnel out there to convince you to leave."

"You think you can sneak by that many guards, sir?" Michael asked.

"With two distractions covering both sides, I think so. I won't be able to plant a camera inside every room, but I can plant them around the house's exterior and maybe a few inside. That'll do for now. It's a preliminary run. That's why I need you to get me the floor plans, Mr. Miller, so I know where I'm planting them for maximum effectiveness."

"I got them, sir. I'm sending them to Brett's computer now."

"Here we are. Everybody take a seat at a computer. That's what they're there for. I'm going to show you where I want you to plant these."

"I'm with you." Jim sat down in the far seat, leaving the one next to Michael open for Ashley.

She sat down and leaned over to his screen. "You have computer training too?"

"Every Initiate does," Brett said. "It's nothing special."

"There. It should be on everyone's screen now," Michael said.

The floor plans of Charlie's home appeared on every screen.

"Now let's figure out where the best locations for our gifts are," Jim said. "This is a huge plot of land he's got. This won't be easy."

"It never is," Ashley said. "How many men does he have?"

"Unknown," Michael said. "I bet after the shooting earlier, he'll up it another twenty or thirty men. I would."

"Alright. I remembered how to mark the locations I want, so tell me if this works," Brett said. His right hand was moving the mouse with adept quickness around the screen, along with clicks.

Jim watched the screen. Red marks appeared on his screen after a brief pause. "I see it," he said. "I think I see what you're getting at. We want maximum coverage.

"I'm marking your entry point with a blue X," Brett said. "It's the best location to infiltrate from, as it's the least visible spot. It houses a shed near its fence and a garage opposite. The only way someone would notice you is if they're directly in front of you. That's a chance we'll take. All you'll do is climb over a wall. It shouldn't be much of a problem with a grappling hook. You can use one of those I know."

"Are we going to be armed?" Ashley asked.

"No," Brett said. "You are just distractions. If the guards spot armed random people wondering around the property, they'll get more suspicious than they already will be. We can't afford that. Just play up the romantic young woman angle. You can manage that, can't you?"

"Can I?" Ashley asked. "Sure, I can. Do I want to? Not really?"

"Tough," Jim said. "You think I wish to head into a compound with dozens of armed hostiles with only two distractions and a computer operator as backup? Not really, but I'll do it. By comparison, your job looks like a cakewalk. While you're pretending to birdwatch or whatever, you get to record the place. Seems relaxing to me."

"I doubt I'll be able to relax knowing you're in there without me," Ashley said with a frown.

"Your concern is appreciated, but concoct a method to cause a scene. You don't want them too agitated, but drawing more outside would be appreciated."

"I can think of a couple ways," she said.

"Good. I want you two to strategize before we head out tomorrow morning. Don't worry about Ms. Summers. I have faith she'll draw enough attention on her end."

"Nobody goes bird watching anymore," Michael said.

"That's not true, but with young people, it probably is," Jim said. "You need a viable reason to possess a camera to record the villa with. Come up with a believable reason on top of your act. I have faith you can manage it."

"What about Charlie's camera system?" Ashley asked. "Smart cash says if he's paranoid, he's installed security cameras."

"I'll disable them remotely," Brett said. "He'll suspect foul play, but he'll be blind. Now, as for Jim's escape plan once you're finished in there. I'm marking that as a green line. Tell me what you think. I have three ideas. Tell me which you like best. It all depends on the order in which you plant the cameras, which escape route you can take."

Three green lines appeared on the screen, all originating from different quadrants of the villa area. They were labeled A, B, and C.

Jim studied the floor plans with total concentration, trying to imagine the building and property he was soon to be trespassing on.

"B has me retreating the way I entered. Ideally, it'd be the one I take. C is for if I'm found I'm assuming? It's a straight line through the front gate. I'd rather not take that. A reminds me of route B but it's in the opposite direction. I don't see any cover over there to block sightlines."

"B is the best choice, by far," Michael said. "It's also the first place they're likely to look if they suspect someone is on the premises."

"How do you know that?" Ashley asked.

"It's where I'd look. It's a great route for someone to hide or break in from, between two buildings. If I figured it out from a quick two-minute inspection, the guards who've been there for months would quickly grasp it."

"At least you're not totally useless with your analysis," Brett said. "Let me devise even more escape routes. You never know which ones might become unavailable. I'd prefer a minimum of two on each side of Charie's property for safety's sake."

"Good idea," Jim said, keeping a close eye on the new marks on the floor plans. "Wait. Route D here is through the garage?"

"According to these plans," Brett said, "there's a second floor to this garage, and it has windows. If worse comes to worst, you climb up, bust out through the window, and book it. You might have some glass inside you, but you'll be fine."

"Or just open it like a civilized person," Ashley said. "If you're not being chased, that's what I'd do."

"This won't be easy," Jim said. He leaned closer to the monitor. "I've never been good at memorization. Just ask Cynthia about high school."

"Cynthia?" Michael asked.

"Forget the name," Brett said, his voice stern. "It's his girlfriend. They grew up together."

"You'd best study these long and hard then," Ashley said. "You can't afford to get lost inside when you're searching for an escape route."

"That's assuming these plans are accurate," Brett said. "I imagine these plans are not the entire story. You may need to think on your feet. Now I'll be nearby. I'll take care of the cameras for you, but you'll have to be quick. Once cameras shut down, they'll grow suspicious and flood the place with men."

"Understood," Jim said. "It'll be like a game of cat and mouse."

"Yeah, with you being the mouse planting intel gathering tech. Except the cats have automatic weapons and a poor attitude," Michael said. "This seems extraordinarily dangerous. Are we positive this is our best move?"

"You doubt me?" Brett asked. "What do you propose, Mr. Miller?"

"I don't know. This seems risky, though."

"This whole life is risky. If you have nothing constructive, shut the hell up," Brett said.

"Why are you nicer to Jim lately?" Ashley asked. "You used to treat him the same as you're treating Michael now."

"Because he's proved himself a warrior. I don't know shit about Mr. Miller here. He's an initiate, which means he's proven some loyalty, but this is his test to become a full-fledged member. Isn't that right, Mr. Miller?"

"It's true. What an assignment to receive as your test."

"Alright, people," Brett said. "Ashley, Michael, you two go plan and scheme. Jim and I have to talk about tomorrow. I'll help him memorize all he needs to for tomorrow."

"Cramming before a test is never a smart idea. Ask me how I know," Ashley said while getting up from the computer. "I'd go with the time-honored method of writing your route on your arm."

"Or in this case, carrying a handheld device that has the map already pre-installed with all our route marks," Michael said. "Shall I set that up, sir?"

"Get on it," Brett said.

"This is going to suck," Jim said. "I'm not a subtle man."

"You will be tomorrow morning..."

8

———

Jason walked along the track. Many inmates followed behind him and in front of him as they walked along during their daily recreation time. He, Eustace, Ralph, and Benny were all walking side by side. They were approaching some empty workout equipment after their latest circuit around the track surrounding the enormous yard.

"Let's get some reps in while we're here," Ralph said. The huge, muscled inmate wore a smirk on his face. "Besides, I bet when I'm done with Walton, he'll be able to out- lift Eustace here."

"No one's on it, boss," Eustace said. "Besides, Mr. Walton's lean, but he could use some more muscle, like Ralph says. Just look at his skinny ass. He wouldn't intimidate anyone with that frame yet. He needs more than cardio. What he needs is muscle."

"It is true, but inmates should fear what's in here." Jason lifted a finger to his head. "This is what wins fights. In only one instance has pure strength won me a fight, and I'm pretty sure the hammer to the head was what won that, not my muscles."

"That's half true," Benny said. "Fine, let's get a workout while we're here." He looked behind him toward the nearby group and then pointed toward the bench and assorted weights sitting nearby. They nodded back to Benny. "Alright, we're covered. Let's get at it then."

"Come on. I'll spot you," Ralph said.

The hairs on the back of Jason's neck stood up, and he experienced a feeling something was wrong. He looked around them in every direction before he finally did as Ralph said. "Alright, but I have a funny feeling." He and the group moved toward the workout equipment.

"I bet," Eustace said. "Yard's the time you're at most risk. Don't worry, kid. We've got every coalition member on guard duty. To take you out, they'd have to start a riot, and then those guard tower boys you see up there, they start shooting. If that happens, lower to your stomach. Don't test them."

"He's right," Ralph said. "I've watched more than a few dumbasses who didn't follow orders. They got their head blown clean off. It was a hell of a sight."

Jason laid down on the bench press.

"Now you're weak, so let's remove some of these weights," Ralph said. He took off weights until only one hundred pounds remained on the bar. "Let's see if you can bench press that at least." He hovered his hands under the bar, letting Jason do the work, but was ready to catch the bar if Jason lost his grip.

Jason exerted himself and got the bar off its resting place. He held the bar there for a few seconds before he slowly lowered it.

"Good," Ralph said. "Now push."

Jason followed the instructions and completed ten reps until he barely lifted the bar upward.

"Good," Ralph said as Jason sat up. "That's a good start. You've got a long way to progress, but I've seen sissy boys not able to lift even that weight."

"I've been working out for months before I got in here. I may be skinny, but I am not weak, sir."

"Duly noted," Benny said.

"Hey!" a male voice called out. "What the fuck do you assholes think you're doing? Those are our weights."

Jason looked to see a group of scowling inmates approaching. The leader was the one speaking. He was a bulky man. Obviously, working out was his favorite pastime.

"Oh great," Eustace said with sarcasm. "This asshole's just what we need today."

"Let me handle this," Benny said.

The group that was tasked with protecting them had a small circle around the weights, and they were holding their positions between the group and their aggressors.

Benny stepped closer to the front lines of the possible melee. "Come on, Drew. We don't have to fight over weights."

"Our beef isn't about the weights," Drew said. "It's about the job."

Another crowd of inmates on the opposite side caught Benny's attention as he checked over his shoulder. Despite being surrounded, Benny's men held their ground. Many of the men's hands were staying near their waistline, waiting for it to pop off. "You seriously wish to fight in the yard? We'll all receive solitary if we fight out here."

"Just hand over Mr. Walton," Drew said. "We just want to talk to him. Right, boys?" The shirtless inmates around Drew laughed.

"That's not happening," Benny said.

Jason checked beside him toward Eustace and then to his left at Ralph. Both members bore a look of grim determination.

"I hope you weren't lying, buddy," Eustace said. "This is about to get ugly."

"Stay near us," Ralph said. "This fight won't last long before the guards fire their rifles. Remember what I told you."

"Now you realize we're going to kill him eventually." Drew and his men on the front side were now within twenty feet. "Why sacrifice your manpower to protect someone like him? Do you really think he's related to Masked Justice? I mean, look at him."

"I know you were paid by the Republic to kill him," Benny said. "Just like we were paid by the Coalition to keep him safe. You want to die today? You keep on walking, big dog. My men do not know fear. We're ready to give our lives for what we know is right. Are you?" Benny reached down the front of his orange pants and pulled free what appeared to be a handle of a homemade knife. "How about it? You want to dance?"

"You got your weapon on you?" Eustace asked.

"I do," Jason said.

"Get it ready," Ralph said. "You watch the other side. We'll watch the front near Drew over there."

"I'm on it," Jason turned around and headed toward the back line of coalition members.

Drew looked up at the towers. He noticed the guards stationed up there with rifles overlooking them. He leaned forward and spat on the ground. "Alright, it appears negotiations have failed. Let's settle this spat the hard way. Let's get them, boys."

Benny stayed near the front lines. "Hold this line, men. We won't allow them through. Is that clear? Cede no ground to these animals."

He barely got the words out of his mouth before Drew and his men charged toward them with knives at the ready in their right hand.

"It's going down!" a distant male voice could be heard.

Jason saw the second group of men rushing toward him. He reached into his pants and pulled out the knife, almost on instinct. He felt his blood pumping, full of energy, but most of all, he felt a familiar feeling - fear. His blood ran cold, and he felt the familiar knot of stress sitting in his gut like a heavy stone weighing him down.

It wasn't long before the lines of humanity approached close and for combat to start, if such a fighting style was called combat. It was brutal, noisy, close quarters, and bloody. Jason had witnessed a man get stabbed before today during assassination attempts and he received an up close and personal viewing for this incident. Men on his team and his attackers stabbed their weapon holding hands at each other rapidly. The sound of grunting, shuffling feet, and cheering of the bystanders was accompanied by screams as they witnessed this struggle across the recreational yard.

Alarms blared once the fighting started. All wandering eyes on the jail's yard turned to the deadly melee taking place that Jason found himself stuck in.

Jason saw one of his allied men close to him tackle an assailant to the ground and start stabbing with reckless abandon toward the man's chest. He took his spot, reforming the line. A smaller inmate with glasses took the prior attacker's spot and was within a few feet of Jason now.

Jason sized the opponent up inside an instant. He reminded him of himself when he was forced to kill that gangster in Mr. Fitzgerald's place not too long ago. His would be attacker was visibly shaking, but he advanced nonetheless.

The bespectacled man lunged his right hand toward Jason, who jumped back, evading the stab. He lost his balance, so Jason grabbed the novice fighter's knife holding hand and pulled hard. He directed the blade away from his body while throwing his attacker off balance. Taking advantage of the opportunity, Jason yanked the man over and forcefully jammed his makeshift weapon deep into the man's chest while twisting the blade. He mimicked the movements of the other fighters around him as he dug the blade out among the panicked screams of the pitched combat erupting all around him. He threw his arm forward and back again and again. Blood came spurting out of the wounds he inflicted and stained his prison wear red. The man's gurgling and begging fell on deaf ears as he finally slumped forward to the grass.

A shot erupted, causing every brawler nearby to freeze and look at the towers. Assorted curses were yelled out toward the guards above, who had rifles trained on the men below.

"Get on the ground!" an irate guard's voice played over the loudspeaker. "There will be no more warning shots. I repeat, get on the ground and don't move. Get on the ground! We won't issue any more warning shots. I repeat, get on the ground and don't move. Any action you take will be interpreted as hostility."

Jason watched every fighter in front of him stop what they were doing and lower to their knees, so he did the same. He got on his belly, along with every man.

"There's never a boring day, eh Mr. Walton?" Eustace

asked from his side. "I hope you like slop, because there's no canteen in the hole."

Jason looked over. "When did you get there?"

"I saw you getting into the fight. I can't let my cellmate catch a blade, can I? You should thank me. See that one?" He motioned with his head toward the exhausted fellow by Jason's victim. "He almost got you while you were dealing with four eyes. You're welcome."

"Thank you," Jason said with sincerity.

"Don't thank him yet," one of the unharmed assailants not far away said. "We'll never stop. You will die eventually."

"We'll see about that," Eustace said. "If this was the best you morons could muster, that's not happening."

"This pointless fight was a senseless waste of life," Jason said.

"You'd best get used to that kid," Eustace said. "Life is cheap inside these walls. Not yours though, you're worth a great deal of money and comfort. Not to mention to the cause."

Jason looked toward the jail buildings and watched a crowd of armored and armed guards flowing out of the doors. "What happens now?"

"Do what the guards order, and this process goes easier. We're all probably going to be thrown in solitary for this," Eustace said. "I hope you like the Bible."

"Why?"

"It's the only literature you'll have back there, and you will read it unless you prefer staring at the wall. Men go crazy there if they allow themselves to grow bored. Take my advice and read the damned thing, even if you don't believe. It'll keep you sane."

"You'll also catch charges for murdering Ike there," the

nasty man said as the guards approached. "If you weren't in for life beforehand, you are now for murder one."

"I'm guessing self-defense won't work for this situation?" Jason asked.

"They'll chalk this up to a gang war. The rules are different for gangs," Eustace said. "I hope whatever connections you have, have a plan for your sake."

"Nobody move!" The guards were now near.

Jason couldn't see much from his vantage point, but he saw quite a few wriggling bodies on the ground. They moaned and clutched at their different wounds, trying to staunch the blood flow from the improvised deadly weapons, friend and foe alike.

"Hell of an exercise regimen. Eh, buddy?" Eustace's nearby voice asked.

"Killer," Jason said, his voice devoid of amusement.

9

Angie stopped at the address Jim had given her last night. "It's almost ten," she said, glancing down at the clock in her car. "What are the odds he gives me the interview?" She grabbed the camera sitting in the passenger seat and took a deep breath. "What's the worst that can happen? They chase me away?"

She climbed free of her car. She found the metal barred gates and what appeared like an intercom system. Angie walked up to it and peered through the security gate. She found a man sitting just inside atop a wooden chair with his back to her. "Hello?"

"Huh?" the man eloquently asked. "Who in heaven's name are you?"

"My name is Angie Summers," Angie said with a hand on her chest. "I'm an independent journalist."

"What do you want, Ms. Summers?" the guard asked, now standing and facing her.

"I'm trying to get an interview with Charles Baskins for the people."

"Let me see your ID, Ms. Summers. You can't be too careful after last night's assassination attempt."

"Here." Angie reached into the purse hanging over her shoulder and pulled out a small card. She handed it through the gate.

"Let's see here." He looked at it before handing it back. "That checks out. Tough luck for you, though. The boss isn't interested in doing interviews now."

"What's your name, sir?"

"I am Gene Gilliam. Now I recommend you return to your office and find a different idea, Ms. Summers. Everyone here is on edge. Wait a minute," Jean inspected Angie closely. "You were at the protest last night."

"I filmed it from a distance, yes. Hey, you were the guy who shot the attacker."

"Yes, I was, and I spent half the night at the DC police department answering questions."

"Are you sure Mr. Baskins doesn't want to give an interview? He's campaigning, and he'd be getting free publicity." She gave him the most pleasant smile she could manage. "I'm sure the public would love to hear how brave Mr. Baskins was in the face of danger beyond my meagre description from what I saw, not to mention his handsome security."

"This is a bad idea." He reached down to his belt line and removed a radio looking device. He brought it up to his mouth and pressed a button before speaking into it. "We have a journalist wanting an interview at the front gate."

There was a momentary pause before a gruff male voice answered through their portable radio. "Just a moment."

"You heard him," Gene said. "I wouldn't get my hopes up, Ms. Summers. Everybody's shaken up today. You seem like a nice lady, and I respect your trying."

"Aren't you sweet? The people are worried about Mr. Baskins. I'm just trying to soothe their concerns. There's a rumor he was hit with a bullet from the gunman. He was rushed out so quickly, I can see why they'd think that."

"I can assure you, Mr. Baskins was unharmed. Thank God," Gene said. He was interrupted by the device and voice speaking.

"Mr. Baskins is not conducting any interviews this morning. Send her away immediately."

Angie looked up at the camera pointing downward at her. "I figured as much. Alright, I'll give up on interviewing Mr. Baskins, but what about you?"

"Me, ma'am? Nobody would want to hear from security."

"Are you nuts? You don't think folks want to hear from the brave soul who kept their hero safe? Can I at least interview you, so I don't go back to my readers and disappoint them? It'd mean a lot to a young up-and-comer journalist. It'd be a fluff piece. I swear. Wouldn't your mother love to read about her strong, handsome son saving a life?"

Gene looked at the mansion behind him for a second before returning his gaze to Angie. "I don't think there are rules against that. I suppose I could answer some questions if you really want to ask a grunt like me."

"Fantastic!" Angie bounced in place and dug out her camera. "Do you mind if I record this? It's a lot easier than transcribing every word on a notepad."

"Go nuts," he said.

"Hello, sir," Angie said after clearing her throat. "What's your name and occupation?"

"I am Gene Gilliam, and I work security for Representative Baskins."

"Everybody saw what happened last night. It's plastered all over the national news. What they're worried about is whether Mr. Baskins sustained an injury. There's been a nasty rumor saying the crazed gunman harmed him. Is there any truth to that?"

"Negative," Gene said. "Mr. Baskins was unharmed. A coworker of mine caught a bullet, but he was rushed to the hospital soon afterward. To my knowledge, he's recovering and in no immediate danger."

"That's a relief to hear. That will put our minds at ease. Now you were present at the protest, weren't you?"

"Yes, ma'am. I was by the crowd when the entire event happened."

"So, you saw the attacker up close?"

"I was scanning the entire crowd. Unfortunately, I didn't see him until the shooting started. After that, my friend who was standing beside me ran and tackled him to the ground before I could."

"What happened next?" Angie asked.

"I unholstered my weapon, angled it at the attacker's head, and let him know to put the gun down. He did not comply. My friend lost his grip on the weapon wielding hand. I saw the barrel of said weapon point toward my friend, so I fired, ending the threat permanently. Unfortunately, we couldn't end it before someone got hurt, but that's the nature of security. We put our lives on the line every single day to keep others safe."

"I know I speak for others when I say this. You and your friend could have a bright future in the Secret Service."

"No, ma'am. We're already employed by the best security firm in the country, and we'd have it no other way."

"Fair enough." Angie sidestepped and saw a group of security members marching toward the front gate. "It would appear we have visitors who also want in on this interview, sir."

"What?" Gene looked over his shoulder. "Oh crap," he whispered, but loud enough to be heard on camera.

"What's so difficult about sending her away?" the one in front asked. "Get out of here, lady!" he screamed while shooing her away.

"It appears the rest of his cohorts do not share Mr. Gilliam's charm," Angie said loud enough for the camera to hear. "I gave up on interviewing your boss. What's wrong with interviewing the hero from last night, sir? He agreed to it. Nothing illegal is happening."

"You are trespassing after being ordered to leave."

"I am not on your property though," Angie pointed the camera down to show that indeed, she was not on their property. "We're having a pleasant conversation here." She raised the camera back to face the angry security. The camera caught sight of a masked soul facing away from her with his hands above his head in the distance, behind the angry faces. He looked like he was planting something. He turned around and waved at Angie's camera before he snuck off while the guards were all firmly focused on her.

"This interview is over," he said with a tone of finality. "As for you, Mr. Gilliam," he glared at the young man, "I'll deal with you later."

The camera saw more guards filing out of the mansion and walking toward the front gate.

"Are you going to leave, or will we physically force you to leave?"

"Hey now," Angie backed up from the gate. "There's no need for that. I'm not hurting anyone. This is public land, and you can't force me to leave."

"You want to bet?"

"You realize this is being filmed, yes?" Angie asked.

"Are you threatening me?"

"I'm informing you of the consequences of your actions is all, sir. We don't need to turn this into a bloody drama because of your foolish pride."

"You turn around and get back in your car, or we take your camera and destroy the footage."

"I'd like to see you try to destroy the footage," Angie said with a smirk. "Livestreaming is a hell of a thing."

"Livestreaming? God dammit," the angry leader of the guards said. "Get the hell out of here!"

The opposite side of the security gate teemed with frowning guards. There were at least ten or fifteen guards present. Angie couldn't tell since they were standing in formation and it was hard to count the ones standing behind.

"Fine," Angie said, taking another step back. "The world will discover which of you was kind enough to indulge an independent journalist and assuage public fears of Representative Baskin's medical status. I bet Mr. Baskins will appreciate Mr. Gilliam here when he sees this interview. He gave him an excellent reputation, while you make him appear like an ass. I'd be worrying about my job security right about now if I were you."

"Leave!"

Angie was wise enough to understand when to retreat, so she did. She kept recording as she backed up toward her car. Eventually she felt her butt hit her car, and she finally stopped recording. She opened the car door and tossed the handheld camera into the passenger seat before she climbed inside the driver's door and looked over.

It looked like Gene was getting his ass verbally chewed out, but little else. "Poor guy. Hopefully that works." She started the engine and pulled out onto the road.

Just earlier, on the opposite side of Charlie's house...

"She's arrived," Brett's voice said over the earpiece. "Are you in position?"

Michael and Ashley emerged through another tree line and saw the mansion in question, along with a large fence surrounding it. "We're here, sir," Michael said. He brought the camera up and snapped a photo.

"This looks like a wonderful place for a picnic," Ashley laid out the blanket she had tucked under her arm before placing the basket beside it. She spread out the blanket over the grass below and sat down on top of it. "Come on, dear."

"What? Oh," Michael followed her hint and sat down on the blanket.

"You think they can see us from here?" Ashley asked, opening the picnic basket.

"I'd bet anything," Michael said. "There's a camera pointed in our direction perched atop the wall."

"You spotted that from this distance?" Ashley asked.

"The zoom function is a hell of a thing when taking photos, dear," Michael winked at her. "They know we're here. I'm positive of that conclusion. The question is when they will rush outside. I'd bet within a couple of minutes we'll have angry guards marching toward us."

"Then we should enjoy it while we're here. Oh look," she pointed up toward a bird flying toward the compound. "I think that's a red-tailed hawk."

He quickly turned and snapped a shot.

"Did you get it?" Ashley asked.

"I believe so. Along with all the other bird pictures I've accumulated in here on our little hike, they should buy that we're out on a date."

"Don't look, Romeo and Juliet, but I think you'll have company soon," Brett said.

"What makes you say that?" Ashley asked.

"Average response time for a security firm is short, maybe only a few minutes. Ample time to mobilize their standard grunts and direct them where they need to investigate. You've been on their timer for a minute or two. Common sense says they'll be showing up soon. Just remember, this is not a combat operation. Don't harm them. It'd put Baskins on even higher alert."

"This isn't a suitable spot for a gunfight anyway," Michael said.

"There they are," Ashley said. She scooted closer to Michael and laid her head on his shoulder. "Wrap your arm around me quick, honey."

Michael followed the orders and used his free hand to grasp her hand. "Don't tell me holding hands is pushing my luck?"

"It's not my acting skills I'm worried about," Ashley said. She quickly stole a kiss, never glancing at the approaching crowd of bodyguards. "Now follow my lead, honey bunny."

"Hey!" a female voice called out once they were close enough. "You can't be here." She and her cohorts marched toward the pair, undeterred by the public displays of affection.

Both looked at the group approaching closer. "Like what's the problem, ma'am?" Michael asked with a Californian surfer accent. "We're enjoying a nice morning picnic out here, away from all the problems of the big city. What's the harm in that?"

"You are on private property, sir." She and her group came to a stop a couple of yards away.

"I'm pretty sure the internet said this land was public

though," he said, looking genuinely confused. "Can't we just eat our lunch before we get moving at least? We've been walking all morning, and don't mean anyone any harm. We even made extra if you'd like to join us."

"No," she said. "Look. You two seem like sweet kids and all. That's why I'm being nice. You need to get moving, though."

"We just got the blanket down," Ashley whined. "Are you seriously forcing us to fold it again and trek through the forest for an hour before we get to another clearing? It took us like forever to find this awesome spot. It's perfect for our little picnic." She giggled and looked over at Michael. "This was our relaxation day, and we wanted to enjoy a perfect date. Surely you know what it's like to be in love, Ms."

"Ma'am," one of the younger guards at her side said, "what possible harm could a sappy couple like this accomplish? Technically, they're not even on the property. We have no legal authority."

"Be quiet, you fool," she snapped.

"See?" Michael pointed toward the young man. "It is public land out here. We won't hurt anything by sharing our sandwiches. Right?"

"Then why do you have that camera?" She pointed toward the camera hanging around his neck.

"This?" Michael grabbed it. He removed it from around his neck and changed from the viewfinder to the built in album of saved pictures. "Here, look. They're all shots of birds native to this region. See, I'm a bit of a birder."

"You made that word up." She marched over and snatched the camera. "Let me see that."

"Go ahead, but I want that back. There are still further specimens I'd like to snag a picture of."

Her men gathered around her and looked over her

shoulder. "It looks legitimate, ma'am," the younger one said. "He's a bird watcher alright."

"The proper term is birder, young man," Michael said. "Bird watching is for people who aren't as serious about the hobby."

"Don't get him started with the term, please," Ashley rolled her eyes. "Just nod and smile. Trust me."

"Look, kids," she said. "Pack up your little blanket and head like a hundred feet in that direction, alright?"

"Seriously?" Ashley asked.

"Ma'am, you are dangerously close to the home of a House of Representative member the morning after someone tried to assassinate him," she said. "What would you think if you were his security firm and found you two loitering nearby?"

"Oh damn," Michael said. "This is Mr. Baskins' place? Oh shit. We had no idea. Maybe we should follow their orders and move on, honey."

"Oh crap," Ashley puffed out her cheeks. "This was such a good spot too. I guess we can if it's so important."

"We appreciate your cooperation." The head guard of the group snapped her finger and reached out to grab the younger guard's shoulder. "You will help show them to a suitable picnic area and then report back as soon as they're settled. Is that clear?"

"Crystal clear, ma'am," he said.

"Good, we have additional plans to accomplish today, so don't take long."

"I hope your boss stays safe," Michael said with a wave toward the retreating woman. "I'm certain he's in excellent hands now."

"Sweet talk with her will get you nowhere," the left-over young guard said. "Trust me, I've tried. Once she's made up her mind, the matter's over. Now come on. I know the perfect place for you two to have your picnic. There are always birds there whenever I sneak off during my break."

"Hurry up!" The group of guards stopped by the rear gate of the property and watched the group packing up the picnic supplies.

"We'd better hurry. They won't leave until you do," he said.

"Oh, no! where's my bracelet?" Ashley sounded panicked.

"Bracelet?" the mid-twenties guard asked.

"I had my bracelet on when I sat down and, oh my God, it's not here." Ashley got on all fours, searching the surrounding grass. "Help me find it. I'm not leaving without it. It was an anniversary gift."

"Oh, no." Michael mimicked her actions. "Come on, man. Help us out here."

Soon, all three souls were on their knees combing through the grass. They spent so long looking that the guard group returned, and this time she didn't sound cordial.

"What the fuck is taking you folks so long?" she asked. "What are you all doing?"

"The lady lost her anniversary gift, a bracelet," the guard said.

"Who gives a damn?"

"I do," Ashley said. "I'm not leaving without it. It's a symbol of our love, and I won't leave it."

"It was also quite expensive," Michael muttered loud enough to be heard. "Please, ma'am, I know you have a heart. Help us find it. We'll be gone immediately after. It's important to us."

The senior guard took a deep breath. "Fan out and look nearby. It might have dropped off while they were walking."

"Yes, ma'am." Assorted voices acknowledged the command.

"As soon as it's found, you're gone."

"Understood," Michael said.

Just earlier near the property...

"According to the front camera, Ms. Summers just pulled up," Brett said over the earpiece. "Their cyber security is no joke. Give it a few seconds, and then you can climb over. Your personal camera on your chest is up and running. I should be able to observe where you are. Thank God Mr. Baskins' Wi-Fi password wasn't too hard to crack for my little program."

"Looks like I won't need the grappling hook," Jim said, looking up at the wall. He estimated he could jump and reach the top to pull himself up and over.

"You have the quick acting adhesive and cameras on you?"

"They're in my fanny pack here."

"Don't let anyone catch you," Brett said with a hint of amusement in his voice. "You'd never be able to explain the fanny pack accessory. Your reputation would fall into shambles. Alright. Go inside now."

Jim jumped as high as he could manage. His hands reached the top of the wall and he pulled himself upward. His feet scraped against the wall, trying to propel himself upward. He soon could see above the wall and the narrow alleyway of sorts he was to enter. He quickly vaulted over the wall and landed on the soft grass below with a soft noise.

"You know the drill and the route. Begin your operation, and Godspeed."

Jim didn't respond audibly for fear of being heard. He stepped forward slowly until he was near the exit of the tight space between buildings. As he approached, he stopped when he heard the crunching of grass. He pressed himself up against the wall nearest the noise.

A couple of guards were heard conversing. "What is it now?" one asked.

"I don't know. They didn't say. Someone's at the front gate. It's probably a reporter. They've been calling and asking for an interview, but this one's probably a real go getter. Too bad for her," he said.

Jim saw the two guards walking away. They quickly disappeared toward the front of the house.

Jim reached toward his fanny pack that was already open and pulled out the small container of adhesive and a camera. He deftly covered the bottom of said camera with the adhesive and stuck the camera on the garage wall, low to the ground, almost on the grass. He held it in place for a solid five seconds before removing his hand and listening for any more guards.

"Camera one is up and running," Brett said. "The batteries will work for days, which is more than we likely need. You couldn't have picked a better spot? I know it's slim pickings inside, but try to get a little more altitude next time. It'll be able to see guard patrols, but it's not pretty. I'd head toward the front of the place next. Angie will be the first to be chased away. If we want a camera there, now's your ideal time."

"Wish me luck," Jim said once he was sure nobody was near enough to hear. His voice was barely above a whisper anyway. He finally mustered up enough courage to duck out of his cover after peeking around the corner and finding nobody.

He stayed low, but moved quickly around the side of the mansion. When he reached the corner of the house, he could hear voices again.

"You are trespassing after being ordered to leave," one of the gruff voices from before spoke.

"I am not on your property though," Angie's voice said. It was barely audible.

He peeked around and saw a veritable crowd of guards huddled near the gate. All of them were facing the journalist. He prepared another camera, along with the adhesive, and felt a knot in his stomach, knowing that one mistake, one sound, could result in him getting caught.

Jim turned the corner and stepped slowly but steadily. He saw Angie through the open bars and quickly got to work, not wanting to tempt fate further. Reaching above his head, he affixed the camera to the side of the building high above. He turned and waved toward Angie before retreating around the side of Charlie's mansion.

"This talk is over," one guard behind him said. He surveyed his new surroundings on the opposite side of Charlie's dwelling, searching for any location out of sight he could use. His eyes fell on the shrubbery sitting just below the windows. He could hear voices behind him getting closer, so he did what he had to. He hunkered down and crawled into the bush.

It irritated his skin with every movement. He was pretty sure he got a twig or two to his eye and he could feel wood poking him all over, but it was worth it. All he could smell was the chlorophyll inside the leaves. He could hear another set of guards coming toward him, heading toward the front of the property.

"This bitch doesn't know when to leave, does she?" one asked.

"She's the remnant of a dying breed of actual journalists," the other guard said. "She's dogged in securing that interview. Come on, she'll shit herself when she sees so many guns and angry men looking at her."

"Camera two is up and running. It looks like you got it high enough to get it out of their sight lines. No one noticed it. Stay where you are," Brett said. "They're dispersing from the front. It looks like they're heading toward the back now. It looks like they just noticed the young couple."

"God dammit," the same guard from just earlier said. "Now idiots are trespassing on the rear of the property, hosting a blasted picnic. Something's wrong here. We never have this much trouble."

A female voice spoke up with authority. "The rear exit is my business. Trust me, they'll be leaving soon. It's probably just two idiotic love birds. They said they saw a picnic basket. Regardless," the voices sounded like they'd just passed Jim and were now in front of him, "we can't allow random strangers to be so close to the boss. It's not good business. They could be scouts."

"I think they're just idiots, ma'am."

"They don't pay us to think, young man. You'd best learn that quick."

"Okay. Give it a few seconds and you can plant a camera near the side you're on. I don't see any guards heading your way from the front. Just watch the back. We don't have eyes there yet."

"Understood," Jim said, nearly under his breath. He got up quickly, snapping a few twigs in the bush. He looked forward and saw no one in front of him. *Thank God,* he thought. *I'd be toast if there was.* He quickly extracted another camera and attached it above his head on the side of the home.

"It's up and running," Brett said. "Head toward the back of the house. Be careful there. The camera on the lovebirds shows a humongous group of guards stationed out there. They're staring out toward them right now, but that could change at any time."

"Got it." Jim approached the end of the mansion and peeked his head around. He saw the group of guards beside the back gate. He looked closer to the home and found no guards gazing his direction. Looking upward at the balcony overhead, he spotted a woman. She was obviously not security, judging by her apparel. She looked like a normal woman. He preemptively fished out a camera and slathered a generous portion of the adhesive to the bottom. He turned the corner and quickly worked on planting another automated scout.

"You'd best hurry," Brett said. "They're stalling as best they can, but they'll be heading back soon."

Right, Jim thought.

"It's up to you where to go next," Brett said. "If you believe you can sneak inside, all the better. If it's exceedingly risky, return to the garage and shed. It's the best exit point you have."

Jim finished with the camera and saw a nearby door leading inside the home. *Fuck it,* he thought. *I came all this way, I'll try.*

He moved over and tried the door, only to find it locked.

"There's no time to pick your lock. Retreat immediately."

Jim followed the order and turned the corner leading to his original infiltration point. There was just one problem, and it was a big one. A guard was gazing outside the nearby window he passed by. He knew this because he turned, and the pair locked eyes.

Jim's fight-or-flight response took over. He dashed

forward toward the garage and shed. He could hear radio white noise along with indistinguishable speaking, but he knew what they were saying, regardless. They were reporting an intruder on the premises - he knew that much. *I'm on the clock now,* he thought.

By the time he jumped and was pulling himself over the wall for the second time, he could hear rapid footsteps coming from behind him.

"He's by the garage and shed!" one male yelled. "He's probably jumping the fence. Get units outside the property immediately! Don't allow him to escape. Consider him armed and dangerous. We believe he's a vigilante, judging by his appearance."

"Fuck," Jim said aloud. Hopping down to the grass below, he took off in a sprint toward the nearest tree line. He didn't get there before he heard shots behind him and felt an impact in his back that caused him to tumble forward and roll. He managed to get back on his feet in one swift motion and keep running.

"I hit him, I think!" one young man yelled.

You sure did, Jim thought. *It hurts like a bitch. It's a good thing Brett taught me how to keep my balance.*

What followed next was a desperate run through a forest.

"You got an entire train of admirers trying to catch you," Brett said. "Get to the car. The motor is already up and running. I know you can outrun them. I trained you for endurance and speed."

You didn't train me to run at full speed after having the wind knocked out of me, Jim thought to himself, feeling anger, fear, and a burning sensation in his chest. He gasped and coughed as he ran, sputtering as he dodged trees and tried to keep his speed constant. Sticks, logs, and rocks made this difficult, messing with his footing. He stayed upright and kept sucking air despite all the impediments.

More shots echoed behind him as bullets shot off splinters from a tree in front of him. Jim covered his face with one of his arms, then felt the splinters embed themselves in his arm; however, that pain was overshadowed by his primal need to run and distance himself from the angry gun toting guards chasing him. He instinctively ducked with every crack of a gun behind him.

Jim finally broke free of the tree line and emerged within viewing distance of the car Brett was in. He could hear the chattering of guards behind him. He understood there was no time to waste, so he ran to the open driver's door and climbed inside, then pulled out without putting on his safety belt and burned rubber.

"You alright?" Brett asked.

Jim gasped, trying to catch his breath as they drove down the road away from the property. "I think so," he said.

"You look like you're bleeding. Did a bullet clip you in your arm or something?" He grabbed Jim's right arm, allowing him to keep his left on the wheel. "It doesn't look like it. What caused this?"

"I believe it was a tree that got shot. It would have been my face if I hadn't raised my arm."

"We'll get that treated when we get back. Just focus on driving. You're not bleeding too bad. You'll be fine until we return. Just to be safe..." He reached into the rear seat, grabbed a white plastic sack, and pulled out a wrap of gauze and some tape. He wrapped the gauze over the bloody wound and then ensured it wouldn't fall off with the tape. "It's primitive, but it'll stop some of the bleeding. We need to disinfect this soon. We can't have you getting an infection from this."

"Are the other two alright?"

"Oh, they're fine. They're having a lovely picnic as we speak, probably flirting and carrying on."

"They best not be carrying on," Jim said.

"You're worried about her?"

Jim glanced over at Brett. "Obviously I am. We don't know this Michael guy. I don't want her falling for some jerk who's not genuine."

"You sound like you want to be her father or something. Is that how you see yourself?" Brett asked.

Jim was silent for a few moments before answering. "I don't know. I suppose so, since I'm the closest thing she has to a father. She's young, pretty, and impulsive. What am I supposed to think when you said they were flirting?"

"It could've been an act for the guards."

"Possibly. She's been known to do impulsive things for the sake of our mission; even so, I can't help but worry."

"That just means you're still human. Worry about her later. For now, just worry about getting us home."

10

―――――

"It's a beautiful morning," a female said.

Charlie looked over with a genuine smile. He walked over to her in front of the sliding glass doors leading to the balcony overlooking the backyard. He wrapped his arms around her waist and pulled her close. "It sure is, but it's nothing compared to you."

Her voice was playful. "You're such a sweet talker for someone who's insisted on keeping me a secret these last few years. I swear, a girl could feel like her man was ashamed to be seen with her." She let her hands fall and covered Charlie's. "Come on. You know I was scared last night."

"I know you were. Hence the me embracing you situation we've got going on," he said with a chuckle. He leaned forward and kissed the back of her head. "I'm sorry. It's a risk of my job."

"I don't understand last night," she said with a smile. She looked out over the forested land. "Why would a vigilante show up at your protest?"

"You expect people who run around in masks and play

superhero to make sense? He probably thought it'd kill the movement I've built. He felt threatened."

"I'm just saying, tactically it doesn't make sense."

"I'm a target. Vigilantes across the country want me dead. I know you harbor a soft spot for one masked madman, but let's not allow that fact to cloud the reality of last night. One tried to kill me for their cause."

"That was not Masked Justice."

"I know that, obviously." Charlie blew air softly over her ear.

"Stop. That makes me feel funny." She reached a hand up and laid it softly on his chin. She turned his lips away from her ear. "You know why I like him. He's actually accomplishing wonderful things."

"He's breaking the law, Daphne. Regardless if we agree with his motivations, he's not trained as a law enforcement officer and doesn't know when to apply deadly force. He has no authority. I will admit that it was fortunate that he helped your cousin, and that is one thing I will always be grateful that he did."

"Oh," she said. "I know what you're saying is true, but I can't bring myself to want him hunted down."

"We'll agree to disagree, alright?" Charlie took one hand away from her hips and brought it up to her hand on his chin. He brought it up to his lips and kissed it. "I have a surprise for you this morning."

"A surprise? Babe, we need to talk about yesterday."

"Oh," Charlie unwrapped his hands from around her and backed off further into the luxurious bedroom. "Isn't it enough that I'm alright?"

"What if you're not next time?" She turned around with tears in her leaking eyes.

"I've increased security. I don't know what else I can do.

It's not like I want to be in danger, but running away and hiding won't win me the election. I can spearhead serious change for our country and get the streets under control again. Surely you agree that's worth the risk?"

"No," she said instantly. "I do not agree, you idiot." She sat on Charlie's bed, reached into her purse, and grabbed a tissue to wipe her runny nose. "I love you. To me, nothing is more important than your safety. You are the reason I wake up in the morning and look forward to bedtime, because it means I'll see you sooner. I love your passion, intelligence, kindness, and so much more. When I saw the broadcast, I burst into tears. I had to rewind it twenty times, double-checking if you were shot or not before they rushed you off."

"Can we please not rehash yesterday for the hundredth time? You know my job is important to me, and I will not give it up. Just trust my security to keep me safe. You know I had my vest on like always."

"If my job had me getting shot at, would you be just fine with it?" Daphne asked.

Charlie paused. "No. I probably wouldn't. It still doesn't change my mind, though. It doesn't change that I love you, or that my job has to be done."

"I know. I just don't like it."

Charlie's phone ringing in his pocket interrupted the heartfelt moment. "Oh crap. One moment, baby." He dug the phone out and looked to see who was calling. "It's your parents."

"They always ruin our moments," she said with a laugh.

He answered it. "Hello, Mr. Kelly. How are you this fine morning?"

"Charles, are you alright? The missus and I were worried after seeing the news last night. Are you hurt after that crazy shot up the protest?"

"Mr. Kelly, I appreciate your concern, but I was unharmed. I've been trying to convince your daughter of the same, but it's not taking." He winked at Daphne, who stuck her tongue out at the remark.

"She's a gentle soul, Charles. She loves you, don't hold it against her. Now I know I told you to call me Barry."

"I would never hold it against her. In fact, I find it adorable." He walked to Daphne and used his free hand to caress the side of her face. "How is Sharon doing?"

"We were both worried sick. We were worried our future son-in-law was harmed."

"I appreciate that, but as I was telling your daughter, I'm perfectly fine. Unfortunately, one of my security personnel was injured. I'm personally funding his treatment so the family can take the proper time to heal."

"You are an upstanding man, Charles. Not only are you pulling our country away from the brink of destruction, but you're one of the bravest souls I know. If I'd been shot at last night, I'm not afraid to say I'd still be quivering in my boots."

"Truthfully, sir, it is a little harrowing, but a leader cannot show fear. That would only embolden my attackers into more action. I'm sure a man of your caliber understands."

"Of course," Barry said. "Oh, hold on. Sharon wants to talk to you."

"I understand, sir." Charlie smirked at Daphne and whispered to her. "Your mom wants to talk."

"Charles!" a sultry female voice came on. "Barry tells me you're alright."

"Yes, ma'am."

"I keep telling Barry you need to get one of those bullet-proof glass wall things that some politicians have for their speeches."

"That's a brilliant idea. In fact, my security is already ahead of you. For every speech ahead, I will use that. I always knew where Daphne gets her intellect from."

"Oh, I don't know about that." Sharon laughed. "We hardly got any sleep, though, Charles. I know poor Daphne didn't either. She called us as soon as it happened, and when you returned, she hung up and I got the impression she was going to rush into your arms as soon as you were out of the car."

"That she did. It was one of the happier moments of my life to embrace her after that horrific event."

"That's sweet of you to admit. Now, when will you accept our dinner offer? We'd love to share a meal with you soon, but we know you're on the campaign trail. How about tonight? You're not going campaigning so soon, are you?"

"How about you two come here?" Charlie asked. "I can cook for you two. I may not look it, but I am an excellent cook. My security chief insists I not leave the property except for official functions or speeches."

"That would work, but I'd hate to force you to cook for us."

"Don't even worry about it. Come over about six, and I'll have a meal prepared for us."

"Alright, it's a plan. Can I talk to Daphne real quick?"

"Sure thing." Charlie handed the phone over to Daphne. "She wants to talk to you."

"I bet she does," Daphne said, taking the phone. "I'll take it on the balcony. Be right back."

"Sure thing."

Daphne pulled the sliding glass door to her side and stepped out into the fresh, warm air. She slid it closed behind her and brought the phone up to her ear. "Yeah, Mom?"

"We are coming over for dinner tonight. I expect you to be in proper attire."

"Mom, this is my home now. I don't have to dress up."

"A man of his caliber wants his future wife to look nice. He's too nice to mention anything, but I know. Now I want you to wear the dress I picked out for you a few weeks ago. I know you still have it."

"Mom, he's not that type of guy at all."

"I will not have you screw this opportunity up for this family because you're lazy. I know you love him, but he is a very important man. We are moving upward in society because of him, and we will not allow you to screw it up for us."

"Gee, thanks, Mom. Here I thought you were concerned about my relationship because you loved me or something and wanted what's best for me."

"Don't be such a drama queen. You know we do. It's just you don't always know what's best for yourself sometimes. If you're with him, you're a high-class lady. That means you're expected to dress formally more than you'd like. He's worth such an inconvenience, wouldn't you say?"

"I don't think he's that kind of man, though."

"Just wear the dress I picked out, would you?"

"Alright fine, Mom, I'll do it. Is my dress all you wished to speak to me about? Or did you wish to kiss up to Charles further?"

"I am simply trying to help you. Men like it when their girlfriend's parents are nice to them. You should thank us. Many men in your father's position would give your boyfriend a hard time. Not him though. He wouldn't sabotage you."

"We both know he wants admission to that golf course

Charles told him about. He's buttering him up to get what he wants."

"Why not?" Sharon asked. "He just wants to play golf with his future son-in-law."

"You all keep saying future in laws. You know he hasn't proposed to me yet, right?"

"We're optimistic. You should try to plan for that. You'll answer yes if he asks, right?"

"I don't know."

"We both know you've imagined it in your head hundreds of times. Don't lie to your mother."

Daphne rested a hand on the railing and gazed out over the seemingly endless green forest. She could hear the chorus of insects and birds in the distance from here. "Maybe I have. I'd say yes."

"Now, be the best girlfriend you can be, for everybody's sake. Alright?"

"Alright, Mom."

"You've been dating for two years already. I'm surprised he hasn't asked you yet."

"He said he had a surprise waiting for me. I doubt that's what he meant, though."

"Then stop talking with me and go find your surprise. You never know. If it is, then you're making him wait. I'll talk to you later. Goodbye."

"Bye." Daphne hung up and took one last lingering look over the pristine landscape before heading inside. She saw Charlie at the door to his bedroom, holding the door open and talking to one of his security.

"Do it now," he said. "Do you understand?"

"Yes, sir. I'll be right back."

Charlie closed the door and turned back to see his girl-friend walking toward him. "Ah, how did that go?" he asked.

"You know how they are. She told me to dress up real pretty tonight for dinner."

"You're dazzling no matter what you wear. Now remember when I said I had a surprise for you? It's on its way right now. When I tell you, I'll need you to close your eyes and let me guide you. Alright?"

"How mysterious," she said with a smile. "Alright then, Mr. Baskins. What do you have up your sleeve?"

"You'll need to wait and see."

Daphne laid a hand on his chest. "Your heart is beating so fast," she said.

A knock at the bedroom door behind Charlie caused him to jump in place. "Alright. Close your eyes and keep them covered. I don't want any peeking, alright?"

"Alright." She closed her eyes and used a hand to cover them. "I'm in your hands."

Charlie reached over to the door and opened it. The same security man from earlier was standing there with a large, decorated cake. Charlie pointed toward the empty desk at the side of the room.

The man nodded silently and brought it over there and placed it down before quietly exiting his employer's room.

"Now let's turn around slowly." He had his hands on her shoulders and guided her. "Stop. Let's step in this direction," he whispered in her ear in a sensual voice. Once she was in front of the desk facing away, he backed away a few steps and reached into his pants pocket to retrieve a box.

"You can open your eyes now." He got to a single knee and extended the box toward her. He opened it to reveal a beautiful engagement ring.

Daphne opened her eyes and looked down at the desk in front of her. A cake sat there on top of it. Ornate flowers decorated the cake along with four words that she'd never forget for her entire life. The icing text read. 'Will you marry me?'. She turned around with tears in her eyes to see Charlie already kneeling with the ring extended toward her.

"How about it?" Charlie looked up at her, waiting for her answer.

She vigorously nodded yes. She barely got the verbal answer out for all the tears, but she managed it. "Yes, I will," she said. Her shaky voice showed tears were imminent, but she forced her words outward.

Charlie rose to his feet and removed the ring from the box. He grabbed her hand and carefully slid the ring onto her ring finger. "You have no idea how long I waited to hear you say those words."

She barely let him finish putting the ring on her before she rushed to him and wrapped her arms around his neck. She put her head into his chest.

He returned the hug. He could feel her heartbeat was giving his a run for its money as their chests touched. "Some female guards guessed the cake writing was a bridge too far. Were they right?"

She shook her head no.

"Good. I never was much of a romantic. This was my attempt at it. Did I do a good job?"

She looked up at him. Their faces were only a few inches apart. "It's a dream come true. It's like something out of romance movies."

"Good, because that's where I got the idea," Charlie said. "Some of them were worried you'd think it was trite. I tried my best."

She cut off any further chatter with a kiss on his lips. A loud alarm blaring suddenly undercut the tender scene, with a great many voices yelling outside.

A female security agent opened the door quietly. "Sir, we

have a-" she cut herself off at seeing the tender scene. She saw him waving her away. "There's something you should know." She had the good sense to leave the pair alone as gunfire erupted outside. Frantic yells accompanied the ominous sound of war outside.

Charlie grabbed her by the shoulders and dragged her away from the windows. He brought her to the opposite side of his bed. "Get down."

"What's happening?"

"You got me. It must be important if she intruded here when I gave strict orders not to be disturbed. Judging by the gunshots, I'm guessing some idiot was on the property."

"You think they're hurt?"

"Maybe. Just stay down, alright? I don't want you anywhere near the windows."

"Don't leave me." Daphne reached out before Charlie could stand up. She had a firm grip on his arm. "Please. You can't leave. Not right now. I beg you."

"Okay. Don't tell your parents or friends about this, please. I'd rather they think it was just a romantic proposal, not one filled with alarms, yelling, and gunshots. It's never a dull moment with me though, huh?"

11

———

Angie watched the footage that she'd captured at the protest again. She stopped the frame on the assassin's face, struggling on the ground with the security guard. "Who is this man? Nobody on the mainstream news is reporting on that. That's highly suspicious. It means they either don't care or they're hiding something at someone's behest. I'm betting on the second. But who?"

She looked over at her laptop sitting a few feet away. "Our first step is to find this assassin's identity. The news did at least give a name. That's a good place to start. Let's see who the hell Erin Jules was."

A quick search yielded a bunch of social media profile links with the name up first. She clicked through, sorting through which links were created after the shooting by attention seekers and which looked legitimate. The process took only a few minutes with her undivided attention to the task.

"Let's do a little virtual investigation, otherwise known as cyber stalking." She scrolled through the legitimate accounts that weren't already preemptively closed by the websites. Most of the websites yielded nothing outside of the ordinary. He hadn't been active for years. Once she'd dug far enough back, though, things started jumping out at her.

"What's this now?" She clicked on a particularly nasty message he'd posted years ago. She read it out loud to herself. "I will never forgive the monsters who took my babies away from me. Some people don't deserve life." She scrolled further down and got further clarification. She saw links he'd posted to a local news station across the country in a small town. It showed a woman and two children caught in a deadly crossfire between a criminal and vigilantes. Ballistics analysis revealed that the bullets that killed the girls were fired by the vigilante.

"Wait. He hates vigilantes, right?" She scrolled back up in a hurry. "Then why shoot up an anti-vigilante demonstration? It makes no sense." She kept up her search, combing through various profiles and timelines. The more she traveled backward, the more pictures of his family she saw. Everything past May 5, 2017, was all about hatred of those who killed his family. "This reads like a textbook example of a fall into extremism. The ending just confuses the shit out of me."

She scrolled up into the current year's time line and saw a message she'd scrolled by in her rush to find anything pertinent. "So, he was interested in politics." She read the entirely capitalized paragraph. "Our world is falling apart. There's only one hope in our government who knows how to fix it. Everybody needs to vote for Charles Baskins."

She leaned back in her chair. "Tell me that's just a coincidence. It's no surprise he'd like his platform after all. Something smells off here. He was a fan of Baskins, but then he tries to kill him? Let me archive this page for future reference and print it out. My intuition tells me this will be deleted in the coming days." She made sure she saved the examples.

Her next virtual stop was Charlie's campaign donation page. She scoured the website until she found the list of donors and the date they sent them. She noticed a huge influx since the incident. Many donations totaled over twenty dollars from people all over the country. "That's a motive if I've ever seen it. I need proof and I have no clue how I could get it."

She leaned backward in the chair and brought her hands up over her eyes. She rubbed them and yawned. "I'd need access to bank records. There's only one way I can imagine that happening. It's not legal either. You know, I helped him. Maybe he owes me. I may as well check if he can. It's my best chance. He's got to have a computer expert or experience, right? Before that, I need to finish and ensure I have my ducks in a perfect row."

"What else should I know that would shed some light on him?" she asked herself. "How about the official story? I haven't kept up to date on what the mainstream's saying about him. Let's see here."

She navigated to one of the major news sites that she'd come to abhor ever since starting her own news company of sorts. It didn't take long to locate the front-page story she searched for and what Charlie himself said.

"It says here that Baskins is claiming the guy was a vigilante nutjob. They're repeating his line as if it's fact, too. Let's check the other websites. Maybe one of them actually did some journalism." She found her way to another mainstream website and checked it, too. "It's the same drivel." She went to another one. "They're all the same message. It's coordinated. Either not one of them did an ounce of research into the guy, or they fell into lockstep with his story for financial and political reasons. I'm betting it's the latter."

She folded up the laptop and took the cord to charge it before stuffing it into a nearby bag she had sitting beside her feet. "I'll see what Justice says about my research. He owes me for helping his little breaking and entering." She threw on a coat and carried everything out to her car...

Later that afternoon...

"We have someone outside," Michael said, bursting into the computer room in a hurry.

"We have a camera watching the front of the house?" Jim asked.

"I'm pulling it up now," Brett said. A small window appeared on the screen showing the feed of a camera they'd placed on the outside.

"I recognize that car," Jim said. "If she's here again, she's found something. I want everyone in their masks."

"Why?" Brett asked. "You're not planning on having her in here, are you?"

"Why not?" Jim asked. He pointed toward the small picture. He saw she had a laptop tucked under her arm. "She's got something to show us. It could be the break we're looking for."

"She's a reporter, not a scout. Whatever she has there probably relates to the protest," Brett said. "It's not our concern."

"I beg to differ," Jim said. "She's found evidence that we want, or she wouldn't show up."

"If she's inside, I want her supervised at all times and never left alone."

"I'll do that," Jim said. "Don't worry about it. I'll tell

Ashley to mask up. You two should too if you don't wish her to know your identity. Have no personally identifiable things on your person. She's quick and perceptive, trust me." He left without further word and moved to Ashley's room. He knocked on it and opened without waiting for an answer.

"Hey!" Ashley said, texting on her phone. "I could've been changing."

"Mask up. We have a familiar visitor. Who are you messaging, anyway?"

"Skye. She's pissed, you know."

"I imagine she is." Jim entered her bedroom and dragged her up and out of bed. "Now get ready. I don't want her seeing your face."

The sound of the place's doorbell echoed in the background. "Get ready, and come downstairs," he said, pointing at her as he backpedaled toward the door. "That's an order."

Jim shut the door behind him and rushed down the stairs. He reached into his pocket and put his own mask on while he stood beside the door. He ensured it was firmly in place before he opened the door.

"I was beginning to wonder if you'd hide inside, away from poor old me," Angie said.

"You caught us by surprise. I'm not complaining, but why are you here?"

"I found intel I needed your help with, or at least, you should know."

Jim looked over his shoulder at Ashley hurrying down the stairs in her mask. Brett wasn't far behind. He was riding the chair down the stairs with Michael behind him, taking up the rear.

"I think we're heading to the computer room, boys and

girls. Don't relocate downstairs," Jim said, looking down at the device in Angie's grasp.

"Thanks for telling me." Brett stopped the automatic chair and redirected it to go upstairs again.

"I just got down here," Ashley said.

"Don't complain," Jim said. He turned back to Angie. "Well, don't just stand there. Come on in. Touch nothing inside, don't go wandering off by yourself, and don't publish anything inside. You agree to that, or you don't enter. It's to protect everyone in here. Do you agree?"

"You always ask that. I'm not going to write about anything inside. I came to ask for your help, not to piss you off."

"Alright. Enter then." Jim stepped to the side and let her enter. "It's up the stairs. Follow me." He closed the door behind her and led her to the computer room upstairs, keeping an eye on her as they walked.

"You own this place?" she asked as they climbed the nearby stairs.

"That falls under questions you don't need to discover the answer to, doesn't it?"

"I'm sorry. I'm an investigative journalist. It just comes naturally. I promise I'll be good."

"It's in here," Jim said, showing her the door. Muffled voices were heard behind the door, but it was impossible to tell the words spoken. He opened the door and held it open for her. "After you."

"I don't know who you are, miss, but understand if you mention a word about any of this, you'll regret it," Brett said.

"Easy," Jim said. "I've given her the security rundown. She won't publish or tell a soul about anything, right?"

"I won't. Masked Justice here saved my life. I owe him my life, and I'd never inconvenience him."

"I don't trust you yet, but fine," Brett said.

"Try not to mind him. He's a bit of a hardass." Jim led her toward the line of computers. "Take a seat and let's start. To what do we owe the pleasure of your company this afternoon?"

"I've been digging into the shooting that took place at the infamous anti-vigilante rally. There are quite a few inconsistencies. I'm convinced there's some foul play going on."

"We are not the police," Michael said.

"True. The problem is, they're satisfied to toe the official story according to their official reports. They're not interested in the truth either. Now, I looked up the attacker."

"I believe the official story is that he was some whack job vigilante that gives us all a bad name, yes?" Ashley asked. "What's so odd about that?"

"What's odd is this," Angie pulled up the social media feeds she'd looked at earlier and showed the rest of the group. "See? He was an ardent Baskins' supporter - a genuine believer. He was trying to convince everyone to vote for him to save this country from vigilantes. Why would he shoot up the rally of a cause he believes in?"

"You're thinking it was a false flag operation?" Michael asked.

"You're quick," Angie said. "Then there's this." She went further back, only to find the relevant messages already deleted since she'd seen them before. "Wow, they move fast. Not to worry." She reached down to the bag she'd placed beside the chair. She pulled out her laptop. "I archived the messages and saved them, just in case they tried to erase it."

"What did they delete now?" Brett asked.

"The messages that showed that his family was killed by vigilantes. To be specific, I'm talking about his wife and two daughters. Here we go." She logged into her laptop and got to the folder she saved the screenshots in. "Look at this."

The others grouped around her chair and looked over her shoulder at the heartbroken man's messages.

"He must have hated vigilantes with a burning passion if they shot his family during a shootout," Ashley said. "Why would he shoot up the protest? It makes no sense."

"That's what I'm saying. Now look at this." She went back to the desktop and went to Charlie's political donation site where it showed all the donations his campaign had received since last night.

"That's a huge spike in donations after the shooting," Michael said, eyes widening.

"You think Baskins is involved," Brett said. It wasn't a question, but a statement.

"I do. There's just one problem. I have no proof."

"That's why you approached us," the wheelchair bound man said. "What do you expect us to do?"

"I need bank records. I thought maybe one of you was a computer hacker extraordinaire of something."

"Ha," Brett laughed. "You expect me to hack two different banks and compare them to see if he paid this guy off?"

"It was my hope."

"Can you do it?" Jim asked.

"Of course I could," Brett said. "It would take hours to set up, though. I'd need help with it, so you would have to help." He reached up and grabbed Michael's arm. "It's irrelevant anyway. We know what awaits Mr. Baskins. Does his paying this poor sap off truly matter that much?"

"For public image, it sure might," Michael said. "If we had proof of his crimes, it'd go down a lot easier for the public."

"It'd also bolster the coalition's support in the upheaval following you know what," Jim said.

"Seriously?" Brett asked. "You think that'd matter to the public?"

"Do it," Jim said. "Make the necessary preparations."

"I don't even know where the hell Baskins keeps his money. This guy, it wouldn't be too difficult. I'd just have to find his hometown and find which bank was his. Baskins could have his money offshore. If he's a self-respecting politician, he's already obfuscated his money to people looking."

"I can help with that," Angie said. "I know which bank Mr. Baskins uses for his personal accounts."

"We don't even know if he used his personal money or if he used political donations to pay him off."

"People get investigated every year for misusing campaign funds," Michael said. "He'd avoid the headache and use his own. I'd bet anything."

"How do you even know where he keeps his money, Ms. Journalist?" Brett asked.

"You don't keep up with the news much, do you?" Angie asked. "He's been donating to various causes for the past few months. It's a matter of public record. There may have been paparazzi that followed him to his bank on the days before those donations cleared, and I might know one personally."

"You think they'd tell you?"

"I paid them already for the information before I rushed here. I should have an answer soon. For them, it's all about the money. If you pay, you get the story or information. They have few scruples."

"Not like you," Brett said, light sarcasm evident in his voice. "You're as honest as the blasted day is long."

"I realize few people trust so-called journalists nowadays. I'm just tracking the story from beginning to end. People deserve to know the truth."

"Uh huh," Brett said, still not sounding like he believed her. "Well, what's the verdict? You know where he keeps his money domestically?"

She pulled out her phone and checked to see if she had any messages. "As a matter of fact, I do," she said with an enormous smile. "He sent it while I was driving with a little smiley emoji there. See? He's happy to do business. Here's where he keeps his money." She handed over the phone to Brett. "Can you find out or not?"

Jim, Michael, Ashley, and Angie all looked at the masked Brett. He wheeled himself over to the computer he'd claimed as his own.

"Fine, dammit. Give me a few hours. Breaking into a bank isn't something that happens quickly. I need the proper security preparations so they don't trace it here. Then we'd all be fucked, including little Ms. Investigative Journalist here. I assume you'll want to be present when we find the answer to your little hunch?"

"It'd be nice," she said.

"Then you need a chaperone to ensure you don't cause trouble," Brett said.

"I can escort her around," Jim said.

"Don't show her anything sensitive. You know one room I'm talking about, I hope. Nothing inside interests an honest journalist."

"Come everybody, let's not slow his progress," Jim said. "Blind, Angie, you're with me. Let's allow our resident techies to work without distractions."

Ashley and Angie got up and let Michael sit down beside Brett.

Ashley's phone rumbled in her pocket.

"Another message?" Jim asked. "Is this message from the same recipient?"

"Who else?" Ashley asked, peeking at the phone while making sure Angie didn't notice.

"I don't mean to cause trouble by coming here, but I have a bad feeling about Mr. Baskins," Angie said. "You know what I think? I think he paid off that poor man to essentially cause his own death. He knew that a shooting in a public place on national television would aid his political career, and it did."

"That's a hefty accusation," Jim said as Ashley fiddled about on her phone. "It would fit his MO, though, at least if you ask me. He doesn't care if innocents are killed if it advances his agenda. I believe you're correct, but I have no proof yet. You don't mind doing this?"

"Why would I?" Brett asked. "I assume our Pulitzer seeking journalist here is going to cause a mess of bad publicity for our dear friend."

"It's a real shame," Ashley said.

"We'll let you all know when we're ready. Go somewhere else." Brett shooed the rest of the group toward the door. "We need to concentrate. Don't allow her where she doesn't need to visit. The world doesn't need to hear about our hideout in intricate detail."

"I already told you I wouldn't so much as type anything I see inside," Angie said. "I won't cause trouble, whoever you are."

"Just get lost and allow us to help you."

"Come on." Jim guided Angie toward the door. "I need to talk to you in private."

"Fine, I'll just go to my room then," Ashley said. She pulled out her phone and continued texting.

The three left the room. Ashley turned and abandoned

the pair to enjoy their alone time. She closed and locked the door behind her and released a deep breath. She checked the phone to see a familiar number and avatar. Her last message she had received read 'I'm here. The camping trip is fantastic.' The message had a picture attached of Skye's latest selfie out in some woods and winking at the camera.

Jim would blow a gasket if he knew she was outside, Ashley thought. *Hell, I knew she wouldn't stay back there. I hate to imagine her outside last night in a tent and sleeping bag.*

The next message had a simple question. "When are you heading out next?"

She typed back a reply with her thumbs and spoke to herself quietly. "I'll tell you later. We're still deciding when we'll head out."

A chirping indicated she'd received another message from her friend. "You will tell me before you depart, right?"

"Of course."

A few hours later...

"It's already four," Ashley said, whining to the group of two. She saw Angie staring at Jim while he stared off into the distance, pleasantly unaware of the attention he was receiving. "Ms. Summers, are you truly intent on publishing a story about our findings?"

"Not so much accusing him of anything, but I'll start asking questions he doesn't want answered."

"It'd be dangerous," Ashley said. She brushed some stray hair out of her eyes. "You know he'd come after you, right?"

"He's on the campaign trail," Angie said, as it was the most obvious answer. "What's he going to do? Send a hitman after me and totally tank his career if it's ever found out?"

"Hitman? I'd imagine not," Jim said, turning to face her. "He wouldn't want to have a paper trail or witnesses to his deed. He'd do it himself."

"Charles Baskins, the politician?" Angie couldn't stop a giggle. "He doesn't look the type."

"Looks are often deceiving, Ms. Summers," Jim said, calm as can be. "You should understand that better than anyone."

"Speaking of looks," Ashley reached up and messed with the mask over her mouth and nose. "Why don't you have yours on?"

"She already knows what I look like and who I am, but not you. At least I hope she hasn't put it together." He met the journalist's gaze. "Have you?"

"No, but I gather you're important to each other." Angie looked between Ashley and then to Jim. "Are you family?"

"It's irrelevant. We are no relation, technically speaking."

"He's the closest thing I've had to a father, though I would never have admitted it years ago," Ashley said. Her sudden admission earned Jim's surprised look. "I used to bitch at him for trying to be my dad and trying to keep me safe, but now he's the one that needs my help."

"I don't need your help with this mission. You insisted on going."

Rapid footsteps erupted from the adjoining room housing the stairs. Michael reached the bottom and called out. "We found it!"

"Found what?" Angie asked as she got up.

"You'd all better see," Michael said. "I couldn't believe it when I saw it."

Jim and Ashley weren't far behind Angie as she nearly

pushed poor Michael forward in her haste to get her story that much quicker.

They finally got into the computer lab to see Brett still in front of his workstation. He didn't turn to address them. "I've still got it," he said. "I told you I am as skilled as Jason - better in some digital areas."

"Yes, you're very skilled," Jim said. "What did we find out?" He sat down beside his mentor.

"I'm putting it on the screens now, so take a seat, folks, and enjoy access to highly illegal bank accounts of a government official. For the record, even if you did act like an idiot and published this, you'd be in a prison alongside us for employing our aid."

"The point is moot anyway, you stubborn fool," Angie said, "since I said I wasn't going to do that."

"You get used to him," Ashley said.

"Hopefully she won't," Brett said. "I don't like news types. We don't get along. They always want to find more than they deserve. It gets them or you in trouble. No offense, Ms. Summers."

"That attitude isn't uncommon from souls that house stories that need revealed. Now stop stalling already." Angie bounced in her seat.

"Keep your panties on," Brett said with a cocky grin. "Here." He grabbed the mouse and did his work. "I'm even so nice that I prepared a nice little photo spread for you all before we called you. Here." He clicked.

A picture of two bank accounts and varying amounts were placed side by side. Names on the accounts were made visible as text added by Brett. "Take a detailed inspection."

The group leaned forward. They stared at the numbers for four minutes before Ashley spoke up first. "All I notice is a bunch of numbers."

"No kidding," Brett said. "What about them? Look harder. Don't let your boyfriend down. He told me he likes smart women. Maybe Ms. Summers is more his type."

"Sir, I don't remember..." Michael was cut off.

"Quiet," Brett said.

"There are two matching amounts here." Angie took the mouse and moved the cursor between the two sizable matching amounts on both sides of the screen.

"Right, but there's more." Brett clicked, and the pictures changed. "The payments have occurred every month until last month. He'd been paying the guy in increments of five thousand dollars a month for the past two years. I guess he figured smaller transactions and continued support would instill loyalty in the mentally frail victim. It seems his plan worked to bloody perfection, too."

"It looks like once the money hit our beneficiary's account, it was promptly sent off to another," Ashley said.

"So she possesses some tech knowledge," Brett said. "Color me impressed. Yes, correct. He was sending it off to his brother. I have no clue what he told the man, but if I had to guess by the social media posts of the family, I'm assuming it's for his niece's education. They seem to have a strong uncle and niece relationship. I think it was his closest relative that he still had remaining."

"This makes me sick to my stomach," Angie said, still reading the confirmation of her suspicions. "Combined with all I discovered, this means he had this tragedy planned for years. He wanted someone to die - to essentially be a martyr to solidify his power grab."

"He's just running for reelection," Ashley shrugged. "What's so big about this?"

"You're thinking short term," Angie said. "He's gained tremendous political clout, popularity with the people, and his own party. A presidential run wouldn't surprise me in six years. Think about it."

"The hero who rid America of blood thirsty vigilantes was shot at, but still showed up afterward like an authentic hero," Brett said. "It's a perfect plan to gather sympathy and smear the other side in one go. Not to mention he'd have untold power if he won. God help us all if that happens."

"None of this surprises me," Jim said. "You have your confirmation, Ms. Summers. Do with it what you will, but exercise caution. Your foe is heartless and won't hesitate to exercise deadly force."

"We should give her a number to call," Brett said.

"Worried about me?"

"Fine, don't give her a number," Brett said just as quickly.

Jim reached down under the desk and pulled out a small bag. He reached inside and grabbed a cell phone. "Someone grab me a piece of tape, please."

Michael stood and rushed across the room to fetch the tape.

Jim placed the piece of adhesive on the back of the cell phone and then recorded his number. He gave her the phone. "Call the number from this phone only if you require help. You got it? We'll come running."

"That's assuming we're not in the middle of an operation," Brett said.

"You really think he'll come for me?" Angie asked.

"You make a big enough stink for him, and he'll want it stopped," Jim said. "I have no doubt in my mind. Now keep that phone on your person."

"Odds are he'll ambush you before you realize what's happening, but make the kid feel calmer and take it, alright?" Brett asked.

"Aren't you a ray of hope?" Angie asked. She filed away the phone and stood up. "Ladies and gentlemen, I have an article to write that raises questions about dear old Mr. Baskins. If you'll excuse me."

"You really don't care, do you?" Ashley asked.

"The citizens deserve to understand who they're voting for," Angie said, now standing up. She grabbed her laptop and purse. "I bid you farewell."

"I'll escort you out. Someone we know would have an aneurysm if I let you wander around unattended," Jim said. He got up and followed her out the door into the second-floor hallway.

"I don't think your friend likes me too much."

"He doesn't like many people when he first meets them. He grows on you, especially when he sacrifices his mobility for your mother's life."

"That was him?" Angie stopped mid-stairwell and faced Jim with wide eyes. "That jackass was the guy?"

"He was the guy. You can't judge a book by its cover or its first impression."

"Apparently not." Angie continued down the stairs. She reached the bottom and opened the front door. "I'll keep this number handy then."

"You think you can make it go viral, whatever you're going to write?" Jim asked.

"It wouldn't be the first instance my articles have reached the mainstream news and trended. I aim for total visibility tonight. Baskins won't enjoy my plans. He won't want people asking why a loyal supporter of his on social media shot up the protest and then had their social media pages deleted before anyone noticed. He won't want anyone asking about why the guy did what he did and digging into it."

"Then he'll quiet it however he can," Jim said. "Where are you staying in DC?"

"Mr. Benning, are you worried about me?"

"Maybe I am. One person close to me is in jail already because of me. I don't want another dead."

"Sorry to burst your bubble, but we all make our choices. Thus, we all take responsibility. It's not all on your shoulders, hero. To answer your question, I'm staying at a hotel, though it is murder on my pocketbook, staying there very long."

"Would you want to stay here?"

"I couldn't do that. Aren't you worried about my digital footprint drawing attention here?"

"We both know that manipulating digital traces is possible, and we have the expertise."

"You clear that with your friend up there? He seems to be the one in charge here."

"I don't have to clear it with him. I'm the boss here, since I'm the one sacrificing everything at the end of this. If they don't like it, then they can bitch to me about it. It won't change my mind about a friend staying over if she's in danger."

"You consider me a friend?"

"Obviously I do. You know my name, where I live, and what I do. You haven't said a word about it to the public. That makes you a friend where I'm from. A real friend knows how to keep a secret and when to shout news from the proverbial rooftop. From where I'm sitting, you fit that description to a tee."

"I doubt your buddies in there want to wear a mask the whole time they're here on my account, though."

"You can stay in your room if you'd like. We won't be here too much longer - hopefully anyway. Then you can return home or to your hotel if you're not done yet. I have a sneaking suspicion that when I'm done, you won't have much left to report on."

"I'm a little afraid to ask what that means. Fine, if you don't think it'd cause trouble, I'd love to have built in security."

"You need to fetch your belongings from the hotel?" Jim asked.

"No. The possessions worth a damn are my laptop and my information, both of which are inside my purse."

"Apparently, she doesn't view clothes as important. That's interesting and revealing," Brett said with humorous sarcasm before his voice turned serious. "How did I know you'd offer?"

Both turned to view Brett and Ashley in the open doorway of the mansion.

"If you're going to stay, I'll need to brief you on the seriousness of the situation. You'd be sworn to more than mere secrecy. You'd also be swearing on your life, as well as your family's."

"Alright then," Angie said.

"Then get inside and prepare to listen," Brett said.

12

———

"**M**r. Baskins," Mr. Trevelyan said. The old politician straightened his tie as he spoke. "Do you mind explaining this disturbing news?"

"Yes," Ms. Leary said. The young woman had a sour look on her otherwise cute face. "People aren't buying the story we had the media print. Why is that?"

"Independent journalists aren't taken seriously," Charlie said, sitting at the enormous table everyone sat around. He gazed at his coworkers. "The media narrative is alive and well. Don't panic. She's a social media influencer, that's all."

"A social media influencer who claims to be an investigative journalist," Mr. Trevelyan said. "She has quite a large following now. My grandson showed me just how much pull she has. Folks are talking about the man who shot up the protest you attended."

"Let them talk. It's rumors. That's all they have. There are stories around every single politician in this room, I might add."

"True Mr. Baskins," Mr. Trevelyan said. He reached up and rubbed his clean-shaven face. "There's just one difference. You are the face of our party. That has its advantages and disadvantages. You are carrying the banner, so to speak, for us. If your credibility is questioned, then ours is too. That's the negative of our strategy. You need to fix this."

"I can't just neutralize her," Charlie said. "That'd look even worse."

"It couldn't look much worse," Mr. Benjamin from Charlie's right said. "People are questioning it more deeply than you realize. Some even theorize that you had him paid off to sacrifice himself for political clout. If that were proved, that's the kind of rumor that ruins a man's political career and lands him in prison and any connections wouldn't mean shit."

"You're threatening to throw the election and our plans down the drain over one little journalist asking questions?" Charlie asked, raising his voice. "Seriously? She's one woman. She has no proof of anything. Let this pass and social media will fixate on the next big thing within three days."

"Don't get so uppity, Mr. Baskins," Mr. Trevelyan said. "We're not abandoning you, merely stating that this is unacceptable. We need this narrative cut off at the source."

"Do you mean what I think you do?" Charlie asked.

"You know what I mean," Mr. Trevelyan said. "Don't act dumb. It doesn't suit you. We're all friends here, hand selected to sit at this table because of our loyalty. We wish to help, but how can we? If we weigh in publicly and further incidents release, then our own reputations are in the gutter."

"Seems to me if I'm carrying the banner, then I should get some support," Charlie said.

"If I remember correctly, you were given help," Ms. Leary said. "Hans springs to mind. Whatever happened to him? He's fallen off the face of the Earth. No one's heard from him. Did he die on whatever job you sent him on? Rumors fly around, Mr. Baskins. What did you send him to do?"

"I've been meaning to ask just that," Trevelyan said.

"Masked Justice killed him," Charlie said after a pregnant pause.

"Masked Justice?" the other occupants at the table asked.

"You've been battling with Masked Justice this whole time? What on Earth for?" Mr. Trevelyan asked.

"He knows who I am and what I do," Charlie said.

"God dammit, Baskins," Trevelyan said. "You never mentioned this before!"

"You'd never have given me said banner if I told you. He can't tell anyone about it unless he wants to go to prison, so I thought the best course was to have him eliminated. How was I to guess Hans would get himself killed?"

"Now he's after you," Ms. Leary said. "Is that right? Is that why you had an intruder?"

"Possibly," Charlie said.

"Damn it all," Mr. Trevelyan said. "You have an assassin vigilante chasing you, and you're dealing with that?"

"I can handle the reporter and Masked Justice," Charlie said, as he reassured the council. "I taught him how to fight. Thus, I can end him just as easily."

"You'd better," Mr. Trevelyan said. "We cannot afford you getting killed. It'd set our party back two decades or more if you fall."

"Then help me."

"Then we risk ourselves," Mr. Benjamin said.

"You're at risk either way," Charlie said. "It's a matter of how much you want to win. If you don't help me, you're risking your political career being set back two decades. If you help, you're risking your current position for a greater chance at said power."

"We will not be helping anymore," Mr. Trevelyan said. "We've given you support and assassins for your secret little missions. Look what it's accomplished - less than nothing. We've lost good men in your secret war with Masked Justice. If you fall, we will be crippled, but we won't be in prison awaiting trial. No, Mr. Baskins, you are on your own with this one. You're a man of means. I have faith you'll complete your last task."

"What task is that?"

"Don't be purposely dense," Ms. Leary said. "It doesn't suit you."

"You are to kill this Masked Justice when he tries to take your life," Mr. Trevelyan said. "God knows you have enough security after your last move."

"What about the journalist?"

"You are to shut her up," Mr. Trevelyan said. "How you go about it is at your discretion. Just don't use official personnel. It's on you to keep this quiet."

"I understand. Any further restrictions before I ride to war?"

"Don't be an overdramatic ass," Mr. Benjamin said. "Your war chest is overflowing."

"We can get you a list of independent contractors to help your little silencing," Mr. Trevelyan said. "That's as far as we go. No more official PHR members for you. Inform them only what they need to understand for the job. Hell, don't let them know who you are. They work off anonymous clients and payments for a living. They know if we gave their name away, the client is trustworthy enough."

"So I am getting operatives?"

"You're getting one," Mr. Trevelyan said. "That should be

sufficient for a journalist. We realize you sending one of your own after her would look problematic, shall we say? We're sparing you that pitfall at least."

"You started this war with Masked Justice," Mr. Benjamin said.

"You'll be the one to finish it," Mr. Trevelyan finished the thought.

"Congratulations on your engagement," Ms. Leary said and a grin.

"Gee, thanks."

"Don't complain," Mr. Trevelyan said. "You want to be the big leader, you do the shit jobs. You knew that when you started. Maybe next time, you'll bring us into the loop when you start a war with the folk hero of the coalition. This war is both political and physical."

"So, the winner of the fight determines the fate of our nation. Is that what you're saying?"

"I hope you've kept up with physical training," Mr. Trevelyan said, "for all our sakes. If I were you, I'd let my men deal with him."

"I aim to have him dead before he ever approaches me. He's always been slippery though, so I'll be prepared, regardless. I can't cut corners or assume anything with Masked Justice."

"You're going to keep campaigning?" Mr. Benjamin asked. "I can't imagine trying to stay on the lookout for him while speaking."

"I can't take a break. We've built too much momentum for me to stop and campaign from my basement. It'd also send the wrong message to the people."

"They value strength and bravery," Mr. Trevelyan said. "You're right. You'd look weak hiding right after the assassination attempt. It looks like you've painted yourself into quite the corner here, Mr. Baskins. I know you're displeased at hearing this, but I must make our position clear here. You wanted to be our next president, and we can accommodate those desires."

Ms. Leary spoke up next. "There's just one thing. If you lose or die, we may lose politics for the next decade or two, but we'll keep our jobs and our lifestyle."

"The ambitious rise to stardom was always going to be rife with deadly risks, friend," Mr. Benjamin said with a toothy grin. "If you win, though, we only stand to profit. We do sincerely hope for your victory."

"Not enough to help me though."

"Risks are a part of success. Show us you can keep yourself alive and popular enough to win. We've sunk enough into this campaign of yours already. We have faith in you."

"I'm sure you do." Charlie's voice was even, but clearly annoyed.

"Congratulations on your impending marriage," Mr. Trevelyan said as he stood up. He cleared his throat. "I hear your bride to be is lovely. I'm jealous. Don't make her a widow already."

"It'd be an outright tragedy," Mr. Benjamin said as he and Ms. Leary stood from their chairs. "Is she a redhead, by chance?"

"Why do you care?" Ms. Leary asked with a giggle. "You never were the classy sort."

"Just wondering in case."

"Your concern is touching," Charlie said.

"Come, ladies and gentlemen," Mr. Trevelyan said. "Our friend has some issues he needs to work on. Let's hope he manages."

Charlie got up and followed them out of the building

before making a beeline for his car. He got in and saw Henry already there with a drink ready for him.

"What did they say?" Henry asked.

"I'm on my own. They're covering their own asses." Charlie raised his voice so the driver could hear. "Take us home." He turned back to Henry. "It seems you'll finally have reason to call yourself an operative after all."

"Right away, sir," the driver said.

The vehicle started, and they waited for the other politicians' vehicles to leave first.

"They aren't happy I was going after Masked Justice for one. As a result, they won't allow me access to the PHR's manpower. It's literally do or die for me now. Oh yes. I almost forgot. They want a certain journalist taken care of quietly. It must look like an accident. A gas leak or something or other."

"I'll take care of it tonight, sir," Henry said.

"I'll oversee your preparation. Be in my basement at eight tonight. That's an order."

"Understood."

After dinner...

Charlie escorted Daphne's parents to the door with a beaming smile. "It's always a pleasure to have my future parents-in-law over. You should visit more often."

"I'm so happy you decided to help me with my newest business venture," the stout man said. "I owe you."

"No, sir. You gave me your daughter, and that's worth all the money in the world. I'll see if I can help you get that business set up correctly. Be on the lookout for my accountant to call. Alright?"

"You indulge my Klein far too much," the wife said.

"Grandma Lana would be proud to know her memory will live on."

"Don't mind Ophelia," Klein said.

"I'm happy to help." Charlie wrapped an arm around Daphne's shoulder at his side.

"We'll get out of your hair now. Don't you two do anything we wouldn't," Ophelia said. "Try to help Mr. Baskins relax, dear. It's good training for being his wife."

"Thanks for the advice, Mother." Daphne watched as her parents left the house.

Charlie moved forward to close the door behind them. "And then there were two remaining," he said after closing the front door firmly.

"What are your plans for tonight?" Daphne asked. "Don't tell me you're working again tonight. I thought for once I'd follow my mother's suggestion and help you relax."

"That sounds wonderful, babe, but I have important work to do tonight, sweet pea."

"Oh, come on," she said while grabbing his hands in her own. "I know you are stressed today. We both know you're less productive when you're wound up. Let your future wife do her job and help her partner relax, even if he is too stubborn of a fool to want it."

"Alright, but I have a meeting at eight that I cannot be late to. After that I'll let you help me relax. Not a moment before, deal?"

"Deal." She wrapped him in a hug. "I'll be up in the bedroom when you're ready. It's almost eight now. I'd like to head home by midnight. I don't want to obstruct, but understand I'm always here."

"What brought this up?"

"You just seem like you're hiding something here."

"Nonsense," Charlie said, trying to show his best smile. "I'm just a little shaken at getting shot at."

"I don't know that I totally believe that, but since today is a happy day, I'll let it drop for now. Let's not argue on the day we were engaged. Just know that I'm keeping an eye on you, buster."

"I'd rather your eyes be nowhere else, beautiful." Charlie stole a quick kiss. "Now I have a meeting to attend before I head upstairs. What am I looking forward to?"

"A candlelit massage with relaxing music. How does that sound? I've been getting better."

"That you have. Will there be a happy ending?"

"You want there to be one? I might consider it if you don't take too awfully long. A girl doesn't like to feel neglected, Mr. Baskins. What was that saying my father always said? A happy wife equals a happy life. You'll learn that in time." She gave him one more kiss on the cheek before backing off and heading toward the stairs leading upstairs. "Hurry on up." She gave him a seductive wink and a small wave before she turned and climbed.

Charlie watched her butt as she climbed the stairs until she stopped. He raised his eye level to see her looking back at him.

"Looking at something?"

"Yeah. You have a great ass."

She shook her head and laughed. "Don't just stand there, big guy," she said before continuing her journey upstairs. "You have a meeting that precedes your fiancé. It must be important enough to make her wait."

Charlie watched her disappear upstairs before he muttered to himself. "It sure is." He shook himself out of the lascivious fantasies that wormed their way into his mind's eye and headed for the basement door in the kitchen.

Opening it, he could see Henry already downstairs waiting for him. He closed the door and cleared his throat. "It's good to see you're prompt. My guests didn't see you or your car, did they?"

"I parked around the back. They didn't see me. I have interesting news, sir."

"What's that?" Charlie got to the bottom of the stairs and adjusted his wrist cuff links. "Did our dear independent journalist end up killing herself?"

"Not quite," Henry said. "I've used the livestream footage she had at your rally. During the chaos, there were two frames that showed her license plate number clearly. I froze the frame and wrote it down."

"Good. Now where is she staying? I know she doesn't live around here. She lives near Denver, where Jim does. Come to think of it, you don't think she's working with him, do you?"

"There's a solid possibility, sir," Henry pointed over toward the one desktop in the basement that was already on. "I tracked where the computer in the vehicle with this license plate is. It's in the middle of the nearby forest, staying at a multiple story house, with at least four bedrooms."

"You think that's where Jim's staying?"

"Possibly. If I were the coalition, I'd want my wildcard operative to have privacy to do whatever they want. That location fits the bill perfectly."

"You also think Angie Summers is staying there, of all places? That'd be crazy, even for Jim's dumb ass. She's a journalist. He wouldn't want her getting too cozy with them. He'd be scared shitless about Ashley being uncovered, even if he's not worried for himself."

"Unless she's helping them and they want to keep her

safe. I don't think it's a coincidence that she's shacking up with them the day her viral story about the guy who died goes live all over the internet. She's scared, by my estimation."

"It's not out of the realm of possibility that they're working together." Charlie snapped his fingers. "Didn't security mention that she visited just before they found the intruder on our premises this morning?"

"I'll pull up the security footage, but I believe you're correct, sir," Henry started working, and a few moments later the color footage showed the front gate with a time-stamp on the bottom right, showing it occurred at ten a.m. that morning. "Here it is."

Charlie watched the young journalist approach the gate and engage the nearby guard in conversation. In the latter part of the conversation, he noticed her looking past the guards. "There," he said, pointing at the screen. "She saw something behind him. I'm willing to bet our intruder was already on the property by this time."

"This was approximately five minutes before the intruder was spotted. It would match time wise. I'll just tell you now, sir, I don't think I can take Masked Justice if push comes to shove tonight."

"Then you won't do that. It needs to appear like an accident, not a murder. Shooting up the address or slicing them open, while satisfying, would raise too many questions I don't want to answer. If someone were to add something to their ventilation, and they were to die in their sleep, people might assume it was foul play, but they'd never be able to prove a damned thing."

"That should be easy enough. I'd park a few miles away, walk through the woods carrying the solution, and then put it inside their air conditioner. I'd sit there until it's empty and then pack up to leave. They'd never realize I was there."

"That's the plan," Charlie said. "For safety's sake, though, I want you wearing a mask, a vest, and I want you armed. You never know what surprises you might run into. If we're lucky, we can deal with both problems without firing a single shot or swinging a blade. They normally stay up late to do their operations. Who knows if they have anything planned for tonight? You'll act at three a.m. or later to ensure they're asleep."

"That's not a problem. I'll grab a nap before I head out. You've still got the sleeping bag down here somewhere, I hope."

"Of course. Before you head off to dreamland, let's finalize the details. Do we have a map of their property?"

"Just a satellite top-down image from the search engine," Henry said, pulling it up. "Here it is."

"Alright," Charlie leaned down and pointed at the screen. "You'll approach through this vector here." He traced his finger through the nearby forest and circled around the back of the villa. "Can we zoom in to see where their AC's positioned?"

"That's as far as zoom goes, sir," Henry said. "It shouldn't take long to find."

"You think they planted cameras around the place? I do. If they're smart, they've hooked it up to an alarm to wake them. That means you'll need to disable the one camera before you approach it. If they're asleep, they won't notice, and it won't set it off. That'd be child's play, assuming I'm in range of their network. I'd rather not see you take a dirt nap because of my laziness. It's so hard to find good help these days."

"I can do this, sir. It should be easy."

"That's the same sentiment that Hans claimed," Charlie said. "Observe what happened to him when he went to kill Masked Justice. Be careful out there, buddy. You're my right-hand man. I'd normally never send you, but I don't have a choice here."

"I swore service to you years ago, sir. If I'm honest, being an aide has been boring. I'm not complaining about getting a little hands on, especially if it secures us a win."

"Bravery was never your issue, nor skill for that matter. Just don't be overconfident. Keep your head on a swivel. Something about this doesn't seem right. It's too easy."

"You think it's a trap?"

"He knows my security is tightened up. It'd be suicide to try to get in now, and he knows it. This reeks as a setup, but I cannot afford to let that woman keep stirring the pot. In fact, I think I'll go with you tonight and take care of the technical side, so I know you're safe."

"If you insist, sir. I assure you I'll be fine by myself, though."

"I know, but indulge me, won't you?"

"As you wish."

That night after three am...

A couple of security still sat inside the car alongside Charlie. He had a laptop on his lap and a headset on that held a microphone in front of his mouth. "I'm barely getting a signal, but it's strong enough to gain access to their camera network. What's your position?"

Henry was out in the forest, trudging as quietly through the underbrush as he could manage with the jug of chemicals and hoses he carried in the backpack slung over his shoulders. "I'm almost in position. I've arrived at the house from what I gather through this overgrown foliage. Give me another five minutes, and I'll be ready."

"Roger that," Charlie said. "I'm not disabling it until you're ready. In case anyone's still up and watching, I'd rather give you as much time as possible."

"No one's up from what I can tell, sir." Henry inspected the multi-story villa and saw no lights on anywhere. "There are no lights on inside and no noise."

"Keep a watchful eye out in the forest, too. The last thing we need is for a killer animal to tear you to bloody pieces before you complete the mission."

"There are relatively few man eaters around, sir, but I'll take the advice to heart." Henry stepped over a larger log and managed to not stumble in the dark. It was almost pitch black under the tree cover, so he had to go one step at a time and feel out his next step before he committed.

Time passed in silence as Henry circled around the building. He finally arrived in position and hid behind a suitably large tree while peering through his binoculars. "I'm in position and see the air conditioning unit. It should be easy to feed the chemicals into it. This model has easy access."

"Good. Stand by and go on my signal. They've updated their systems. It's not a problem, it's just taking a little longer. I suppose Brett has had plenty of time to reinforce this since his last incident. What else is he going to do, walk?" Charlie chuckled to himself as he worked.

Henry heard a twig snap behind him. He looked in that direction but saw nothing but trees and wilderness. He shook his head and returned his attention to his objective.

"Go now," Charlie said.

Henry didn't need to be told twice and emerged out of the tree line and ran toward the air conditioning unit attached to the building. He got to a knee when he was close enough and unpacked his bag. He pulled out the canister of chemicals they'd prepared.

An arrow flew out of the nearby tree line to his side and punctured the container. A fine mist exploded in his face, causing him to retch and dive away. He scrambled to his feet. "Shit," he coughed.

"What happened?" Charles asked. "What was that noise?"

"A damned arrow." Henry ran, abandoning his pack and objective in favor of trying to get away. He witnessed another arrow hit the tree he was about to pass, along with a female voice that called for him to stop.

"Stop!" Skye yelled, making Henry stop in place. She emerged from the tree line and gave herself a free line of sight. "You move again, and I shoot you. I do not miss. Do you understand me?"

"Yes," Henry said.

"Who is that? Is that Ashley? Hold, I'll be there inside a few moments. Try to keep them talking. I'm already suited and ready."

"Negative," Henry whispered. "You'd be a massive disadvantage out here. There could be more. Let me deal with it. You return home if something happens."

"Who are you speaking to?" Skye approached, an arrow already nocked and ready to fly. "Answer me." She lowered her aim to Henry's leg. "You have three seconds."

"None of your business," Henry said.

"She'll kill you," Charlie said. "Just hold on. I'll be there soon."

"Fine then," Skye said. She released the arrow. It flew forward and embedded itself deep into the front of Henry's leg.

He fell on his butt. One of his hands clutched the wound while the other disappeared behind him. He grabbed the pistol from where it rested. "Just hold on a minute. I have no ill will to anyone."

"Then care to explain what you were doing with that canister?" She readied another arrow and took aim. "It looked an awful lot like an attempt at killing the occupants to me. Now bring your other arm slowly to your side. I want to see what you're reaching for."

"Here." Henry brought his hand out and quickly tried to fire a shot toward Skye, using his pistol, but not before she fired the arrow.

The bullet impacted Skye, and she fell backward onto the dirt below.

Henry looked down at the arrow in his chest. He sputtered out some blood from his mouth. "Leave now," he barely managed to get out.

"Damn it," Charlie said. "Did you at least get them?"

Henry stayed silent. He was still shivering and shaking, sure, but the ability to form words with all the blood entering his lungs was making it impossible. Henry hacked and sucked for air as best he could. He saw his attacker roll behind a tree. He tried to hit her, but his aim was off.

"You bastard!" Skye yelled. "You hit me in my ankle. What kind of shit for aim do you have? Son of a bitch, that hurts." She hissed in pain, gasping sharply.

Henry couldn't answer her with anything beyond more lead projectiles coming from his pistol, still aimed toward her wooden cover.

"Guy, you've got about a minute of useful consciousness left before you pass out from asphyxiation. Use it more productively than trying to hit me, please. Might I suggest praying?" Skye huddled, keeping her head low behind the tree. She looked to where she fell and the trail of blood leading over to her location on the leaves below.

Henry managed to climb to his feet, but he couldn't breathe. Although his lungs were on fire, and his chest was in earth shattering pain, he couldn't rest yet. He took a few stuttering steps as he grew dizzy, but stumbled as he tried to bring new oxygen into his body, leaving a puddle of blood as he moved slowly forward. He was within maybe five feet of the tree Skye was behind when his vision darkened at the edges.

"Just go down already, you stubborn idiot," Skye could be heard from nearby. She heard the crunching of leaves in the darkness behind her slow and eventually stop. A loud thump caused her to jump in her hiding place as she looked to her side and saw Henry lying beside her. She reached out and grabbed the gun holding hand and found it easy to disarm the now unconscious, dying man.

She heard a door slam nearby, along with voices too distant to understand what they said. "They'll be here inside a few minutes." Skye looked down at her ankle, laying on the forest floor in front of her. "This will be a fun conversation."

She could hear Ashley's voice call out. "If someone's there, you'd best say something now."

"I'm here. Don't shoot," Skye called out as loud as she could manage. She raised a hand above her and waved her arm back and forth to get her attention. She saw Ashley getting closer. "You all had an unexpected visitor."

"Holy shit." Ashley got close enough to see the pair in the dark. "What happened to you? Oh, no. Were you hit?"

"I was hit in the ankle. This dumbass tried to trade shots with me, and I guess he wasn't a good shot."

"You should be grateful he didn't hit you in the stomach." Ashley stopped and kneeled next to Skye. She reached toward Henry and laid a few fingers on his neck. "Yeah, he's dead alright." She checked his ear and pulled out the ear bud before smashing it underfoot.

"What gave that away? The massive blood loss, the arrow in his chest, or the pool of blood I'm marinating my ass in?" Skye asked. "Now help me up. I need a bath."

"You probably need medical assistance," Ashley said. "Here." She helped her up from the ground. "I found the disturbance. It's on the north side."

"You're telling them?"

"It's unavoidable at this point. You need to get that bleeding stopped. You're carrying two."

"Don't remind me. Ironically, my nausea saved all of you. I couldn't get to sleep and heard that asshole stomping around."

Rapid footsteps approached the trees they were in.

Ashley helped Skye take a few tentative steps toward the house. They stepped out of the woods to see two masked armed figures stop when they noticed the pair of girls.

"Who is that?" Jim asked, obviously angry.

"A friend," Ashley said. "Take it easy."

"Easy?" Michael asked. "That canister beside the AC unit would have killed us all."

"You have her to thank for it not being administered." Ashley looked at Skye.

"Oh, don't tell me." Jim marched over and leaned forward to inspect the mask-clad face of Skye. "Escort her inside and get her medically tended to. We're going to double check that there are no further surprises outside and take care of the body. This address houses shovels?" He looked at Michael.

"Yes, sir."

Just afterward...

Skye laid on the bed, and Ashley tended to her wounded ankle. Jim and Michael had yet to come inside, presumably still burying the remnants of Henry outside. A knock at the bedroom door interrupted the ladies.

"Come inside," Ashley called out without a second thought.

The door opened and there stood Angie.

"Who the hell are you?" Skye asked.

"I was going to ask you the same question. I heard yelling and shooting outside. Then I witnessed you two coming inside."

"So, this is why you insisted I not take my mask off," Skye said, giving a momentary glare toward Ashley. She looked back at Angie. "Yeah. you all were nearly poisoned to death by who I suspect was a lackey of Charles Baskins."

"Poison? You mean like the water supply or something?"

"No," Skye said with a hiss of pain as Ashley wrapped the ankle up. "He was planning to put airborne chemicals into the ventilation system. You'd all have died in your sleep if I wasn't there."

"Who are you anyway?"

"Aren't you curious? The question is, who are you, lady? I have seniority here."

"I'm Angie Summers, an independent journalist working on something huge."

"If you're here," Skye said, "that doesn't surprise me. Does it have to do with Baskins?"

"As a matter of fact, it does."

"Then he was probably trying to have you killed. It's probably how they knew where we were to boot. Your car's new, isn't it? It is lovely. I saw it out front earlier."

"How would my car lead them here?" Angie asked.

"Every new car past 2025 has computers in them," Ashley said. "They would've had a history of its signature when you stopped by Baskins' address. Hence, all they needed to do was follow its signal here."

"Bingo," Skye said.

"Oh, I didn't mean to cause more trouble."

"Ease up on her," Ashely said. "She's giving Baskins hell online and forcing his hand. This could be just what we need, if you catch my drift."

"Maybe, but you're all lucky I was outside awake," Skye said. "Where's the rolling bottle of sunshine? I figured I'd be getting an earful from him already."

"He's probably awake now," Ashley said. "It was quite a commotion you two had outside."

"I wanted some answers, and that's why I got shot. I thought I had him dead to rights. Turns out a bow and arrow aren't as quick as a gun. I knew that, but I was greedy for details. I thought he might be the break we needed."

"You're here with them?" Angie asked. "I never saw you around yet."

"Technically, she was supposed to stay back in Denver," Ashley said, finishing the wrapping of the fresh wound. "You're lucky this thing grazed you or it'd have been worse."

"I disobeyed a direct order from Masked Justice. This shouldn't have happened under my watchful gaze."

"I'm under sworn oath to never publish anything I hear or see inside this place," Angie said. "Why are you here?"

"Mama told me to never talk to reporters when you commit illegal acts," Skye said. "Sorry, sweetheart. I'm sure you're nice and all, but I don't think it best I talk to you."

"Her boyfriend's locked up, and the powers that be

promised to get him out if we complete our mission," Ashley said while getting up and dodging a swipe from Skye.

"Damn it." Skye scowled at her friend.

"You're here to make sure the job goes well," Angie said. "That's kind of romantic."

"Yes, well," Skye said, "the boss didn't think so since I'm expecting."

"What?" Angie's eyes widened. "You were out fighting some assassin with a baby?"

"You can thank said baby if you want for your being alive. I was having nausea and couldn't sleep. While I was out vomiting, I heard him tromping around as quietly as his loud ass could manage."

The door burst open to reveal an irate-looking Brett wheeling into the room.

"Speak of the angry little devil, and he appears," Skye said. "Don't blow a gasket, old man. You'd be dead in bed without me."

Brett slammed the door as best as he could manage and approached closer to Angie. He stopped at her side. "You're not supposed to be here."

"You're welcome for saving your life," Skye said, obviously not caring for the direction of this conversation. "I would think you would be grateful."

"Am I happy you killed the assassin? Sure," Brett said. "I'm even impressed you did so. Don't get too full of yourself. That was a pencil pusher that was given an honorary title by Baskins. He was his bodyguard in name only since they were friends. He wasn't a fighter, by any means. You know I won't be able to stop Masked Justice when he yells at you. The same rule I mentioned before we left applies now. You think about that."

"The vest?" Skye asked. "Yeah, I got it."

Ashley moved over to the window. "Masked Justice is coming back in alone. Get ready everybody."

"I'm going to leave you to face this reckoning. I don't want to get involved in whatever this drama is," Angie said. She left the room, leaving the three.

"He's pissed and rightfully so," Brett said. "He was trying to keep you safe, and you pissed all over that."

"His job isn't to keep me safe," Skye said. "That's my and Jason's job, not his."

"I wouldn't let him hear you say that." Ashley finished the wound dressing and gazed outside the nearby window. She saw Jim slam the mansion door closed and disappear inside. "He means well, and you know it."

"Where is she!?" Jim's angry voice was audible even inside the closed bedroom.

Ashley rolled her eyes and moved to the door. Opening it, she yelled back. "She's up here! Prepare yourselves," she whispered to the bedroom's occupants. She left the bedroom door open and retreated further inside.

Jim pushed the door open and immediately stared down at Skye. He closed the door behind him. "I knew deep down you'd be here. I guess I hoped you respected me more than this."

"It's not a matter of respect," Skye said.

"Yes, it is," he said.

"It's a matter of love," Skye said. "We both realize if Cynthia was in prison, you'd never stop for anything until she walked free. Why would it be different for me?"

"You know the answer to that question. It's the same damned reason I've got Cynthia begging me not to go on this mission. She pleaded for me not to go because of our child. I looked her straight in the eyes and told her I needed to fight. You have a choice. You know I'll free him, and you still endanger your child's life."

"That's not enough," Skye fired back. "Besides, without me, your mission would have indeed failed, and Jason would be in prison for the rest of his natural born life. So I was proven right."

"It's not about who's right!" Jim yelled, causing the room to fall silent in its wake. "Get over this childish notion of rebelling. I'm not here to repress you or whatever. I'm trying to do what's best for you, especially because I don't have that luxury. It's me that got Jason and you all in this. I'll get him out."

"It doesn't change the fact that if I hadn't disobeyed, you'd all be dead in your beds and Baskins would have gotten exactly what he wanted," Skye said. "My nausea had me awake at this hour. Without this baby, you'd be dead. Just take the L here, dude."

"You are infuriating," Jim said, pacing in the room. He stopped and looked down at the tended wound. "How bad was the injury?"

"That thing?" Ashley asked. "It was a graze to her ankle. It bled quite a bit, but it wasn't too hard to dress. She should walk inside a day without pain."

"That should make it easy to drive home then," Jim said.

"No way in hell," Skye said.

"Let me handle this," Brett said. "You want to be here and help. I understand the sentiment, truly." He patted what was left of his legs. "I understand wanting to feel useful. I know what it means to want to help a partner."

"What's your point?" Jim asked.

"She can guard this place," Brett asked. "It'd still help our mission, but be a lot less dangerous than what you're planning to do." He looked to Skye still laying on the bed. "We can't put a vest on you, given your circumstances, so you can't go after Baskins. Think of yourself as the rear guard so our forward forces can attack without fear of ambush. Is that acceptable?"

"So long as I'm helping the effort, I don't give a shit," Skye said. "Though I'd prefer to go along when you do it."

"Unacceptable," Jim said. "There's very likely to be a large explosion. I won't have you there. I will not let you kill yourself and your kid when I know I'll get it done one way or the other."

"By killing yourself," Skye said. "Maybe I don't wish you to do that either. Did you ever think that's why we don't want you to fight by yourself? Wearing that horrible vest is just asking to die. With my arrows, Ashley's sword, and your skills, he can't win. We don't need to sacrifice you to accomplish this if we work together. That's my point in this. I know you want to be the hero and sacrifice yourself. It all sounds so noble when you say it out loud, doesn't it?"

"I am not trying to kill myself," Jim said. "I'm just prepared for that possibility, as any warrior should be. This is the right play. It puts you and Ashley in the least amount of danger. I'm prepared to accept the risks."

"Well, we're not," Skye said. "You might think yourself expendable, but you're not."

"Not to us," Ashley said. "I don't fancy you going there and not returning either, you know. I'm supposed to keep you alive, or Cynthia would kill me when we return."

Brett wheeled over close to Ashley and pretended to look out the window near her. His right hand snaked into her pants pocket and picked out the phone. He quickly turned it on and input the password.

"Hey," Ashley finally noticed when her hand snaked its way into her pants and noticed the phone missing. She looked downward and saw Brett with it. "How the hell do you even know my password?"

"I notice and pay attention. You unlock your phone a lot, you know. Well, look here. You two have been talking this whole time I see."

"Is that true?" Jim asked, now turning to Ashley.

"She was already here anyway," Ashley said. "I figured it'd be better if she was nearby instead of sitting in a dirty motel somewhere. It was the correct decision, anyway."

"You went behind my back too?"

"Easy," Brett said. "There's no use crying over spilled milk. We can only move on. Bitching and moaning isn't a productive area of discussion. Yes, they both disobeyed. Let's move forward to their upcoming jobs. Rehashing this argument will get us nowhere."

"You're not accompanying me when I go to kill Charlie, and that's all I'm saying about that subject," Jim said.

"Fine. You should know, I've been conducting my own surveillance while you were busy having your little breaking and entering. Her name is Daphne Kelly."

"How could you know that?" Jim asked.

Skye smirked. "I followed her back from Charlie's. She stopped at a clothing store, so I went inside and made acquaintances. She's too nice for him. We should tell her what her boyfriend's into if you ask me. That's if you're not too busy playing home invader. I saw that too from my vantage point. You did well - until the alarm anyway. I think they're engaged now, judging by the cake they brought in this afternoon."

"Good," Brett said. "Now, let's figure out where you're going to sleep. You're our night guard apparently, so you'll need somewhere to sleep during the day."

"You expect me to walk on this?"

"Would you like one of my spare chairs?" Brett asked. "You wanted to come along so bad. Don't complain when you are given a job. It's in poor form. I doubt we'll receive anymore unwanted guests. He'd never come here by himself. He wants the home field advantage."

"Where am I sleeping then?" Skye asked.

"I'll show you in the morning," Jim said. "Have fun tonight. You've still got a few more hours before it's light. If Charlie wants to pay us a visit, I'm going to pay his girl a visit tomorrow morning." He stormed out of the room, leaving Brett and the girls.

"What is wrong with him?" Skye asked.

"There's nothing wrong with either of you from where I'm sitting," Brett said. "Just because he's right about keeping you safe, doesn't make you wrong for wanting to save Jason, or at least help. Life isn't that simple. The sooner you understand, the better. Now if you'll excuse me," he backed the chair away from the bed and toward the door. He looked over his shoulder at the two girls. "I need to sleep tonight. You also need to meet the new guy, Michael something or other. I can't remember his name."

"It's Miller," Ashley said.

"You'd know better than me. Do you truly like the sound of Ashley Miller, though?" Brett asked as he wheeled out. "It seems pedestrian to me." He shut the bedroom door, and the room fell quiet.

"What does that mean?" Skye asked. "Do you like the guy or something?"

"No."

"You're lying," Skye said.

"Maybe."

13

———

Daphne rolled over in her full-sized bed. She swore she felt someone's gaze on her. She sat up and rubbed her eyes. As she opened them, she noticed a masked man with a sword tied to his hip. He had a finger over his lips.

"Stay quiet," he said. "If I wanted you hurt, you would be already. You realize you need an alarm system?"

"I own one."

"You didn't arm it then. Too busy after visiting your boyfriend Baskins' place, were you?"

"Who are you?" she asked. She reached over toward her nightstand beside her bed.

"If you're looking for this," the man showed a gun he housed atop his lap, "I took it for safekeeping while I'm here. Don't worry, I'll leave it when I leave. I'm not a thief. I do bad things, but I don't steal from the innocent. As a matter of fact, I make it a point that they're not harmed under my watch. You may know me as Masked Justice."

"Are you serious? Why would you be here? Don't you live out west?"

"Is it that hard to believe? I go where my work takes me. You have a wonderful home."

"If you're truly Masked Justice, why are you here in my house? Is it because of Charles?"

"Yeah, you could say that. I understand you're engaged to him as of yesterday?"

"That's right. He's a kind man."

"No," Jim said, his voice stern, "he is not, ma'am. I know he's charming and charismatic. You know how I know?"

"Don't tell me you've had dealings with him?"

"I grew up with him since grade school. It all started a few years ago when I started this business of mine. Surely you remember when the news started talking about me? You are aware of his political party, I assume, but there's something you don't know about him."

"What's that?"

"He's not just a representative for his party. Tell me," Jim said, crossing one leg over his other as he leaned backward in the seat beside the exit. "Did you wonder how he received his start in politics?"

"I assumed he busted his ass and did all the things a normal politician does."

Jim imitated a buzzer. "Wrong. I was there before he started his career, you know. Would you care to learn how it all happened? He'll deny all of it if you ask him, but I'll be happy to tell the truth."

"I'm still not convinced you're even Masked Justice, so how can I believe you?"

"I realize you're under a lot of stress right now. Getting engaged, having a vigilante show up in your room early in the morning - these are scary developments. We cannot have a heart to heart if you don't believe me though."

"Fine, let's say I believe you. How did it happen then?" Daphne asked.

"First, realize nothing I say to you is a lie and things will start making sense. Before he was in politics, he was part of the PHR, a little known offshoot of his current political party. You know the type, extremist in their frankly justified ideals. I even joined them when I first started this hobby of mine. In fact, your fiancé trained me."

"My Charles?" Daphne laughed out loud. "He trained you? That's quite the tall tale. He can't even hurt a fly."

"I beg to differ," Jim's voice stayed even as he patted his sheathed blade handle. "He trained me how to use this blade. He taught me how to break and enter. Charlie taught me how to work out properly. He taught me many things since he was my partner and first mentor. He taught me when to kill and when to spare."

"Why would he work for this PHR?"

"The Pedophile Hunting Republic is a steppingstone for those ambitious enough, say if one desired to jump straight into national politics after never having held any local office before. Sound familiar? Now our first adventure drew to a close because I took in a girl whose parents sold her into slavery. There was just one problem."

"Sold her into slavery? Good Lord," Daphne said.

"Quite. Charles feared what would happen if the higher ups discovered her. I'll give Charles one thing. He was always quick-witted and resourceful, to the liability of everyone around him. He betrayed me and turned my girlfriend over to his boss and kidnapped her. That was the beginning of his war against me. We've been at odds ever since. That's not even the worst he's done to me." He stood up and let his voice raise as he stomped his foot, startling the poor woman. "He had my family member killed!"

She flinched from the sudden voice raising. "Family?"

"You remember when he went back to Oklahoma a few months ago? That was for appearances. We grew up together, and he returned to supposedly pay his respects. It was horse shit. He gave the order that killed my father. After those years of eating with my family, talking, and belonging, he had him killed, all to anger me."

"This doesn't sound a thing like my Charles. I think you might have the wrong man, with all due respect, Mr. Justice."

"Oh no, ma'am." Jim shook his mask covered face side to side. "You know that scar he has on his cheek? I gave that to him the night he tried to kill me and that little girl I told you about earlier. Yeah, he tried to have us killed to propel his career forward. She was only sixteen."

"He said that wound came from some lunatic vigilante when I inquired."

"He told you a half truth, which is the best you'll squeeze out of him. What did he tell you he was planning yesterday evening? Let me guess, he claimed he was working, yes?"

"Yes, why?"

"He lied to you, dear. He was at my place last night, trying to kill me and four other people, one of which is the unfortunate journalist who's making your fiancé's life a living hell."

"You have proof of this?" Daphne asked.

"Are you very good with tech, Ms. Kelly?" Jim asked. "Do you know how to check the GPS history of your car? I recommend you check his. It'll corroborate my story. Now let's return to the history lesson so you know who you're pledging your life to. He returned to Oklahoma a few months ago. That was for my father's funeral. He hired a

PHR assassin called Hans who stabbed him to death in his own living room. I killed him eventually through a hard-fought duel. The point is at the funeral he and my mother got to talking."

"Is this the police officer he said Masked Justice had killed?"

"He told my mother face to face that Masked Justice killed her husband while I was standing right there. I wanted nothing more than to rip his throat out with my bare hands right there on the spot, but since I'm not an animal, I restrained myself. I want you to tell your Charles that Masked Justice paid you a visit. You'll see him panic and squirm, probably asking all kinds of questions."

"Why? Is it just to scare him?"

"He killed my father. Why can't I get a little justice? He wanted to scare the piss out of me then, so I shall return the favor. The difference being I'm not going to hurt you. I'd sooner kill myself than harm an innocent. He won't though. He knows what it's like to be capable of such a despicable act. One thing about the guilty, Ms. Kelly - If they're capable of something, they assume everyone else is too, since they tell themselves they're not a bad person. He will jump straight to me threatening you. You watch."

"This is a lot to absorb," Daphne said, looking at her pajama clad body. "Especially in my pajamas."

"Our shared history needed to be mentioned, and this seemed the ideal time. He isn't what he seems. He's a psychopath, or maybe a sociopath. I'm not a mental health expert, but there's something wrong with him. Take it from his best friend since childhood. You don't want to get involved with him. He'll turn on you when it's convenient. Mark my words."

"Can I ask you something now?" Daphne asked.

"I suppose it's only fair," Jim said. He moved to the door and leaned against it. "Shoot."

"Is it true you've taken down multiple syndicates?"

"If you'd call those half-assed groups syndicates, sure," Jim said. "They were slaver scum is what they were. They bartered people's lives for money. Why?"

"My cousin called me a few years ago. She told me a wondrous story of Masked Justice and his partners saving them from a container with a bomb strapped to it or something like that."

Jim turned away, vivid memories of screaming and scratching at the sides of the container flooding his mind. "That night wasn't all sunshine. The bastard in charge of the containment lied to us about the codes to one container. We opened it, and it went off, flooding the inside with poison. We had to shut it to keep the rest alive. I still hear the screams and scratching. I'm glad your cousin got out, for what it's worth. Anything else?"

"If your story's true, why chase Charles now? Why not earlier? Why now?"

"That is a long story with countless players involved. Suffice it to say, one of my family is in dire trouble and someone with the power to carry through on their promise of freeing him has made me an offer."

"Jason Walton?"

"You know of him?"

"Everybody in the country has watched television in the past few months. They're always claiming about how Masked Justice's collaborator has still yet to say a single word."

"They arrested him because of a single mistake. My benefactors seized on the opportunity to coerce me to do this. If I do, he goes free. I can't deny I wanted the job, anyway."

"You're telling yourself you're to kill Charles to free your partner? Murder is still murder."

"The sky is blue too. The world is the way it is. It doesn't matter if we condone it or not. I've made my peace with that. I have no hangups on murder if the victim deserves it. Baskins is the most worthy piece of shit I've ever hunted. I don't care if we were friends. He tossed that aside when he gave up my girlfriend to that animal Dillon of the PHR. He solidified my will when my father's dead body hit the floor. Do you understand? It isn't just business; this is personal. I realize that's dangerous. I've never had an emotional connection until now, but I am trying to keep you from being hurt as bad as if you were blindsided. You want my advice, run screaming from that sorry excuse of a human as soon as you can. It'll only bring you sorrow and ruin."

"An eye for an eye makes the world blind. Are you prepared for the consequences of chasing vengeance? Make no mistake, this is not justice you're chasing, it's vengeance."

"I've made my peace with dying," Jim said. "Now research what I told you and inform him if you insist on talking to him. You'd be smarter to run and never second guess yourself."

"You're not at all like I imagined from my cousin's stories."

"Really?"

"Yeah. Is your girlfriend alright now?"

"She's pregnant and we're expecting. Thanks for the concern, though it's no thanks to your boyfriend, Baskins."

"You're willing to risk your life when you know you have a kid coming?" Her eyes went wide. "Why for God's sake?"

"My partners in crime aren't just cohorts or sidekicks,

you know. I think of them as family. Jason's like that little brother who wanted to tag along. You know the type? He looked up at me with such undeserved hero worship. I can't help but feel responsible for what happened to him. If I can do anything to free him, it's done."

"I can't tell if you're insane or if you just have a huge hero complex."

"Why not both? Now don't forget to tell dearest Baskins about this conversation and watch his reaction. I guarantee he'll be scared, thinking I'll hurt you to get at him. Mark my words. I thought I knew him, but I know that much of him." He opened the door, only to pause and check over his shoulder as Daphne reached out to him.

"One last thing," she said. "You mentioned a job earlier."

"Yes, I did. You don't desire the answer to the question you are about to ask. Nobody gets to cheat fate, Ms. Kelly, not even your boyfriend. He will receive what's coming to him because he's hurt a lot of innocent people, including those close to me. That's all the answers you're receiving today. Take my advice and run away from that animal for your own benefit." That was the last Jim said. He placed the gun down on a nearby dresser and slammed the door.

Rapid footsteps were the only sign that Jim had left. Daphne stared down at her wrinkled bed sheets and just stared, processing all she'd just heard. The ringing of the cell phone on her bedside table shook her out of her reverie. She reached over and grabbed it to see it was Charles calling. "Hello. Yes, I understand, but I kind of need to talk to you. No, it can't wait. Seriously? You can't spare twenty minutes to talk today at all? Alright, well I'll be over quickly then. I know you like getting an early start to work. I'd hate to hold you up. Bye."

At Charles' place after...

Charles had a formal suit on with a tie when Daphne was practically shoved into his room by his security. He turned around with a beaming smile. "There she is, my adorable future wife."

"We need to talk about something."

"Now those are words every man dreads hearing," Charlie said, turning back to the large mirror and adjusting his tie. "What's the problem?"

"Where'd you go last night?"

"I met a colleague and discussed policy. You know I'm bound to secrecy when discussing state secrets.

"State secrets, huh? Out in the middle of the forest? I checked your car's GPS history earlier because you're so tight-lipped."

"My colleague enjoys his privacy. We all deal with crazies, and he's built himself a regular fortress. Now, is there anything else? I can't reveal anything further."

"I had a visitor this morning," Daphne's casual tone undercut the upcoming revelation.

"Oh, one of those religious proselytizers? I know how annoying that can be."

"Not one of them." She walked over and sat on the already made bed. "He claimed you knew him personally."

Charlie stopped what he was doing and turned around immediately. "Who?"

She looked away. "Would you believe me if I told you it was Masked Justice? I woke up in bed, and he was sitting across the room from me."

"Masked Justice?" Panic was evident in Charlie's voice. He rushed over and wrapped his arms around her. "Did he hurt you?"

"No, he did not. Why would you think he would? His credo is that he only harms the guilty."

"He's a crazy man who goes around killing people. You ask me why I'd be worried he was in your house?" He kissed her forehead. "I knew I should have gotten you security too. It was lazy of me, and it's my fault. I'll make sure by tonight you have some security at your place too. I swear it. Did he say anything that'd lead to his whereabouts? We'll call the police right now."

"He did not," she said, pulling away gently. "He just told me a lot about you."

"Me?" Charlie asked, trying to play innocent. He released her from his hug and looked away before wiping away a bead of sweat. "What could he say about me?"

"You know, for a politician, you sure suck at lying," she said bluntly. "You truly wish to know what he said?"

"I'm sure it was all lies anyway, but it should prove interesting to hear."

"He said you two grew up together, at least until you betrayed him for something called the PHR. He said that's how you got into national politics after never having won a single local election in your life. It makes sense when you think about it."

"Nonsense. My message simply resonated with the voting populace is all, sweetheart. They don't want vigilantes running around anymore than I do."

"He also said you betrayed a girl to a guy named Dillon."

"Dillon? I don't know anybody named Dillon."

"I got the impression Dillon was dead. You don't want to know what he revealed regarding how you received that scar." She reached upward and ran a soft small hand over the long thin slice on his cheek.

"I'm sure it was all lies."

"Did you betray him because of a sixteen-year-old girl, for fear of reprisal from the higher ups of this PHR? Tell me the truth. You didn't, right?"

"Of course not. I'd never join any group that hurts people. Don't you know me better than that? You're putting too much stock into the word of a lunatic who is a notorious serial killer. You know how I feel about those like him. It probably wasn't even Masked Justice, just some pretender."

"He said he remembered the night my cousin was rescued. His details match up with the exact story that my cousin reported, too. It was the real Masked Justice. I'm sure of it."

"That's precisely why you should be scared and suspicious. The man hates me. You remember that?" he asked. "I'm leading a movement that would eradicate him and his ilk. Is it any wonder he'd lie and go after those closest to me? This is an intimidation tactic, plain and simple. Trust me, I know men like this."

"You know murderers?"

Charlie didn't have a quick retort to the simple question. "People leading our country are not saints, sweetie pie. You know what I meant. I'm used to the type of man who uses fear to get what he wants. It's called politics. Hell, I'm going to have dinner with Mr. Benjamin next Sunday. Don't tell anyone, but there are rumors regarding him you wouldn't believe. My point is, please let me deal with this degenerate. I want security for you."

"I don't want strange guards hanging around my home all night."

"You prefer the types with swords and masks, though? Just not guns."

"What's that supposed to mean?" she asked, her voice even and dangerous.

"It means you should be more upset that a murderer casually snuck into your place. Why am I the only soul upset by this horrifying revelation? Do you not care if you die, or has it not sunk in? You were in mortal danger. Why is my being concerned a bad thing, exactly?"

"It just feels like there's something you're not telling me is all. We're engaged now. We shouldn't have any secrets. Why is this guy showing up at my place if he's lying?"

"To sow dissent. He wants to put pressure on me is all."

"Maybe you're right. I can't imagine you having his father killed."

"Is that what he said?"

"Yes. He also said you taunted him in front of his mother at the funeral." She laughed. "That doesn't sound like you."

"Because he's lying. Now will you let me post some security around your place? They wouldn't be inside your house."

"You think they'd stop him?"

"It's either that or you live here from now on."

"Is this your method of asking me to move in? You know I'm an old-fashioned gal. That's not happening until we're married. As far as security for my place? Only if I can give them orders. I don't want them digging around my things."

"I can make that happen. Wait here." Charlie stood up and ran for his door. He opened it and talked to the guard stationed outside for a minute or so. It was impossible to hear what he was saying from the bed. "Make it happen. I want at least six men."

"Yes, sir," the guard said loud enough for Daphne to hear.

She got off the bed and walked closer to Charlie. "I have security now, huh? They better not peek when I'm changing or anything."

"Don't worry about them. You'll forget they're there until you need to go somewhere. Then they'll escort you there. I don't want my precious at the whims of that crazy man again." He met her halfway to the door and grabbed her hands. He squeezed them and looked deep into her eyes. "Come, let's eat already. All this talking has made me hungry and I've scheduled a rally this afternoon. I can't attend that hungry, can I?"

"I suppose not."

14

"Hello, everybody. It's me, your host Josie Bradley," the female host said, looking straight into the camera with a beaming smile. "Welcome back to VIP Guests, where the hottest trend-makers come to talk. Today we have a special guest with us that's causing quite a stir on the web. Many of you may already know of her stories." She held a microphone in one hand and cards in her other. She extended her card holding hand off stage. "Please welcome Angie Summers."

Upbeat music played, and the studio audience burst into applause along with a smattering of boos. Angie waved toward the audience as she walked to the host. They met and shook hands before Josie escorted her to the desk with chairs sitting beside it.

"Please take a seat there, Ms. Summers." Josie sat down behind the desk as the applause died down. "I understand you're making a big splash online."

"You could say that. That's not what's important. What is important is what I'm saying that's causing the uproar. People wish to hear the truth, and that's what I report."

"There are those who say you're nothing but a vigilante sympathizer. I understand you were saved by Masked Justice himself not too long ago. Is that true?"

"I am not a sympathizer, as you word it, to anyone but the people. It is true he saved my life from another masked crazy. That does not mean I will abandon my journalistic integrity, even if many of my cohorts have done precisely that."

Murmuring in the crowd interrupted the two.

"Let's not delve into the independent journalist versus mainstream journalist debate again for the millionth time. Let's focus on why you're here. You made quite a claim last night. Can we pull up the message I'm referring to on our screen behind me so the audience can view it, please? Now this was posted last night."

A social media post showed up behind the pair of women on the screen.

"To be precise, Josie, this morning around three a.m. Yes, that's right. I found the timing to be odd, seeing as yesterday I started publicly asking questions that Mr. Baskins refused to answer. He ignored my tagging him and kept his publicist in control of his account."

"For those unfamiliar, can you give us a summary of said questions? Context is important here."

"I couldn't agree more. I asked questions about the shooter of the recent anti-vigilante march in our nation's capital. After doing research into him, I found some interesting facts."

"What's that?" Josie placed both arms on the desk and leaned forward on them.

"I found out that the attacker was a rabid anti-vigilante activist, for one. When I discovered that, I wondered why a citizen like him would shoot up an anti-vigilante event."

"That does strike me as odd. Why do you think nobody is talking about it?"

"If I said why, we'd cut to commercial faster than you could utter taxes," Angie said with a laugh. "Suffice it to say, they don't wish to speak about it because they have received orders to remain silent. It's as simple as that. Frankly, I'm surprised I received a call from your people to be on this show, considering what I've said."

"We never shy away from the truth, inconvenient as it can be. I started my career as an independent content creator like yourself you know. That's why you should feel free to speak your mind, and don't censor yourself."

"If you say so. It's because mainstream pundits are paid by powerful elites to only ask questions about certain subjects."

"That's not hard to believe. That's how the business has worked for decades. I suppose your average Joe might not know that. Let's delve into what you were asking before this assassination attempt."

"Besides the fact that Erin Jules was an ardent Baskins supporter, his entire family was murdered in a shootout between vigilantes and cops. Coroner reports show the bullets originated from the vigilante side. Answer me this. Why would this unfortunate soul, whose family was killed by vigilantes, shoot toward the very politician he believes can fix this mess? It makes no logical sense to me or many of my dear subscribers."

"These are hard-hitting questions. You have proof?"

"I left a copy of said proof with your editor, as you requested."

"Jerry, show the relevant messages then. Don't be shy." Josie looked over her shoulder at the screen perched above her shoulder.

The screen showed the archived website of various social media posts before their deletion.

"I had to archive these since I figured social media sites would delete them. I was correct. You may search for these messages, but they're deleted and censored. For those at home or with their phones, you can verify this by visiting the archive link at the page's bottom. Now why would that happen so fast?"

"It does look suspect. Social media sites have been caught deleting suspect things before. We know they have. I'm beginning to understand why no other shows clamored for you to be their guest."

"Starting to worry about being canceled?" Angie quipped with a smile.

"Never. I started my career to pursue the truth and I will proverbially die on this hill. Please continue."

"Last night I witnessed users all over the wide internet asking the same questions I posed. I never found a satisfactory answer. Some made excuses for Baskins. Some claimed I was libelous and slandering the man. How that works with questions is anyone's business, apparently. Anyway, in the middle of the night, someone tried to kill me."

"That's a tall accusation. You're sure of this?"

"As sure as the canister of poison they tried to put into my house's ventilation. I have it here if you'd like to see it. They didn't have the guts to come inside and try to stab me. They wanted it to look like a natural causes death. Now who would want that?" She reached into her hoodie's front pocket and pulled out the small canister. It housed a giant hole in the side.

"What is that hole from exactly?" Josie leaned forward, trying to inspect the container. "That doesn't look right."

"Heck if I know. All I understand is when I went outside

this morning, I found this beside my beloved air conditioning unit. If you want my opinion, the idiot got a lungful of this compound and retreated in sheer panic."

"I notice you've not lobbed accusations as to who may have tried this. Do you have any guesses?"

"Sure, I have guesses," Angie said, turning from the host and gazing directly into the camera. "They know who they are. I know who they are, but if I say it, I'll be the one in legal trouble. Isn't that something?"

"You're not talking about who I think you are?"

"Probably. I can't legally say."

The audience interrupted the pair by talking loud enough to be audible.

"Please. Please calm down everyone. We're not done yet." Her words caused the studio audience to quiet down. "What do you plan on doing now, Ms. Summers?"

"I'm going to stay the course, obviously. I will not allow myself to be silenced. The people deserve the truth."

"You're not worried about another attempt?"

"Of course I'm worried. I won't allow fear to run my life or stop me from doing what's right. If I quit, I'd be ashamed of myself, and I'm more afraid of that than my wannabe killer. If I gave up, my family would be embarrassed."

"You're a brave woman, Ms. Summers. I pray that no harm comes to you. We need more journalists like you. It shouldn't matter which side of the aisle you're on politically. We need more truth seekers inside this grim world. You have my respect, and you'll always be welcome on this show."

"That's excellent. All the other shows I've been on have called me and informed me I was no longer welcome."

"That does not surprise me. You speak your mind and don't play word games. They don't like that. Unfortunately, we need to take a commercial break. We have more guests after these messages."

Backstage at Charlie's rally...

Charlie turned the channel away from the talk show. "This is bull," he said.

"You think she really had someone try to kill her?" Daphne asked. "She didn't look like she was lying, from her body language.

"She could have gotten that canister anywhere, and then she goes on national television and implies it was my fault? The nerve of the woman is infuriating."

"It would be mighty convenient for you if she had died, though. She's causing a big problem for you, isn't she? What will you announce to your supporters?"

"I'm going to tell them what I always do, the truth." Charlie stood up from the couch and moved to the tall mirror in the corner of his dressing room. "Is my tie straight?"

Daphne came up behind him and peeked around him. She snaked her arms around and fixed his tie. "There," she said, after fixing the apparel.

"Thank you." Charlie turned around to face her. "The woman has a vendetta against me. She loves Masked Justice, and I get why. She was saved by him, but I think she's not nearly as professional as she pretends to be, if you catch my drift."

"You think she and him - you know?" Daphne asked.

"It wouldn't surprise me with how much she runs interference for him. You saw him. Do you think a normal woman would find him attractive?"

"I don't know. He had a mask on. Sure, his voice was sexy

and deep, but I couldn't tell anything else. I suppose if he had saved my life and carried me out of the building bridal style while the place blew up, my tune might change, though."

"Exactly. He's got her under some type of influence, mark my words."

"I hope you're right."

"You know I'm right. This is all politics, baby cakes," Charlie brought his hands up to either side of her cute face and tilted her head to gaze at him. He caressed the sides of her face. "I'd never hurt a fly or even try to. You know me."

"Yeah," Daphne said.

Charlie leaned down and planted a kiss on her lips. "This will all go away once I'm reelected. Trust me. This is all about trying to stall the movement by discrediting me. It's a coalition plot. You trust me, right?"

She stared at him and answered after a few seconds pause. "Yes, I do."

"Good."

A knock at his dressing room door interrupted the pair. A male voice came through. "You're on in five minutes, Mr. Baskins."

"That's my cue. I want you to stay here, and I'll come fetch you when I'm finished."

"I don't like big crowds, so that suits me fine. Good luck out there."

"I don't need luck," Charlie said. "I have the truth on my side."

That night at Daphne's...

Daphne entered the home and shut the door behind her. She took a deep breath and searched her living room. She jumped in place when she saw Jim standing beside her by the door.

"Evening," he said in a calm voice. "I see you've upped your security. They're not skilled, so that's a promising sign. I assume they're Baskins' team?"

"Yes. He insisted on me having them after I told him about you. Why are you here again? How did you even sneak by them?"

"It wasn't difficult. They have a predictable pattern, and I already knew my way inside. What do you think about your fiancé? You still trust everything he says? I can personally vouch for Ms. Summers' story."

"You can?"

"My team was the one who stopped them from finishing the job. You saw that hole in the container? That was an arrow from our sharpshooter. They were partially correct on the talk show. The wannabe assassin did receive a nice lungful of his own cocktail before he promptly dropped it and took off running. I have reason to believe your Baskins was his operational support, too. Tell me, did he chase you off that night? I suspect he did."

"He said he had work. He claims he met a colleague, and they were conversing about state secrets."

"They weren't," Jim said. "He was planning Ms. Summer's death. That's a fact. Did you check his car's GPS? Did it go into a nearby forest at night?"

"Oh God," Daphne walked further into the living room and plopped down on the sofa. "What am I going to do? If what you say is true, he's a horrible man."

"He is," Jim said.

"If you're correct, what do you think he would do if I dumped him? I'm stuck."

"Not for long. Tell me, how committed are you to finding the truth behind Mr. Baskins?"

"I need to know before I marry him. What are you proposing?"

"Nothing too bad. Would you be willing to plant devices in his home? You have free access. It's simply for information gathering. That way we can prove his wrongdoing. Would you help?"

"Yes," she said. "I've got to tell you, though, that I'm not good with electronics. I'm not sure how much good I'd be planting listening devices or whatever."

"It'd be cameras. Surely you can find some spots out of sight that would help us gain insight. Preferably you'd plant them where he spends the most time. Additional rooms and hallways would be our best chance to see what all he's devising."

"What are you planning if I comply?"

"If I told you he killed that civilian at his protest for political points, would that make a difference? You already know it's true. That's why you're even considering helping me."

"You know me that well, huh? You're as bad as he is sometimes, thinking you know me."

"Sure, but at least I'm honest," Jim said. "Now, will you help us?"

"Are you going to hurt him?"

"The same way he had my father hurt. We're on a timetable here. If our plan is to work, it's imperative those cameras are set before the bugs we planted run out of power. That's a few days, max. After that, more people die."

She covered her eyes with her arm and leaned her head backward. "It sounds like people will die either way. It isn't fair asking me to help you kill him. You know that."

"I don't really care what's fair. I'm concerned about my own agenda. You should be concerned about your agenda. If I were you, I'd either do this, or break it off with him and run away for your own safety. If you don't want to do this, I won't hold it against you or harm you. I won't force this on you."

"You've already forced it on me. Don't you understand? Now I'm uncertain if the man I love is a murderer. Do you understand what havoc that inflicts on a person's psyche? It's torture. Then you inform me if I don't hand him to you on a silver platter, more lives will be lost. You're manipulating me as much as him."

"Yes. I've never said I was a saint. I get results with brutal efficiency. Now this is happening. It's just a matter of how many souls die. Besides, don't you want to learn the truth about him? You can slip one of them into his pocket, and then we'd both have the audio proof you want. Then you won't feel bad for helping me."

"It's not like I have a choice. Fine, I'll try to divert some of his guards. I don't want Madison, his security guard, to die stupidly. I'll tell Charles that I want more security. The big bad Masked Justice showed up at my home again. I'll play the scared little maiden, if that'll save more lives. I'll need a number to call to inform you when they've gone with me, though." She looked over at Jim, still standing by the door. She watched him peek out the blinds of the nearby window. "Besides, I can't sneak into some of the rooms around his home. He keeps them locked. I don't know what he keeps in there."

"It's probably his warrior equipment. His old suit, his sword, his guns, and probably gadgets. The man is a contract killer. I should know. He taught me everything I know about the business of murder. Trust me when I say he's not counting on his security forces. He's counting on his own skill on besting me. Now, I already took the liberty of placing the equipment in your bedroom on your bed. There's a folder in there with the floor plan, and where we recommend putting them inside. There's one parcel that I'd love to get into his locked room, but that'd be an extra if you could manage it. I trust you'll look at the instructions before you go improvising where you put them."

"I hate homework, but fine, I'll do it."

"You will?"

"You heard me. Now, I need one last thing before you depart. You see that desk near you?"

Jim looked to his right. He saw a desk sitting beside the coat rack. "Yeah."

"Open it and grab a piece of paper and a pencil, please."

"To what end?"

"My cousin insisted on getting your autograph one day for what you did for her, and by God, I'm not letting you leave again until you sign one for her."

"Seriously?"

"Just sign the damned thing, would you? She'd kill me if I ever told her I'd met you and didn't get one. Also, write down a phone number. I'll tell you when more of the guards are gone."

"This is not a game." Jim's words didn't match with his body language as he did indeed go over to the desk and open one of the drawers. He pulled out the notepad inside, along with a pencil. He quickly wrote on it and tore the page off before placing it atop the desk. "There. I hope your cousin enjoys it. It's the first and only Masked Justice signature. She can probably get quite a bit of money for that. Can I leave now?"

"Did Charlie really kill your father?"

"He also tried to kill my mother. In the process, he crippled a friend of mine who defended her while I went out to save Miss Summers from a madman. I'll never forget that night. Now this is important. Don't be at Charlie's place tomorrow evening. Make up an excuse. I don't care what you say, just do it. Alright?"

"Fine. I won't be there. Be careful. It'd be dumb if you snuck inside, only to get shot on your exit."

"Your concern is appreciated."

15

"I'm sorry about before," Daphne said. She looked down at her own feet. She saw Charlie's feet in front of her before his hand reached and gently grasped her chin to angle her head up to look at him. "I don't know why I acted the way I did. With last night's surprise visit, I've been under tons of stress."

"You're talking about yesterday? Don't even worry about it," Charlie said. "You're under a lot of stress right now. Not many souls live through a meeting with Masked Justice once, never mind twice. I can't believe he had the guts to sneak inside with security present."

"I wish to make amends. Let me clean the place for you. I know you hired a maid and all, but there's a difference between an employee cleaning it and me."

"Sweetie, you don't need to worry about anything. The reason I hired the maid was so we didn't have to clean. I'm not so petty that I'd make you clean this giant place because you got a little heated yesterday. Now I have a meeting to attend. Please, stay here and relax, alright? You deserve it after what you've been through."

"Alright then. Can you send in Madison before you go?"

"What do you want with her?"

"Maybe I wanted to fetch you something as a surprise and I wanted her advice on how to surprise you. Anything else, or do you want to completely spoil the surprise?"

"I'll send her in, but you don't need to do anything," Charlie gave her a quick peck on the cheek before moving toward the door. He stopped at the door and checked over his shoulder. "You already gave me the best gift a man can get. You said yes." He blew a kiss and then exited the room.

"Yeah." She moved over to Charlie's bed and sat down. "It's quite a gift, too." She felt sick to her stomach for what she was about to commit, but she'd decided beforehand. She looked upward as the door opened again and a female security guard appeared.

"Yes, ma'am?" Madison stood at attention. "You wanted to see me?"

"Yes, I want to plan a surprise for Charles. I need your help to make it perfect. Are you too busy to help? It's okay if you are."

"It depends on the job. One of the benefits of being in command is you create your schedule. I can probably help." Her serious expression faded to a smile. "What do you need?"

"I want to give him the biggest surprise of his life after he gave me the same with that cake."

"Did you enjoy that? It was my idea. Mr. Baskins was nervous if you'd like it or think it too much."

"It was lovely, thank you." Daphne reached inside her pants pocket and grabbed one of the devices that Jim had left her. She walked over to Madison. "You know those rooms that he keeps locked?"

"Yes, ma'am? I cannot open them for you if that's what

you're hinting at. I've promised Mr. Baskins nobody besides authorized staff may enter."

"Aw, really?" Daphne asked. She placed a hand on Madison's shoulder, drawing her attention there while her other dropped the electronic device into Madison's jacket pocket. "Alright then," she said with a shrug. "I don't want to get you in trouble, but I just thought the gift being inside there would surprise him."

"I'll place it inside for you, but that's as far as I can offer."

"You'd do that?" Daphne's eyes lit up.

"Yes, ma'am."

"Here," Daphne said. She hurried over to the bed where she'd dropped the backpack she'd brought. She dug around inside and pulled out the wrapped present she'd gotten ready last night. "This is it."

"What is it exactly?"

"If I told you, you'd tell him. It's nothing bad or dangerous. Don't worry." She walked over and handed her the present.

Madison brought it up to her ear and listened.

"You concerned it's a bomb or something?" Daphne giggled. "I don't know the first thing about explosives. If you must know, it's one of those cute dolls sold at a local market. It's just in a big box for camouflage."

"Ah." Madison transferred the package to under her left arm. "Where do you want this specifically?"

"You know his private office? I want it there when he returns home. So he'll walk inside and see it and know I was thinking of him - that I went so far as to recruit you. He made a grand romantic gesture. I think it's about time I repaid it, wouldn't you say?"

"You're a very kind woman, Ms. Kelly. I'll make sure it

arrives there." She bowed to show her respect. "If that is all, I'll deliver your gift and return to my regularly scheduled duties. Someone's got to keep these slackers in line."

"Thank you. I owe you one."

Madison left the room, leaving Daphne alone in Charlie's bedroom.

Daphne went and picked up the backpack. She dug around in it and found the fanny pack, which she tied around her waist. She unzipped the large container and felt around inside. As Jim promised, the fanny pack contained the surveillance devices he asked her to plant. It took her a while to figure which way to place them to allow their viewers to see properly, but she'd discovered the correct method earlier while experimenting on her own computer.

She pulled one out and moved over to the bookshelf lining one wall of his bedroom. She reached up and practiced the motion of planting it. It was quick, almost like just touching one of the book's spines to the naked eye. She removed her hand and inspected her handiwork. You couldn't see the device unless you were looking for it.

She decided now was the perfect time to fulfill the mission she chose to accept. With Charlie gone, she had more freedom to wander around the property. It didn't hurt that many of the security loved her since she was always kind to them and stuck up for them. They tended to just let her do whatever she wanted.

She headed out into the upstairs hallway. She already knew where she was putting this one. The potted plant on top of the table would do nicely. She leaned forward and pretended to smell the plant while she placed the device.

"It's lovely smelling, isn't it, ma'am?" Madison had just approached out of a locked room nearby and spotted her.

"It's wonderful. Don't let me keep you. I've already taken enough of your valuable time."

"Ma'am." Madison nodded and passed by her.

She wandered around all the rooms upstairs she had access to, not running into anymore security. She planted the cameras and microphones without incident. The security was almost always focused on their ground level.

Time to venture downstairs, she thought to herself. *Just be cool and be natural. They don't know what you're doing.*

She headed down the stairs with her usual pep in her step. She reached the main living room and saw a young man walking through it on a patrol route.

"Good morning, ma'am," he said with a smile.

"Good morning, sir," Daphne said. "Hope everything's going well with you."

"Don't worry your pretty little head about security, ma'am. We'll keep you safe."

"Don't let me keep you," Daphne said. "I was just straightening up a little. I figure it's good practice for being a housewife. Charlie said I don't have to, but I want to."

"I'm sure you'll do a fine job, ma'am." The young man kept patrolling and disappeared around the corner into the dining room.

She was alone in the room now and quickly fished out another device to plant above Charlie's flat-screen television. She wiped the dust that had accumulated off the television and coughed. "Maybe I should clean this more often," she muttered to herself. When she turned around after planting it, she saw Madison passing through. She didn't pay Daphne any more mind. Her mind was clearly on business as she spoke into the walkie talkie, chewing someone out for their incorrect patrol pattern.

She made her way through the first floor, carefully avoiding detection from the guards downstairs. She made small talk with them, distracting from her subtle work. By the time she finished downstairs, she had placed a camera in every unlocked room she had access to. She knew why Masked Justice had asked her to plant these. After all, she wasn't stupid. She understood he wanted the cameras operational so he could sneak in and kill Charlie. *The sole reason I'm doing this is to keep as many of these security personnel alive as possible. I'd rather Masked Justice not need to kill them to get to Charlie.*

"You're quite busy," Madison interrupted Daphne as she was planting the last bug. She jumped in place and turned around. "You scared me there," she brought a hand to her chest. "I just get in the zone while I'm straightening up."

"Sorry, ma'am. I wish my men and women had the work ethic you do. You're not even employed to clean, and you still do it."

"A wife's work is never done. I'm just getting a head start on it, is all."

"An admirable attitude to have," Madison said.

"Do you have any idea when he'll be getting back? I'm just so eager for him to see the surprise you left him."

"I do not know, ma'am. Sorry. If I had to guess, I'd say an hour and a half. Shall I get one of the boys to help you out with this?"

"Their job is to keep us safe. I don't want to distract them. Next is cleaning the floors."

"Shall I recommend to Mr. Baskins that we employ a new maid?"

"God no. I don't want the poor girl unemployed just because I want to clean."

"Very well. If you'll excuse me," she said before making her exit.

Daphne decided if she's cleaning the place, she may as well actually clean, so she hunted down the necessary cleaning supplies and got to work.

16

The little window on Jason's isolation cell opened. A guard spoke through the new opening. Muffled yelling and the sounds of thumping met his ears. "Walton, put your hands through. You're going back to general population."

"So soon?" Jason backed up toward his cell door and stuck his hands through the opening to be handcuffed. He heard the click and felt the cold metal around his wrists. He moved forward after the cuffs were secure and turned around. The door swung open, and he saw the other cells outside. He saw his coalition friends, all of them, banging on their doors. "What about them?" he asked.

"They're fine where they are. Now get moving."

Jason exited the solitary cell and felt his arm grabbed by the guard as they walked side by side outside of the solitary wing of the jail. "I'm surprised. I thought they would transfer me to another high-level facility."

"You're not that screwed yet. You keep getting in trouble for your little friends and that will soon change."

Jason and the guard emerged outside the building and

found themselves on a small outdoor path between a variety of buildings. He recognized the area as he had to pass through here often. "At the least, I figured I'd be inside solitary longer."

"Normally you would be," the guard pushed him toward the building containing his cell block that he'd come to know as home the past few months. "Someone important wanted you to move back to your cell. Guess it's your lucky day."

"Or my worst nightmare," Jason said under his breath.

"You should be grateful." The guard's tone was harsh. "At least you won't listen to the chorus of the damned at all hours."

Jason stepped into the familiar buildings and went through the all too familiar corridors. He finally found himself back at his cell block. Tables and benches filled with inmates dominated most of the ground floor. The ground floor and the second were all lined with cell doors.

"Hey look who's returned," a man said from a nearby table where they played spades. He recognized the clean-shaven man. He was an inmate from Jamaica, according to the banter they'd shared playing together over the past month. "Have fun back there?" he asked as he played a card.

"Good morning, Jerome. It's always good to see you." Jason walked over and took one of the empty spaces. "You know solitary - always a barrel of laughs. The screams of the damned add to the calming ambience."

"You're always the funny man," Jerome said. "You should learn that acting the joker inside here can have lethal consequences if you mouth off to the wrong convict."

"Point taken."

"You should also notice some new faces. Second floor to

your left. There's one guy leaning on the rails. He's been asking all about a Mr. Walton."

"I think he's got a crush on you," another of the players laughed. They slammed the card down. "What do you think about that?"

"I think Mr. Walton is in trouble," Jerome said.

"Yeah, this is about what I expected when they released me early." He glanced up to where Jerome had mentioned earlier and saw the man.

He was shirtless, and it was obvious that working out was more than a mere hobby from his Mr. Olympia physique. His darker skin tone didn't bother Jason, but his serious expression gave him cause for concern.

"He was asking about me? What about the other guys?"

"Repeatedly," Jerome said. "I wouldn't wish to be you now, Mr. Walton, that's for sure. The others were asking too, but not quite as persistently as the larger gentleman upstairs. He may be a brother, but I know nothing about him. He's the one I'd worry about."

"You know anything about him?"

"I know he's new here. Rumor has it that he was moved from his last jail because of some trouble he had caused. I believe he killed his last cellmate."

"Perfect," Jason said.

"You haven't heard the funniest part," Jerome's friend said.

"There's more?"

"You've been assigned a new cellmate," Jerome said. "I assume so anyway, seeing as he put his things inside your cell, and they didn't throw your shit out, only Eustace's. He's your new cellie."

"Fantastic. That means tonight will be eventful."

"That's one word for it," Jerome chuckled and played

another card. "Rumor flying around is that he's wanting to kill you."

"That's a pretty safe bet. Speaking of which, why did you guys start talking to me? I figured you'd want to keep your distance."

"We don't give a fuck what those two gangs want," Jerome said. "We're on our own. Now don't get it twisted. If anyone asks, we don't like you, but we don't want to involve ourselves in their little feud. Besides, you're not an ass about skin color. That's rare in here if you hadn't noticed."

"I appreciate the honesty if nothing else," Jason said, taking another look at his new cellmate. "I need to prepare for the worst. Are there any coalition boys still inside our block?"

"Sure, you'd know them better than I, but the majority are in solitary alongside you. I count two remaining besides you. I'd meet them if I were inside your shoes. Maybe try talking to the big guy."

"Yeah, maybe he'll spare you if you beg kindly," Jerome's friend snickered. "Just get down onto your knees and ensure your lips are moist and smooth."

"I'd sooner die than that."

"That is your choice."

"Thanks for that option," Jason said as he stood from the table. "I need to take care of business."

"You go handle your business then," Jerome said. The rest of the table erupted into laughter.

Jason headed up the stairs to the second floor of the cell block and toward the familiar row of cells that his coalition vigilante buddies inhabited. He knew of the coalition members remaining, but hadn't spoken to them before. He avoided approaching too close to his new cell mate on his way and knocked on the open door as he stood outside the cell.

"What is it?" the occupant asked. One was on his bunk above while the other immediately shut the locker. Both looked over at Jason. "Mr. Walton, nice to see you back from solitary," the one on the ground said.

"Yeah," the one laying on his bunk said. "We figured you'd be back there for another few weeks. You meet your new cellmate yet?"

"I imagine I'll have to fight him to the death after lock-down tonight," Jason said. "He's been asking about me, I've heard. That means he's probably here to kill me."

"That is the preferred paranoid method of thinking."

"Vick," Jason said to the one who closed the locker. "We both understand there are folks who wish me dead. This new arrival is here after killing his old cellmate. You think that's a coincidence? It wouldn't surprise me if they offered him a deal. I bet if he kills me, he gets a boatload of cash or something."

"Or his old cell mate disrespected him. Remember the code. Always give courtesy flushes, clean up the sink after shaving, and don't be a douche. You might just live."

"You're telling me to bank on him not being sent to kill me?"

"What choice do you have?" Vick asked. "You can't run away from the dude unless you run to the guards and tell them you fear for your life. They don't have to move you even then, so you'd cause a ruckus for no reason. I'd say get strapped, be respectful, and prepare for the worst. If he's intent on harm, he'll make it evident. With that physique, I doubt he'd resort to killing you in your sleep."

"Which brings me to why I'm here," Jason looked to his

left and right, looking for anyone eavesdropping outside the cell.

"You're looking for something to defend yourself with," Vick said. "Ordinarily I'd tell you to pound sand, but considering you have the higher ups favor, I guess I can do you this favor." He moved back to the bunk bed and got to a knee, reached under the bed, and felt around for where he'd stashed the makeshift weapon. He finally found it and tore it free, then moved over to Jason and handed him the weapon. "You didn't get that from me. If you tell anyone you did, the coalition will be pissed."

"I understand." Jason stuffed the sharpened metal down his pants and into his underwear, careful of harming anything delicate in the process.

"I'd stash that somewhere in your cell, if you want my opinion," Vick said. "You'll want quick access to it if he wants to kill you tonight."

"I wouldn't keep it on me though," the other occupant of the cramped cell said. "You know how often we're searched. That's unless you wish to return to solitary with another charge for your upcoming trial. I hear that's coming up soon."

"The justice system speeds up for degenerates like me," Jason said. "It's a wonder, isn't it?"

"More like conspiracy. Be careful, Mr. Walton."

"Yes," Vick said. "I hope you'll remember this later. Now if I were you, I'd go find out this guy's motives. Maybe he's just a loner. Besides, it's disrespectful to not introduce yourself, and as you've learned, respect is a currency of sorts in here. Do not underestimate it."

Jason backed up out of the cell. "Have a good one. Don't work too hard," he said as he departed and turned toward his former cell. The man was still standing where he saw him earlier, just in front of his so-called home. He approached the nearly seven foot tall man who looked like a bodybuilder. He stopped a few yards away from the man and cleared his throat, drawing the man's attention.

The man's expression was blank and hard to read. "What do you want?" he asked.

"I hear you've been asking about me. I'm Jason Walton, your new cellmate."

He took his arms off the railings and now stood on his own. He towered over Jason and looked down on him. "You're him?" His voice was a deep baritone.

"You bet I am. You have me at a disadvantage. Who are you?"

"They call me Willy. I expected you to be taller, if I'm honest."

"I don't mean to cut this pleasant conversation short, but why are you looking for me? You understand what that usually means."

"You'll know after lockdown. I'd rather not speak of it until then."

Jason took a step back. "I was afraid you would say that, considering the reason for your transfer here."

"You know of that?" Willy asked.

"You know how inmates are. They're always gossiping, but I don't put much stock in secondhand information. I won't ask out of respect, but don't think I'm a fool, sir."

"I've heard you are many things, but a fool isn't one. Thy told me you were in the hole, so I took the other bunk."

"Before I leave you be, I need to know one thing. Were you sent to kill me?"

"As I mentioned, all will be revealed tonight after lockdown."

"I suppose I'll keep my shoes on before lockdown..."

17

"Where's the journalist?" Brett asked. "She's not listening and transcribing what we're going to be saying, is she?"

"She's in her room along with Skye," Jim said with his arms crossed and a dour look on his face. "I don't know what she's doing, and it's not my business past that. Now, did Ms. Kelly deliver on her promise?"

Brett grunted. "She did. We have cameras in nearly every room inside his house. She even snuck the package into one of the hidden rooms she couldn't get inside because of some magic she used."

"I'm sure he'll love that surprise," Jim said.

"We should have put one of those explosive vests in it," Ashley said. "It'd have made our jobs easier."

"How exactly would we detonate or even realize when to?" Brett asked.

"I don't know, put some sensor in there telling when it's opened? Hell, put a microphone inside, and listen."

"You want to program that?" Brett asked. "Besides, microphones would set off their wands if they inspected it.

"I don't know why you insisted on delivering that message," Ashley said. "It's just going to make him more paranoid."

"He's been messing with my head for years. Payback is more than warranted," Jim said. "He went after Cynthia; I go after Daphne. The difference is I won't hurt the girl like he tried to with Cynthia. He killed my father, so I send him a message saying his pops won't live long. Payback is a bitch."

"I'd be lying if it didn't make me laugh, but we need to focus on the game plan for tonight," Brett said. "The original cameras we planted outside have at max until tomorrow morning before they're out of power. It must be tonight if we want a hope in hell of getting inside without alerting the whole location. To that end, I have an idea of how to accomplish this mission."

"Go right ahead then," Jim said. He took a seat at the computers, as did Brett, Ashley, and Michael. "What's your idea? I don't fancy trying to kill all those security guards."

"It's not advisable to rely on brute force," Brett said. "We know security's tight, and they have a lot of bodies at their disposal. We need a plan to neutralize that advantage. There's one easy method to accomplish that, but it requires Blind Justice or Michael to be a little sneaky. Which of you are skilled at sneaking?"

"Me," Ashley said. "I'm lighter, faster, and shorter. What do you need?"

"We're going to utilize my favorite tactic," Brett said with a grin. "Misdirection is what will get Jim inside with Charles. Jim will make his approach from this direction." He clicked and a red X showed up on the map on the opposite side of where he made his infiltration the first time. "Ashley will approach in this direction." He clicked and a green arrow showed where the young woman was to go.

"What do you wish me to do?"

"Let me finish for one," Brett said. "You're going to apprehend one of the guards, put your blade to his neck, and force him to call in a disturbance on the east side."

"The back gate area?" Ashley asked. "I can I suppose. To what end?"

"It allows Jim to get inside while most of the guards chase this specter we've created. Michael, you've got your blade cleaned and sharpened, yes?" Brett asked.

"It's always ready, sir. What do you need from me?"

"You are going to pick off stragglers as they rush aimlessly in the chaos - quietly. Thinning their numbers is key. When you two are done, you will retreat away from the property."

"You're joking," Ashley said. "You can't expect me to just leave after stirring up the hornet's nest."

"If you like, you can move to aiding Michael after you're done, but I don't want you two getting into a shootout and getting yourselves killed senselessly. You also know the rules of this operation. Everybody involved, myself included, is going to be wearing our specialty vests."

"Oh, don't remind me of those damned things," Ashley said.

"Yours and Michaels will be remotely controlled by yours truly," Brett said. "Don't worry. I won't set them off unless I know well and truly that you're dead."

"That doesn't make me feel better knowing my life's in your hands."

"You knew the rules when you agreed to come," Jim said. "I'd rather you not go along, if I'm honest."

"To keep me safe?" Ashley asked. "You realize how well that works with us."

"Yes, you just go behind my back and endanger your

friend and her kid. I know how stubborn you two are," Jim said. "Now Michael, I expect you to watch her back with your life. If Brett finds out you didn't, you'll have him to deal with."

"That would probably be more effective if I was my old self," Brett said.

"You can still fire a gun." ·

"True that."

"You're always trying to watch out for me, but the whole reason I'm here is to watch out for you, you dumbass," Ashley said. "I don't need your protection. You need to learn when to accept help. You're not invincible."

"I understand your thought process," Jim said. "Now, once I'm inside, I'm going to grab information on where Charles is from Brett."

"With the sheer amount of cameras inside, along with the camera we hid inside the box in Charlie's special room, I should have a general guess where he is," Brett said. "After that, it's all in Jim's capable hands."

"I don't want either of you coming inside once the fight starts," Jim said. "In fact, I want you running away in case the worst happens and I fall. The blast would kill you if you're nearby. Staying close may make you feel better, but it's akin to suicide if I lose."

"You ever stop to think if you had our help that you might not lose?" Ashley asked. "Three on one is a lot smarter odds. I don't care how skilled he is. No one can fight three swordsmen at once."

"That's assuming he lets it end up in a melee," Brett said. "Odds are with three attackers he'd resort to guns, and that's a shit show waiting to happen. It's better if it's just Jim."

"Better for you or him?" Ashley asked, glaring at Brett.

"For the mission," Brett said.

"This is not negotiable," Jim said. "If you're in there, you're accepting death. I hope I've taught you over these years to realize when to retreat."

"Knowing her, that lesson may not have taken," Brett said.

"We're just on crowd control duty, then?" Michael asked. "We can circle around the outer perimeter and pick them off one by one if we're patient enough. We could make it faster if we go on different sides, too."

"He has a point," Ashley said.

"When your adversary is using firearms, it's best to not present too big of a target," Brett said. "I hate to admit it, but the kid has a point. We'd eliminate more guards by having them split up."

"You all knew the risks when you signed up," Jim said. "Do what you feel increases our odds. All I ask is neither of you take too many risks tonight. Keep your head down and swing that blade with all you've got. Your lives will depend on it. Stay quiet and be quick. Once they realize what's going on, they're going to call in reinforcements. You have to be gone before they arrive, or else."

"Or else what?" Ashley asked. "We'll die like you're planning to?"

"It's a possibility. We all know the stakes. As long as I'm leader, you will follow my orders. Is that understood?"

"Understood, sir," Michael said.

Jim looked over at Ashley.

She returned the gaze with a glare of her own.

"Well? I didn't hear you."

"Fine. You'd better not get yourself killed, though, or you'll answer to me."

"It's a simple plan," Brett said. "So long as Ashley here

gets her part done, we have an excellent shot. If she fails, then we're going to have to play it by ear."

"Before we prepare for tonight, I'd like to gather everybody in a room. I have something to say before tonight's operation," Jim said.

"Your last will and testament?" Ashley asked.

"Something like that," Jim said. "Michael, go gather Skye and Angie and bring them to the living room. Then we can gather what we need for tonight and get it ready."

"You want the reporter to hear it too?" Brett asked. "Just be careful of what you say."

"You heard me."

"Right, sir." Michael hopped off his desk seat and rushed out the open door into the hallway.

"You're scaring me with this," Ashley said.

"I'm amazed you haven't said those words before tonight," Jim said. "Just trust in my plan and it'll all work out."

"So you say. If you were so confident, you wouldn't make us all wear those vests. You only wear that if you're afraid we're going to fail and die."

"That isn't what I wish to discuss at tonight's meeting. Just meet me in the living room downstairs. Brett, you stay here. I need to talk before I say my piece."

"Got it."

"Whatever. You two discuss whatever you're planning. It's not like I need to understand. I'm only risking my life tonight."

"Going to tell Skye the plan?" Brett asked.

"Someone has to," Ashley said, sticking her tongue out toward Jim. "She saved our asses once already. She deserves to understand our plan," she said before slamming the door shut behind her, leaving the men alone in the computer room.

"She's hurt," Jim said. "Have I been too hard on them?"

"Maybe. I'm not their nanny. I have no clue," Brett said. "They're adults, they'll get over it. Now what did you need before your farewell speech? I assume that's what you're gathering everyone for."

"We both know there's a good chance I may not live through tonight." Jim reached into his jacket and pulled out an envelope he'd tucked away earlier. He gave it to Brett. "If the worst happens, I want you to give that to Cynthia when you return. Promise me you'll do that for me, won't you?"

"Sure," Brett said, taking the envelope. "I don't guess I get to look in it?"

"You'd better not, or I'll haunt you for the rest of your days, you jackass."

"I was just checking. Don't get your panties in a twist," Brett laughed and shared the rare moment of levity with Jim. "I'll make sure she gets it, don't worry. Try to not make me have to deliver it by coming home alive, alright? We must be prepared for death, but not plan for it. You understand that lesson, yes?"

"I know, but this is a hopeless situation I'm rushing into when you break it down," Jim said. "I'm rushing into a government official's home with nothing but two swords, a gun, and some body armor. Toss in the explosive vests and the lunatic who taught me to fight is my enemy, and you have a situation I'm actually scared of, though I'd never admit it in front of the girls or Jason."

"You remembered to pack the grenades, just in case, I hope?" Brett asked. "I didn't have them stocked for no reason."

"I got it. You know, I think you're the first person I've ever vented to like this."

"Aren't I honored?" Brett asked. "Just remember what I taught you."

"Right, let's attend this meeting. I'm already going to catch hell. It may as well not be for being late for my own scheduled meeting," Jim allowed Brett to go first, after concealing the sealed envelope.

The men departed the computer room and approached the stairwell's pinnacle.

Brett heaved himself out of the wheelchair at the top of the stair and moved himself onto the motorized chair. He pressed a button on the chair and a motorized whir accompanied the chair coming to life and heading down the stairs.

Jim moved the wheelchair out of the way and followed him down. He saw Brett move himself into the wheelchair at the bottom of the stairs. Jim could already hear the murmuring of everyone gathered in the nearby room. He let Brett move his chair out of the way before he reached the bottom. He entered the now populated room. "Thank you all for indulging me."

"What's this all about?" Angie asked. "I was in the middle of writing another article."

"This won't take long," Jim said. "Though after tonight, you should probably head back home or somewhere else. We won't be returning here."

"Noted," Angie said.

"Get on with it," Skye said. "It must be important to drag Ms. Summers to hear it."

"I asked you all here because I have something important to announce before tonight's operation," Jim said.

"Tonight?" Angie asked. "What's tonight?"

"You'll find that out later," Jim said. "I realize I have been a little cold lately."

"More than a little," Skye said. "You tried to exclude me entirely."

"You know why," Jim said. "I stand by my decision in that regard. I'm not apologizing for trying to protect you or your child. Now shut up and let me finish, would you? This is hard enough without the peanut gallery sniping and taking cheap shots."

"Whatever," Ashley said. She looked down at the floor, making a show of not listening to Jim.

"I have something important to mention should the worst happen tonight, and make no mistake, there's a sizable chance it could occur."

"Stop saying things like that." Ashley couldn't help herself. "You've never brought up the chance of dying before. It's like you're planning on it."

"It is a little disconcerting," Angie said.

"Shut the fuck up," Jim said, now losing his patience. "Sit down and listen. This is not difficult." He pointed at Michael. "See? Do what he's doing." He cleared his throat. "Before you made this ordeal harder, I wanted to mention something I don't say often. I'm not sorry for trying to protect any of you. I'd do it again in a heartbeat, even if you don't appreciate it now. You will when you hold your baby in your arms. Do any of you possess the slightest idea why I'm acting like this, or do you think I'm just a power-tripping dickhead?"

"I think that's my job title though," Brett said, trying to draw a laugh from the crowd but failing. "Geez, tough crowd. Go ahead."

"I'm not doing this out of some arbitrary sense of duty. I'm doing this because most of you, excluding Ms. Summers, sorry - I treat you like this because I love you and I consider you a part of my family. Whatever you've told yourself about how I've been acting, I don't do it to make you feel bad or unskilled. I'm scared. Not for me. I'm scared something might happen to you. This job we're doing tonight is the most dangerous we've ever taken on. That's a fact."

Angie raised her hand. "Does that make me the best friend type, not family?"

"Uh," Jim said, "let's just say close friend. Best friend is already taken. Sorry."

"Oh, okay then."

"My point with my embarrassing speech is I'm trying to keep those I care about alive and well, even if there's a good chance I won't. I'm not a superhero, despite what some in the media say. That means you, Ms. Summers. I am not superhuman, or even always an upstanding individual. I got Jason Walton caught up in this, and it's my fault he's where he is. If this is my final accomplishment, freeing Jason, then I'm alright with that possibility. I have one thing to ask you."

"What's that?" Ashley asked, now appearing to pay a bit more attention. She wiped away the corner of her eyes, hiding any signs of tears that may have snuck out from under her watchful eye.

"Please help Cyn with raising my child, should the worst come to pass. She'll need support. If I'm not here, I need you all to promise me you'll keep an eye on her. She's liable to lose herself if I'm gone."

"You damned idiot," Skye said. "That's already a given. Even if I'm pissed by your recent behavior, I still get it. I don't like it, but I understand your reasons. Obviously, I'm going to help her."

"I think the same goes for us all, minus perhaps the new guy."

"If I knew who she was, I'd help," Angie said.

"She could probably use the publicity to get more clients," Jim said. "Make sure it happens." He walked over to Ashley, who stood up when he neared. He wrapped his arms around her in a hug, and that was the straw that broke the proverbial camel's back.

Ashley lost all composure. She leaned into the embrace and stuck her face into Jim's chest, bawling as hard as she ever had before.

"Damn it," Skye said, looking away from the heart wrenching display in front of her. She saw Michael looking away as well, but Angie was openly crying.

"I always considered you like a little sister," Jim said to Ashley. "Maybe a pigheaded one, but I love you nonetheless. I want you to know that. I always will."

"This is not the sort of emotions I wished you to experience before a fevered battle, but I suppose this has its unique merits," Brett said with a roll of his eyes.

Ashley eventually let go of Jim and returned to her seat. She looked downward at the floor and wiped away her tears.

"The same applies to Silent Justice," Jim said. "I don't expect any tearful embraces from you, but just know it's all for a reason. You'll thank me when your kid's born."

"Damn it all," Angie said, trying to stifle the flow of tears. "I can't publish any of this, I take it?"

"Not until after tonight. Even then, only at his discretion." Jim pointed at Brett. "You run it by him and then, maybe."

"My answer is no, straight out," Brett said.

"Aw, but people would love this insight that Masked Justice and the group are all a giant family that's worried for their leader. It's heartwarming."

"We do many things," Skye said. "Being heartwarming is

not one of them."

"I beg to differ," Angie said.

"Whatever. You know I'll be going tonight. Bum ankle or not. I need to keep you all from dying."

"I figured you'd say that," Jim said. "The only way we'll be able to stop you is to tie you up, I imagine."

"You wouldn't," Skye said.

"Are you sure about that?" Jim asked.

"Knowing you assholes, you'd probably try."

"Don't be obtuse," Jim said. "You'll be with Blind and watch her back. That is all. That will aid in my mission - but no further. Understood? I cannot stress that enough. It will be detrimental to me if you all get ideas above your station."

"Right," Skye said. "You want it to be a one-on-one duel. I understand it after what happened. Just one arrow through a window wouldn't hurt, though. Right?"

"It's not happening." He looked downward at his side when he felt a vibration inside his pocket. "I think that's our cue. She managed to divert a sizable portion of security to leave with her. That's our sign. Get ready, boys and girls. Ms. Summers, drive safely to the local motel."

"Local motel? I'm staying here until you all return. That's the end of it. I'll hear nothing else on the matter. I'm invested now."

"You will not want to leave DC until tomorrow morning. Trust me on that," Jim said with a sad smile. "This is my last gift to you. It'll be the perfect story for you. I am counting on you to run with the story you've got right now. It's imperative that Charles Baskins' deeds are known to the world. Do you understand me?"

She could barely manage to get any words out from the constant crying and sniffling she found herself enduring. "Okay," she said with a nod. "I'll do as you say, but please be careful, and don't get yourselves killed. That goes for all of you. The world needs the Justice family."

"Justice family?" Brett asked. "Does that make me the angry uncle?"

"I never heard of this ragtag group being called a family, but it fits," Jim said, appearing genuinely happy for the first time since they embarked on this fateful journey.

"Right, now let's not miss our window of opportunity, people," Brett said. "Saddle up and let's get moving. We're paying a visit to dear Mr. Baskins."

At Charlie's just earlier...

"I need more security," Daphne said, almost the second Charlie entered the door.

"What now?" Charlie asked.

"He was in my home again," Daphne said. "He was waiting when I returned home today while you were busy. I thought I'd stop by my place and grab the recipe that Madison wanted, but there he was, sitting there on my couch."

"Damn it," Charlie said. "Alright, fine. I'll send more personnel with you."

"Can you send Madison? She'll keep me safe. She always does, and she keeps me calm, even if it's not part of her job description."

"Your safety is my topmost priority, babe," Charlie said, playing it smooth and sidling over to her. He rested his arms on her shoulders and gazed deep into her eyes. "I can't allow anything to happen to you, so I'm doubling the amount of security at your place. I don't want to hear any complaints."

"You'll get none from me. He was more menacing this time, threatening me. So, I ran here as quickly as I could after he retreated. I won't let him chase me out of my house for good. I refuse to let a low life like him dictate what and where I sleep because you're my future husband."

"You always were strong," Charlie said, hugging her tight and placing a palm on the back of her head. He played with her hair, trying to calm her down. He reached down and grabbed the walkie talkie strapped to his belt and brought it up to his mouth. "Madison, I want you in my room right now, on the double."

"Right away, sir," Madison's voice said after the burst of static.

"Now I'll inform her to have men inside the house, too. They're professionals. I know you don't like people being inside the house, but I'd rather they be inside than Masked Justice."

"I don't mind that anymore. Do what you have to. Just please, honey, keep me safe."

"I always will." Charlie said with a kiss on her forehead.

The door opened, and Madison entered his room. "You called for me, sir."

"So I did," Charlie said. He looked over at Madison, still holding Daphne. "Masked Justice was at Ms. Kelly's place again today. I want extra security there tonight. In fact, I want it doubled."

"Sir, if we double the security at her place, that won't leave enough for me to confidently say this address is secured."

"I don't care about that," Charlie bellowed. His outburst left an awkward silence. "I want you to head up this team personally. Is that understood? That's an order."

"As you say, sir. I'll round up more men to get it done. When are we to deploy?"

"As soon as she heads home," Charlie said.

"It won't be long," Daphne said. She pulled herself out of the embrace and walked over to Madison. "I don't want that bully to think he can muscle me out of my home. I'm putting my foot down."

"You heard her," Charlie said. "Keep her safe there at all costs."

"Right away, sir. I'll return inside a few minutes, and we'll be ready to move." She excused herself and exited the room.

Daphne walked around the bedroom in a daze. She eventually found herself staring out the large double glass doors leading out to the balcony. "Why does he hate you so much, love? Don't give me the public spiel either. It's not just you railing against vigilantes, is it?"

"Did he say something to you?"

"He said you killed his father."

"That's an outright lie," Charlie said. "He's insane. That's all there is to it. You don't kill that many people and stay sane. He's had to have killed over a hundred victims. He's a maniac."

"I see," Daphne said. "That doesn't make me feel better."

"These security agents are the best in their field." Charlie walked over and grabbed her hand to squeeze. "If anyone can keep you safe, it's them. If you've ever trusted me before, trust me when I say this. I love you and you are my world. I would never allow anything to happen to you. Please stay here with me. It's safer here."

"I won't be bullied out of my home by this killer madman. It's a matter of principal."

"I understand that but, baby, please," Charlie pleaded.

"You know my answer."

"You always were stubborn. Normally it's adorable, but not so much now. Fine, I'll trust Madison and the boys to keep you safe. Just please, if he shows up again, do what Madison says. Don't argue, and don't debate. Just run or whatever she says." He laid a hand on her shoulder and squeezed gently. "Please. I couldn't bear it if you got hurt by him."

"I promise, my love." She flinched as the words left her mouth.

Charlie didn't see as he looked out his bedroom window. "Thank you."

A knock at the door interrupted their tender moment, and Madison intruded without being called inside. "We're ready whenever you are, ma'am. Sorry if I interrupted, but you seemed in a hurry."

"It's fine," Daphne turned to Charlie and gave him the tightest hug she'd ever given him. She got on her tiptoes and kissed him long and passionately. "I'll see you tomorrow, alright?"

"Bright and early, like always." Charlie gave her a slick smile.

She released the embrace after a few moments and ambled to Madison. "I'm ready."

"Right this way, ma'am," Madison nodded to Charlie and led her down the stairs of Charlie's manor. She took her to the vehicle she had prepared earlier. "We're driving your car on the way back. There's a chance someone might see it and target it, so you're right here." She stopped next to the black SUV and opened the back door. "If you please."

Daphne climbed inside and scooted to the side to allow Madison to enter beside her.

Many men filled the rest of the cabin and the two cars besides theirs.

Daphne pulled out her phone and texted a familiar number only one word. "Now."

18

J ason tied his shoes and hopped off the top bunk to the floor below. It was almost time for lockdown, and he realized it. That meant he'd be locked in this cell with his cellmate until morning. He reached down and touched the side of his jumpsuit, where he had the weapon he'd secured earlier that day. *I'm just lucky I could trade for that screwdriver from the garage,* he thought. *I'm just lucky he needed someone to fix his television. That knife from before was too half-baked to kill Willy if push comes to shove.*

He heard footsteps approaching his cell and saw the enormous shadow coming into view. He felt his blood pressure spike with each step closer. His body tensed, and he reached his hand into his pants pocket as his cellmate he'd come to know as Willy approached.

Willy stepped into the cell just in time for a loud noise to echo throughout the cell block. An audible locking sound was heard.

"I think it's time you told me why you wanted to see me," Jason said. "I've been in jail for a short while, but even I realize someone asking about me is a sign of trouble. Did someone send you to kill me?"

"Kill you? No. Nobody sent me to kill you. You're not a target of the Front, are you?"

"The Front?"

"You've never heard of the Front?" Willy asked. "You must be new to the system. No new guy, it's nothing you need to concern yourself about. I am here because my last cell mate pissed me off too many times for his own safety. I was asking about you for a very simple reason. Do you know what they told me when I was getting ready to transfer? They said I was going to the place where they were holding Masked Justice's accomplice."

"You were trying to verify the rumor, is that it?" Jason asked, visibly relaxing. He sat on his bottom bunk and heaved a sigh of relief.

"Precisely. I have no hate for Masked Justice. The inmates I listened to on the ride here did not share that feeling. Apparently, they were former members of the groups the Justices finished, and they seek revenge. They told me of the reward on your head."

"There's a price on my head?"

"This is a surprise to you? Surely you know you've made many enemies in the criminal underground."

"So, a former slaver wants to kill me for revenge and money. That sounds correct for my life."

"Slaver?" the large dark man asked. "I don't know their jobs outside."

"I'm imagining this is one of the guys from the human trafficking organizations we burned to the ground a couple of months ago. That, or the Fitzgerald syndicate."

"He has a partner, and they were fixated on making sure

you are dead by tomorrow night. They tried to get me to join their little crusade for money."

"I take it you said no, or we'd already be fighting?"

"The Front does no one else's dirty work unless we're guaranteed the money, and even then, it's not guaranteed. No one has told me to harm you, thus I won't."

"That means I've got two people to worry about," Jason said. "I don't suppose you remember their names?"

Willy moved over toward the bunk beds and climbed onto his above Jason. His feet dangled over the side beside Jason's head. "One's name is something Fitzgerald, and the other's last name was Laramie, I believe. I think Fitzgerald was the one in charge."

"Fitzgerald? Oh, that's perfect. It makes sense, though. They're the ones who blackmailed me. They were aiming to kill a kid who saw too much of their operation, so they'd grabbed some evidence on me. If I didn't stand down, they said they'd run to the police."

"I take it you did not stand down?" Willy asked. His legs disappeared from Jason's view, showing he was now laying down.

"I wasn't going to allow some scumbag to kill a kid, even if it meant I ended up here. Only one of their men escaped. I have a feeling it was this Fitzgerald man. It's probably some cousin or brother of the late Mr. Fitzgerald."

"Sounds like you're in some shit, then. People told me you're with the Coalition prison gang. You may be in luck."

"I am? How do you figure?"

"The Front doesn't have what you'd call a partnership with the Coalition, but we have a working relationship. It wouldn't be out of the realm of possibility if I helped you. See, I have a personal thing against human traffickers and scum who kill children. I won't bore you with the why, and I'd appreciate you not asking. I, however, want some vengeance on them and their ilk."

"You'd be willing to help a guy you just met? What's the catch here? There's always a catch in jail I've learned."

"The catch? You're right about that. The catch is that you'll talk to your Coalition buddies and get them to accept a little business deal with the Front. You do that, and you've got yourself a partner to ride and die with."

"You know I'm not actually a Coalition member, right? There's no guarantee they'll accept anything. I'll do my damnedest, though, to convince them."

"They will say yes," Willy said.

"I'll talk to the remaining two Coalition members tomorrow. You should come with me to discuss the intricacies of the deal. They'd know how to contact the correct people for your little project, whatever it is."

"That's a deal. Try to stay near me tomorrow," Willy said. "They'll make their move then. You have weapons?"

Jason got off his bed and stood. "I have one. I had to rush because I thought you were the one trying to kill me." He pulled out the screwdriver and made sure Willy saw it before stashing it away in his cell, away from prying eyes. "I can get you something, too. I have more to trade, along with radios and televisions to fix. Though I can't guarantee it'll be the most professional shank ever, at least you'll have one." He dug out the makeshift shank his coalition members gave him earlier and handed it to Willy. "Take this until we find better."

"That's all I need," Willy said. "You should get some sleep tonight. We'll need all the energy we can get for tomorrow."

"Yeah," Jason sat and then laid on the hard bunk. He got under the covers and stared upward at the bunk bottom Willy was lying on. "Last time they started a riot in the yard for me. I doubt they'll be so grandiose this time."

19

Charlie closed the door to his armory and saw the package sitting on his table. "What the hell?" he asked, approaching it. He saw it had Daphne's name under the from part of the tag. "How did she get it inside here? Someone must have helped her. I should reprimand Madison next time I see her, as romantic as this is."

He pulled the ribbon and unwrapped the square. It was a simple cardboard box that was sealed with tape. He ripped it open. A single piece of paper was sitting at the bottom with letters from newspapers glued to it to form a message. He read it out loud. "Are you prepared for the consequences of your actions? I know you had that man kill himself. You betrayed his trust like you did mine. The reckoning is at hand. Poor Daphne is cute. I think I'll start with you, and then hunt her afterward, just like you had Hans do. Or maybe we should start with your father or mother, too?"

Charlie tossed the paper to the table below. "He wants to play it like this? Go ahead." He checked the inside of the box one last time and noticed one more thing waiting for him. He reached inside and took out a plushie depicting Masked

Justice that stores had sold years back, complete with sword and gun in each hand. "Why did he send this toy?"

He inspected the child's toy closely, looking for any irregularities. He couldn't see anything wrong with it. It didn't tick when he brought it close or smell off. It was just cloth, stitches, and excellent craftmanship. He threw it down onto the table and it landed on its back, staring at the bright lights above. "I guess he hasn't lost his sense of humor after all this. It could be an intimidation tactic. I must assume he's planted bugs on the outside of the property. That must be why he broke into my property earlier. The inside should still be secure."

He reached down and grabbed the walkie talkie clipped onto his belt. "We're probably going to have visitors tonight. Watch the outer walls closely. I want everyone on high alert. Repeat, tonight we're likely to have unwanted visitors."

"Roger that," a male voice said. "Shall we send those on the inside out to compensate? We don't have the numbers we did before."

Charlie felt a cold pit in his stomach. A lingering doubt dug at the back of his worried mind, and it wasn't a pleasant feeling. "Yes. The inside is secure. Make sure the outside remains safe."

"Understood," the voice said following a sudden burst of static.

Charlie clipped it back on his belt. "No." He shook his head. "He couldn't possibly have anticipated I'd send almost half my security with Daphne, could he? With Brett, anything's possible. Still, I can't risk him killing her for his vengeance."

His eyes widened as he looked downward at the tag on the discarded paper of the gift and found Daphne's name handwritten on the from tag. "He got to her. Damn it all.

How did I not notice earlier? He made her send this here. My question is, is delivering this gift all she accomplished for Jim? No, I can't suspect darling Daphne. She loves me. That's all there is to it. He must have forced her to do this, probably telling her he'd kill her if she didn't."

He moved over to the mannequins in glass cases wearing his old combat suit. Opening it, he took out the full armored suit. He set to work putting it on with untold amounts of possibilities running through his mind.

"He could've ordered her to thin my guards' numbers. That would explain why she requested more security." He was almost finished putting on the full suit of bullet and blade resistant armor. "I can't doubt her. She was just scared. She's not trained. Daphne really thought he'd kill her. That has to be it. It's up to me now." He finished the cumbersome process of putting on the suit and wandered across the room to the weapons behind the glass display cases. He opened them and pulled free the sword he'd been practicing with for the past years, then attached it to his belt, along with an automatic pistol.

A knock at the door interrupted him. "Enter," he called out.

The door opened to show an older gentleman. "Preparing for combat, Mr. Baskins?"

"You bet your ass I am. I have reason to believe we'll be attacked tonight. Inspect my table there. I received that threatening note today. That asshole has shown up at Daphne's for the past couple of days."

The guard walked over to the table and read the note he'd received. "That explains why she was so on edge today. She wouldn't tell anyone why. She must trust you."

"I'd never seen her so scared. I want all the personnel

outside. Keep him from getting inside. If he does, I'll deal with him myself."

"We only have ten men remaining here, sir. You sent as many with Ms. Kelly. He snuck in and escaped when we had more. You're sure you don't want protection in here for yourself?"

"If you all do your job well, he won't get inside, now will he? Do as I say. I know tactics as well as all of you, I'll have you know. I wasn't always a politician."

"It'll be as you say then, sir. Just please, be careful and stay away from windows."

"I also want every security guard here to draw automatic rifles from my armory." He pointed toward the rows of automatic rifles he had hanging from the wall where he'd gotten his swords and automatic pistol. "This assassin attacking isn't to be underestimated. Pistols will not cut it. Aim for his head. He has a similar armor to mine, but not as advanced or as covering. It only covers his chest and arms. Aim for his legs or his head. Center mass won't work for much other than pissing him off."

"I'll relay the information." The guard walked over to the glass case and grabbed his own walkie talkie. "Every single guard will report to the armory and grab an automatic rifle. Aim for the intruder's legs or head. If you aim center mass, follow it up and make sure they're neutralized." He looked up at his boss. "Do you know who is coming, boss?"

"Masked Justice."

"Masked Justice is coming to pay us a visit? Let's show him our brand of hospitality tonight." He grabbed the two rifles. "I'll hand these rifles out and speed up the process, sir."

"Make it happen. This will be the hardest fight of our

lives, make no mistake. Treat is as the greatest challenge you've ever faced because it will be." He reached down and used his thumb to push the blade hanging at his side out of its sheathe with a metallic slide of metal meeting their ears. He pulled it out in one swift motion, slicing in the same motion as unsheathing it, almost faster than the eye could see. "I will do the same."

"With all due respect, sir, swords aren't going to help in this modern age."

"In close quarters combat, a sword is worth more than a gun, good sir. You'd do well to remember that. Even a knife would be better than that unwieldy firearm you have, unless you'd prefer a bayonet. Do not underestimate the ancient ways of killing. I guarantee he will not. Besides, he's known for his swordplay. Do not presume to tell me how he fights. I'm the only one here who's fought him and survived."

"You, sir?"

"Get out already!" Charlie raised his voice suddenly and roared at the poor grunt.

"Right away." The guard nearly tripped over his own feet as he ran for the door like a scolded dog.

"Fool," Charlie said to the empty room. "Thinking he can tell me how to fight when he's just a young twenty something upstart." He sheathed the sword on his right side and took a deep breath. "Is there anything present I can use to gain a needed advantage in combat?" He paced, inspecting every weapon hanging on his wall. He stopped when he reached the end. "I hope I don't have to use you, but it could come in handy." Reaching up, he took a couple of grenades and clipped them to his vest before heading over to the mannequin he'd gotten his armored suit from.

Charlie reached up to its head and removed the mask. He put it on and adjusted it to his liking. "It's not like he knows what surprises I have in store for him." He brought his right hand up in front of him and made a fist. A small blade popped out from the gloves with a low metallic sound. He made another fist, and it retracted back into the glove. He did the same with his left hand, making sure it worked.

"Oh yeah," Charlie said. "We're ready."

20

———————

Ashley and Michael skulked in the tree line. They could see Charlie's property from their position. "We're in our first position."

"You should split up now. Blind, find a guard by himself and force him to call in a disturbance at the rear gate. M, I want you to stay near the address and when she does, you hop the fence and work. Remember to stay quick and quiet. Never stay in one place for too long. Masked will go on my signal."

"I'm almost at my position now," Jim said. "I'm already in the garage."

"You weren't supposed to head in yet, but fine, that works," Brett said. "Blind and M, get going."

"Why am I called M?" Michael asked.

"Shut the hell up and follow orders," Brett said.

Ashley saw Michael running into the trees. He was following the tree line, trying to circle around the compound out of sight. "I'm on my way to my position now."

"Go for it," Brett said. "The guard I want captured just

passed, so you should have plenty of time. I've looped the camera on that side, so they're none the wiser. Get in there."

Ashley sprinted out of the trees toward the walled off compound and her objective. It didn't take long before she reached the outer wall. She jumped and climbed up and over. Ashley landed softly on the other side. She lowered herself to the ground and saw where she was to post up. She was under the garage now, just below Jim.

"The guard is patrolling around the building. He'll arrive in under a minute. They're on high alert, running around. Masked Justice's message must have been received," Brett said. "Remember, it's the rear end we want them watching. You'll need to kill him afterward."

"I can handle that," Ashley said.

"Be careful down there," Jim said.

"I'm almost in position," Michael reported.

"Don't hop over yet," Brett ordered. "Wait ten seconds and then go. Someone's right where you'll be."

"Understood."

"Blind, your time is approaching. Get ready. He'll be there within fifteen seconds, so limber up."

"I got it," Ashley replied in a whisper. She unsheathed her sword quietly and heard footsteps approaching from around the buildings she was pressed between.

"The old representative's growing paranoid," she heard one of the young men say.

"Shit, it's a pair of them," Brett said.

"I can do this," Ashley said. She waited until they were turning the nearby corner and swung the blade horizontally neck high, catching one of the targets flush. The blade dug deep into the young man's neck and nearly decapitated him. It wasn't though, as the head hung on instead. He fell to the ground around the corner, out of sight.

Ashley didn't give the second guard time to scream or even notice what happened. She grabbed him and yanked him close. She stuck the blade to his throat. "You scream, and you die like your little buddy. Nod if you understand me," she growled into his ear.

The petrified young man nodded in compliance with her order.

"Good boy," Ashley said. "Now you are going to grab that radio on your hip and you're going to call in a disturbance near the rear gate. You spotted masked men with swords running over there. If you say anything else, I cut your head clean off, unlike your friend. Well, cut's a generous word, more like sawing it off. It hurts much worse from what I've gathered when I've done this before. Sure, you'll pass out from blood loss long before the head's clear, but it's more gruesome. Do you understand me?"

He nodded again.

"If I see you reach for a knife or gun, I kill you and grab some other poor idiot. Slowly reach for that radio now. I am Blind Justice. Don't think it would be my first kill."

The young man reached for the radio, but a sudden voice stopped him.

"Kid, where are you? You're lucky to have landed this job, and you wander off in the middle of shift on tonight of all nights?" Crunching of grass accompanied the voice.

Ashley turned him around. "Get rid of him, or you die right here." She kept the blade poking against his neck as she got onto her knees in front of him. Her left hand already had a gun ready, prepared if the unfortunate soul was unsuccessful.

The footsteps stopped, and the scared guard looked over his shoulder.

"There you are," the other said. "What the hell? Who is

that with you? Is that the new girl, Caroline? Oh, you two would be in deep shit if I informed the boss you ran here for a quickie.

"Just leave already," he said.

"You owe me for this one new guy. I'll be collecting real soon." The guard went back the way he came. "Just hurry, you two."

Ashley stood up and looked downward at the radio on the guard's hip. "Now make that call, before any more of you show. You get to climb this fence and then run for your car next. If you do anything else, I kill you."

The guard raised the radio and clicked the device. "I have eyes on two targets sighted near the east gate. They're masked, armed, and to be considered dangerous." He let go of the button.

"Get climbing then," Ashley said.

The young man pushed past Ashley and jumped up. He grabbed onto the wall and tried to climb, but hung there for a few seconds.

This was all Ashley needed to line up her swing. She swung with all she had, and the blade cut through his neck in one motion. There wasn't time for the poor soul to scream from her callous betrayal of trust. His body and head landed with heavy thuds.

"Move, Masked, and be careful. Blind and M, it's your turn for the killing. Good hunting, the two of you. Cover Masked if necessary on his approach."

"Understood," Ashley said and heard Michael over the earpiece. She had her sword in her right hand and her gun in her left as she approached the edge of the garage. She heard rapid footsteps nearby. Looking back toward the dead body, she witnessed Jim exit the building. She turned the corner in time to find a young guard jogging in her direction, coming directly at her.

She dashed toward the guard and aimed her slash at his right hand, which was reaching toward the firearm on his person. The swing landed, and the wrist was cut off. The screaming couldn't be stopped this time as the makeshift amputation caused him to let loose a blood-curdling scream. Ashley raised her left hand and pointed it at the guy's face. She squeezed the trigger and his body crumpled to the ground. She kept moving around the side of the house and heard more gunshots nearby.

Michael could be heard over the piece. "I got a couple here."

"I killed two," Ashley said.

"Blind, there's one heading your way. Watch your front. M, watch your back. Someone's trying to approach behind you. They're by the manor," Brett said.

Ashley didn't slow down with the news of another heading her way; instead, she readied her sword arm and doubled down. She sped up when a young man turned the corner in front of her. She tried to thrust the sword toward the guard, but he dodged to the side.

There was no chance to pull her sword back and try again, judging by the weapon he already held, so she attempted the only sensible action she could. She tackled him to the grass below. His gun fell a short distance away as the two struggled.

The guard tried to push Ashley off of him, while she tried to maneuver the blade to a position where she could finish him off.

He grabbed the blade from under her, causing blood to appear on his hands as he gripped the blade. She leaned forward, trying to use her weight to force the blade where she wanted it.

He used this to his advantage, using his legs to lift her and throw her off balance until she fell forward. He rolled with her and ended up on top of her now.

"Just die already, bitch." He directed the blade toward her throat now that he had the leverage and control. Blood dripped from his hands, but he didn't seem to care for the liquid crimson he was leaking from directly controlling the blade between them.

"I miss one operation with you, and you nearly get yourself killed easily," a familiar voice said into Ashley's ear.

A wet squelching noise and warm wet fluid covered Ashley's face. It tasted of copper. *Blood*, Ashley thought.

The young guard checked over his shoulder to find an arrow sticking out of his back. He redoubled his efforts with Ashley, bringing the blade closer to her neck while she struggled with all her might.

"Stubborn fuck, aren't you? Hold on," Skye said.

Two more thumps caused the young guard's eyes to go wide as he fell to his side off Ashley. He let go of the blade as he fell. All he accomplished was to gurgle and try to gasp for air as more gunshots rang out in the background amid the many yells from the dying nearby.

"I got one," Jim said over the radio. "Mark another one off."

"Sorry. I was tied up." Ashley got off the ground and kicked the dying young man in the ribs that had nearly killed her. She looked up at the wall separating the property from the woods outside. Skye was perched atop the nearby garage, looking down at her. Ashley could see the large grappling hook sitting beside her, answering how she got where she was with a bum ankle.

"The only guards remaining are by the rear gate now," Brett said. "You all should move there and finish them off. Masked, what's your status?"

"I'm inside," Jim said. "I'm looking for the target."

"He's upstairs in one of his secret rooms. I don't know which one."

"Got it."

"We're moving now," Skye said. "Move, Blind."

"On it." Ashley saw Skye pick up the device and toss it over the wall.

Skye took off running and jumped down to the wall below. She ran along the top of the wall toward the rear gate.

Ashley sprinted off, trying to keep up with the wounded woman. She did and stopped around the corner from the rear gate. "How many are there?"

"I spot five," Skye said. "They're heavily armed and paranoid. Recommendation on how to proceed?"

"M, take out your bow. You and Silent start picking them off. Blind, you're going to use your gun and start blasting as soon as you see them go down. We'll overwhelm them before they realize what's happening," Brett said.

"Ready," Michael said.

"At your leisure," Brett said. "They'll realize it was a hoax soon enough if they haven't already from the other gunshots."

Ashley peeked around the corner with her gun pointing toward their targets. She saw two guards go down with horrific screams. She moved her aim to a different target and squeezed the trigger.

Another one fell from the lead projectile embedding itself into his chest. She moved her arm and aimed quickly toward the fourth on the ground. She squeezed, but the guy was quick enough to duck and start rolling.

The fifth fell to another arrow, and the fourth ran after his roll.

Ashley fired again and again, but none of her shots hit the desperate man.

"He's headed toward Blind. I don't think he realizes," Michael said. "Be ready over there."

Ashley moved back behind the corner and tucked away her gun. She gripped the sword with both hands and waited for the rapidly approaching footsteps. She readied a horizontal swing toward the corner as the steps got closer, aiming the swing at chest level.

The man turned the corner and felt cold steel impact his rib cage. The impact knocked him to the ground and to his knees. He did not drop his weapon. Before Ashley could yank the blade free, he aimed it at her.

Another arrow flew. She could feel the wind from the projectile. The young man realized he had an arrow lodged in his neck.

Ashley kicked his gun holding hand, knocking the gun to the grass below. She yanked the short blade free of his ribcage and readied a thrust. She finished him off by penetrating his chest again, this time not being impeded by any pesky ribcage. The blade came out the young guard's back. She could tell he was trying to wheeze, judging by the hatred infused glare he was giving her. She used a foot to kick his chest while pulling her blade free.

The young man fell backward onto the grass and didn't move ever again.

"That's all of them," Brett said. "Masked, you're on your own in there. God speed. Everyone else, retreat immediately. Stay nearby the location just in case, but get into the woods. Reinforcements will take at least fifteen minutes."

Inside with Jim...

Jim had his pistol in his right hand, ready to aim and fire at a moment's notice as he slowly stalked through the dark hallways inside. He'd just climbed to the second floor. His imagination ran wild, making it difficult to discern fantasy from reality. He imagined Charles popping out of many doors to take a potshot at him and aimed at these specters, yet didn't fire. "Damn it," he muttered to himself. He brought a hand to his chest, feeling an extra layer underneath he'd never felt before.

Another mental image of it blowing up didn't help his mood any. He shook his head and pressed onward. He opened every door by getting to their side and throwing it open while behind the nearby wall for the safety of cover. Thus far, none of the rooms had his target inside.

An all too familiar voice invaded his ear. "I finally found the frequency you use," Charlie said. "Are you searching for me, old friend? Shall we play hot and cold like we used to as kids? I think we need to raise the stakes. Loser dies, how about that? You're it first."

"Every man deals with his impending death differently," Brett said. "I never imagined yours would be to regress to an infantile state, but it fits you, Charles."

"Ah yes, the crippled swordsman extraordinaire speaks," Charlie said. "I know your backup's retreated and I'm not a fool as to why. You're touching that puffed out chest extra gently tonight. Wearing insurance, are we?"

"You're dying tonight one way or the other," Jim said. "Even if it's the last act I accomplish, you'll die."

"How simple-minded," Charlie said. "Fine, I don't need any more security to kill you. Find me if you can."

"That transmission came from your front and toward your right. He's in the..." Brett was cut off.

"Now we can't have you ruining the surprise," Charlie said. "I blocked his transmission for the rest of the night. Now it's just you and me, old buddy, old pal."

Jim recognized the location of the secret room based on the information that Brett had relayed. "Found you," he said.

"You're sure about that? Even if you're correct, are you positive you want to bust inside? This is a deadly game we're playing here."

"It doesn't matter if I die," Jim declared as he charged headlong toward the door, convinced that his one-time friend was behind it.

"So, you do have an explosive vest," Charlie said. "God damn it."

Jim rammed his shoulder into the door and rolled once he was through. It was a wise thing he did as bullets impacted where his head was mere moments ago. He found himself behind a large glass display cabinet that shielded him from the hail of bullets. The glass webbed and cracked, but held the bullets at bay.

"Damn it," Charlie said. "I knew I shouldn't have sprung for the bullet resistant display cases."

"This is already over, Charles!" Jim yelled, keeping his head down. "I've stacked the deck. I win either way now."

"You really think I didn't plan for this?" Charlie asked between bursts of gunfire. He pressed a button near the windows, and they moved upward immediately. "I kill you and then jump. It's simple. I'll break a few limbs, but the voters will eat that up."

"If you think that'll save you, you're even dumber than I

am," Jim said, yelling over the deafening gunfire, and hoping his words reached Charlie's ears.

The glass Jim hid behind started to buckle. He rolled to his side to another display case.

"You're on the wrong side of the room, buddy," Charlie said. He dashed over to the large wall of weapons and moved to grab a large automatic rifle.

Jim seized the momentary opportunity and pulled the grenade off the front of his vest. He pulled the pin and tossed it behind him.

"Son of a bitch!" Charlie noticed the explosive rattling toward him and took off in a sprint before he could grab the weapon. He ducked behind a nearby desk before the room shook from the violent blast.

A dust cloud shrouded the room. Both men's ears rang from the blast, and Jim felt disorientated.

"You bastard," Charlie cried out. "Since when did you use grenades?"

"Someone needs to even the playing field if you have all these fancy toys." Jim took the opportunity and ducked out of his cover toward Charlie's last known location in the room.

"Hasty as always, I hear. Approach if you insist," Charlie said. "Once this smoke clears, you'll be in the middle of a desolate island without cover."

"Too afraid to duel me?" Jim asked.

His question was left unanswered as he approached the weapon racks. He couldn't see far through the dust saturated air. Jim heard a sound to his side amidst the ringing in his ears. He quickly aimed his pistol toward the sound and fired.

"Too slow," Charlie's voice said calmly through the clouded interior of the armory. "I have no incentive to clash swords with you, buddy. If you have a vest on, that means it's probably wired to go off when you die. All you've done is turn this fight into a game of keep away."

Jim kept moving, trying to utilize the sound of his former best friend to find him through the dust particles. Though he stayed low to the ground, he moved as fast as he could. He heard a door open, and Charlie disappeared through the fog of war. He took off into a run after his former best friend, and nearly didn't stop in time as bullets struck the door frame. The bullets were low. If Jim had been there, he noted it would have taken his ankles or legs out.

"Don't let me slow you down," Charlie's voice could be heard. "Tell me, where would you prefer to die? I'd recommend this hallway up here. I think you'd love the décor we went with as you slowly bleed out and I escape."

Jim used Charlie's gloating to his advantage and barreled out of the door without warning. He fired his weapon as soon as he cleared the frame and rolled as soon as he was clear of it.

Charlie ran down the rest of the stairs and fired a few more shots upstairs in Jim's direction.

They missed Jim. He sprung up to his feet from the roll and pursued Charlie down the stairs without pause.

A loud intercom system nearby came to life, with Charlie's voice coming out of it. "You always were stubborn. I'm getting out of this alive, and you'll go down in history as a madman who killed his own father. I will lead this country to the greatness it deserves."

"Spare me the drivel and the empty platitudes. You should know you're caught between a rock and a hard place. You may be waiting for reinforcements, but mine are surrounding this place. If you run, they put you down. If you stay, I'll kill you one way or the other."

Jim decided to throw caution to the wind and, turning the corner, immediately started running, aiming to close the distance to his friend if he was inside.

"Getting colder. Your friends can stay outside all they like. It just means more of them will be caught. I just have to run out the clock and hide from you. They'll take you out."

Jim stopped in the middle of the kitchen and examined his surroundings, mentally trying to figure where Charlie had run to. "I guess I could just off myself and take this whole fucking building down with me, including you. Would you like dying that slow and agonizing death? It's either that or come out."

"Don't give up so easily. I'm closer than you think."

Jim moved into a new room on Charlie's ground floor. He kept his eyes downcast, watching for any attempt to take out his mobility. Jim pulled a blade free in anticipation of melee combat at Charlie's words. His forward thinking allowed him to see the blade coming toward the front of his legs. He leaped over the blade and turned to see Charlie standing beside the doorway.

"Can't blame a guy for trying," Charlie said.

Jim didn't allow Charlie to run away again. He thrust a sword toward Charlie, who dodged to the side. He was now in front of the same doorway Jim entered and he backed up quickly.

"This is growing old. Stay still and let's finish this already." Jim recovered his form and gave chase. His blade finally met Charlie's, as the frantic politician was in full defense mode. He backed up through the house, no longer turning his back on Jim.

"Scared?" Jim asked. The two warriors fought as they spoke and moved. Neither would grow tired from this pace, but the stakes were still high with each parry, deflection, dodge, and swing of their swords happening.

"More amazed," Charlie said. "You think using two blades is a good idea? Did you do this against Hans?" He leaned back to avoid a slash Jim had leveled at his throat. "Tell me you weren't that idiotic. He specialized in two blades. I know you don't."

"Willing to bet your life?" Jim asked. He let Charlie backpedal an extra few steps before holstering the gun and pulling out said second blade. "You wish to see how skilled I became? Let's go." He twirled both blades in his hands to show off to his former friend.

"Was this Brett's doing?" Charlie went on the offensive and threw some blows Jim's way. Nothing was aimed at his neck, nor were there any thrusts toward his chest. Every blow was aimed at slowing him down, either aiming at his hands or his legs.

Jim spent more time guarding his legs than actually trying to parry and riposte to gain an opening, even with his two blades. Both blades allowed him to deflect any of the blows, but he knew that one wrong move could result in his legs being chopped, rendering him immobile. Charlie knew how to put pressure on Jim and throw off his battle plan. This infuriating trait from their childhood hadn't faded with age, to Jim's frustration.

"Attempting a similar strategy as your buddy Hans is certainly a risky move," Jim said with a calm voice. "I killed him. You sure you want to imitate him?"

"I beat him in a duel when I faced him," Charlie said. "You had your entire squad there. I'll take my chances."

"Look at you," Jim said as he deflected the single blade of Charles again. "You've forgotten the warrior ways."

"I never taught you anything about being a warrior. I only taught you to kill."

"You're a disgrace to your skills. You cower behind security guards' dead bodies, you run and hide, and then you try to cripple your opponent to run away. These aren't warrior traits. They are the actions of a coward. You disgrace yourself and your honor. Besides, you moron, if you cripple me, I'll shoot myself in the head. You still die. You're fucked."

"What do you know about a warrior's honor, huh?" Charlie's attacks were growing faster with his anger rising. "Being a warrior is all about power. What better profession exists to gain power?"

Jim saw an opportunity in the myriad of blows the pair exchanged. He used his right blade to meet Charlie's single blade and used it to knock it to the side while his other blade tried to stab toward Charlie.

Charlie's right foot moved behind him, effectively turning to the side so the blade grazed his stomach, but little else. He used his free hand to punch Jim squarely in the chest.

Jim stumbled backward, trying to regain his breath from the torso strike.

"You want a lesson about power? Fine. Here's my last lesson as your teacher before you die a lingering death, realizing this was all for naught. A warrior craves power more than anything. Honor is a figment of their imagination. What wiser profession for a warrior than a politician? Name a more powerful man than the President of the United States. When I'm president, I'll do anything I want for this country." He cackled. "Where will your Justice family be then? They'll be hunted like feral dogs and all your honor won't account for shit."

The two resumed their deadly dance of steel, sparks,

and footwork, with Jim taking the aggressive posture of the two.

"It just takes one mistake, Jim old boy," Charlie said. "You taught me that with this scar. I won't make the same mistake twice by underestimating you."

The two men fought through the kitchen. Sparks flew with every clang of blades. Jim advanced, now within only a couple feet of Charlie, as the politician desperately tried to keep himself safe from both blades trying to end his life. There was no more talk right now. He was too concerned with staying alive as he felt an icy knot in his stomach growing. He hadn't felt that icy pit in his stomach in years, and he knew it. The adrenaline helped him ignore the crippling fear and kept him in the fight.

Jim had cornered Charlie now. He had him pinned between the oven and sink. The exit to this kitchen was behind Jim. "Let's end this." He swung both blades horizontally toward each other in a scissor motion with Charlie in the middle.

Charlie fell to the floor, dodging under the two blades. His blade caught a little of the blades above him. He managed to get his blade under control fast enough to thrust it toward Jim's leg while he was on the floor and it hit its mark.

Jim felt the blade enter the front of his foot. He regained his balance and looked down to see Charlie desperately trying to pull the blade out of his foot. He swung downward at Charlie, who leaned to the side, frantically dodging the blade. Jim swung the other blade, compensating for Charlie's move. This one struck flush with Charlie's left arm. The blade dug into Charlie's upper arm a few inches deep. "Got you."

"You don't even realize when you're beaten." Now

Charlie had to wield his weapon with only his right arm. His left hung limply at his side.

Jim could feel that he couldn't put much weight on his freshly injured foot. He could feel his shoe flooding with warm blood. So he committed to the only plan he could devise. He kept attacking while standing in place.

Charlie got low to the ground and rolled to his side, trying to move clear from the now effectively crippled Jim.

Jim summoned every bit of willpower within him to keep up with the combatant below. With every step, Jim felt excruciating pain, but it did not deter him. His muscles had not given out, merely screamed in pain, and that was adequate for him. He kept up with Charlie when he stopped rolling and kept the onslaught going.

Charlie attempted to scramble to his feet, but Jim's downward slashes prevented him from doing so. It was all he could do to stay alive under the added weight of Jim's blows crashing down on him.

"I think you miscalculated, Mr. President. I think you hit my artery with that stab. Good job. We're on a timer." Jim lifted said foot up and kicked Charlie square in the teeth, knocking Charlie back to the tiled flooring. His sword clattered away, out of reach. Jim fell on top of him and sat on Charlie's chest. He pinned Charlie's hand that had been holding the blade to the tile using his left arm. "Come, let's journey to hell together, like old friends should."

"You first." Charlie raised his injured arm toward the incoming sword falling toward him. He made a fist, and his glove's hidden blade punctured his glove, deflecting the point of Jim's sword away from his neck and down to the ground beside his head. He utilized the surprise of his near suicidal defense and punched Jim in his side using his other hidden blade.

The force of Charlie's blow caused Jim to fall to his side, as well as spring a new leak as the blade pierced through the protective vest and into Jim's abdomen.

Charlie tried to get to his feet again, but found Jim holding onto his leg for dear life. He tried to yank his leg free, but realized it was a fool's errand. He noticed his blade still on the ground where he was forced to abandon it to roll to the side. "Get off of me and accept your failure already!" He had lost his cool and his fear was on full display. "I'm going to save this country from you and your kind, and I won't let your stubborn dumbass stop me."

Jim had dropped both his blades, so both were on the floor near him, but his arms were wrapped securely around Charlie's left leg and he wasn't planning on letting go. "I think you'll stay with me as I bleed out."

"Dream on, you delusional psychotic." Charlie reached downward and punched Jim's head using his uninjured arm, but the grip on his leg didn't falter. He couldn't lean forward enough to grab any of the blades without overextending his leg being held in place by Jim. His blood ran cold when he saw one of Jim's arms unwrap from his leg.

"I'd love to gamble and say this will work, but I don't play the odds," Jim said, picking up one of his blades. He twirled it in his hand, so the sharp edge pointed toward Charlie. "I want you to know, I hate you. I hope you burn in hell with me so I can watch you be tortured for all eternity for what you did to those I love."

"Now don't do that, we can talk about this." Charlie was trying to break free of the vice like grip, but Jim's blood loss wasn't severe enough to weaken his stranglehold on Charlie's leg. Nevertheless, he used his free leg to kick Jim, to no avail.

"I'm done talking. Now die so Jason may be free." Jim

first brought the blade behind Charlie's leg and cut deeply, imitating the cut that Hans had given his mentor.

Charlie fell to a knee at his hamstring being sliced open.

"You're not going anywhere. This is how Brett felt. You feel that jolt of fear? I've been living with that ever since you killed my father." He moved the blade to the remaining hamstring and repeated the motion. "You'll bleed out with me at best. Our destinies are truly intertwined now."

The blood pool beneath the two men was steadily increasing in volume as the conversation carried forth. He let go of Charlie finally, knowing he was now crippled. He used his free hand to shove the remaining blades on the floor a good ten feet away.

"You fool," Charlie crawled away from Jim. Every time his injured arm slammed into the kitchen tile, it smeared blood already pooled on the kitchen tiles.

Jim screamed as he stood up from the sheer pain rolling through him, but he did stand. He took an unsteady step toward Charlie, keeping pace with him. "That fear you feel? I'd be lying if I said I didn't share it."

Charlie clawed forward, heading toward the back door. The kitchen resembled a horror movie set, doused with blood from both combatants.

Jim hobbled closer to Charlie's crawling form. He got close to Charlie before his injured leg gave out. He fell, and Charlie broke his fall as he landed on him, pinning Charlie's arms out at his sides. "We're going to die, so if you wanted to issue an apology, now is your perfect opportunity."

"Fuck you."

"I knew that would be your answer." Jim could feel Charlie trying to raise his arms to claw himself further. Jim's blade was in his hand, with the blade pointing away from the former friends. "You're bleeding out, as am I.

When I die, this vest goes boom, and there won't be any evidence remaining. Make your peace with God as I intend to."

"I'm not dying here," Charlie said.

Jim zoned out, but kept his grip on Charlie's hand. He kept them pinned to the ground with great effort as Charlie was using all his strength to get the vigilante off him. *I knew it'd come to this,* he thought. *Deep down when I started this crusade, I knew this was how it was destined to end, dying in a pool of my blood.*

"I've had enough of this shit!" Charlie used all his remaining strength and got his uninjured arm free of Jim. He used it to elbow Jim on the side of the head.

The blow did not weaken his other hand's grip, nor did it cause him to roll off. Jim was still firmly laying on Charlie's back, minus one arm.

Charlie tried to use the breakthrough to escape but couldn't manage the speed necessary to wiggle free and found himself stuck again once Jim recovered.

"Are you through? Recognize when you're beaten. You may be a better swordsman than me, but I don't really care. We both know you'll never run far enough away by the time I die. Not with those hamstrings cut."

"I finally broke through the interference he setup. What the fuck's happening?" Brett asked.

"I got him precisely where I want him," Jim said. "He's not getting away, and we're both bleeding out."

"Sounds like the mission is accomplished then," Brett's voice was solemn. "Everyone return to the vehicle. We're leaving now."

"He's still inside!" Ashley said.

"I'm not leaving," Jim said. "Get the hell out of here, all of you. Keep yourselves alive and out of prison."

"You let me free, you fucking psychopath," Charlie cried out.

"Thank you," were Skye's only words.

"We've got to go!" Michael sounded like he was struggling, presumably to keep Ashley from rushing inside the house he was in.

"Get off of me," Ashley said. "I'm not leaving while he's still in there."

"This is my final order. Follow it," Jim ordered as loud and commanding as his exhausted body could manage with the world swimming before his eyes. "I'm dying, Blind. It's a foregone conclusion now, and I'm taking Mr. Baskins with me to hell. I love you all. Please stay safe out there." He reached up with the hand holding Charlie's injured arm and ripped the earpiece free. "Now it's just us, old friend. Is your vision swimming yet? Mine is. I think I'll be dead in a few minutes."

"God dammit," Charlie kept struggling beneath, never giving up.

"I guess I'll seal the deal now then," Jim moved up and sat on Charlie's lower middle back, effectively pinning him underneath and freeing Jim's arms. "Use those little trick claws if you like. It won't help you." He brought his sword up and pointed the blade at himself.

God, please forgive me for what I'm about to do, he prayed. Before he could muster up the courage to plunge it into himself, he saw images flood his mind.

He remembered rescuing Ashley from that infernal mansion, killing the innocent guard, and escaping with Cynthia in the car. The next memory was seeing Silent Justice for the first time inside that home all those years ago, when they found their target already dead. Flashes of Skye's smiling face as she and Jason grew closer together came next. He felt a flash of pain. Gazing downward, he found Charlie had stabbed him in his leg again. He simply didn't care at this point. He welcomed it with open arms.

Next was Jason. The memory of Jason showing up at his door and attempting to blackmail them to join them was vivid. He remembered Ashley's reticence at the man joining and her eventually warming up to him. He always loved how Jason showed him the respect he didn't deserve. *Jason's like the little brother I never had,* he thought. *I'm sorry, kid. My final sacrifice is for you.*

There was one additional person who forced their way to the front of his mind during these hopeless moments. *Cynthia,* he thought. A torrent of images flooded his mind all the way from childhood. Them sitting on a park bench looking up at the stars came first. The next was them at a local diner, eating pie and drinking coffee after his fateful livestream that kicked all this off. The final was their first night together, along with the words that shocked him before he departed. He heard her voice clear as day inside his mind. *"I'm pregnant with your baby."*

He looked down at the blade pointing toward him with his arms stretched out in front of him. His arms wobbled and shook from the blood loss, his vision was darkening. He knew his life was ending. He looked downward to see Charlie still struggling against all odds to escape. *I'll miss everyone of you and be watching over you, assuming I'm not burning in hell. Please, God, forgive my many sins. I simply wanted to defend the children, misguided as my methods were.*

He thrust the blade into his stomach with everything he had, careful to avoid the explosive vest. He dragged it to the side. The pain was unlike anything he'd ever experienced before. His flesh gave way under his blade's unrelenting onslaught, fueled by his sheer willpower. He eventually could take no more and fell forward, crushing Charlie beneath him. "It won't be long now, Father. I'll see you soon."

"No." Charlie was obviously panicked. "No, no. This can't be happening! Help me! Someone!" He called out, his voice beyond frantic. He clawed at the tiled floor so hard and so long his finger nails were bleeding profusely now, adding to the giant puddle beneath the two men.

The entire house was leveled by an explosion that detonated just behind him, drowning out his cries. Both former friends were annihilated in an instant. The mansion was destroyed, now replaced by a giant dust cloud...

21

The ride to the safe-house was silent. No one had said a single word about what happened when they'd left. They'd seen and heard the nearby explosion, but no one wanted to acknowledge what it meant the entire ride home. Skye followed behind in the second car.

Michael pulled the car into the driveway they'd seen too many times over the past few days. "We're back," he said simply.

"Come on then," Brett said. He waited for their vehicle to stop before he threw the passenger door open. "There's no sense sitting outside all night."

Everyone got out of the car without further word and headed inside the base of operations. Angie was standing just inside, obviously worried. "You're back."

"So we are," Brett said, leading the group inside. "Why are you still awake?"

"I was worried."

"No sense worrying now," Brett said. "You'll have a juicy story for tomorrow. It came at a hefty price, but the job is done. Keep in mind, if you reveal any intimate details after you find out, you'd incriminate yourself too."

"You're still an insufferable ass, I see." Angie looked at the still crying Ashley being guided inside by Skye. She looked behind them to find Michael bring up the group's rear and shut the front door. She took a step back and covered her mouth. Her voice was muffled. "Don't tell me. I don't believe it."

"You'd better believe it," Brett said. "We'll have enough trouble with this girl dealing with the reality of our situation."

"What happened?"

"He accomplished his mission," Brett said simply. "What more do you need to hear?"

"How about the part where he fucking died, you asshole cripple?" Ashley was obviously angry, judging by her tone of voice and words chosen. "How about that he sacrificed himself unnecessarily because of the God damn plan you and he devised? How about he refused to allow us to come inside and grab him because he thought he was already dying? You and he didn't even allow us a chance to save him."

"He was already bleeding out!" Brett attempted to cut this hissy fit off at the pass with a yell, but it only had the opposite effect. His voice softened for one of the first times Ashley had known him. "There was nothing you could have done except die with him, and he didn't want your senseless death. He informed me before we departed that he wanted you to survive and thrive, not be mired in the past.

"You gimp." Ashley broke free of Skye and stood in front of Brett, sitting in his wheelchair. "You believe you knew what he wanted because you were his teacher for a few months, huh? You didn't know shit about him."

"Personally? Yeah, you're right. I know my student's skills and aptitudes better than you though. There was a reason I insisted on each of you wearing those explosive vests. It was for you and your family's best interests, so someone like our reporter friend didn't make your family's life difficult if they found your dead body in there."

"He was my family." Ashley quite literally punched down and snapped Brett's head back from the impact, along with his wheelchair being pushed backward..

Michael rushed forward and dragged Ashley away from Brett.

Brett covered his face, covering the broken nose he'd just received. "You feel better now?"

"No," Ashley said.

"You mean to say that Masked Justice is..." Angie couldn't force herself to complete the inevitable question.

"He's dead," Brett said. "He completed his mission at the cost of his life."

"Those assholes better keep their end of the deal." Skye hadn't spoken before this, but she wasn't in the best of moods either, judging how she spoke through clenched teeth.

"They will," Brett said, taking his hand away to reveal a bloody nose. "Or they'll have me to deal with."

"I doubt they're afraid of you," Ashley said. She broke free of Michael's grip and moved away from Brett. She paced back and forth in the giant lobby, away from the group.

"They know better than to doublecross me, and that would certainly fall under it. I know you don't care for me right now, but Masked Justice was my student. He was my first ever. I know our meeting wasn't exactly pleasant, but I grew to care for him in my own way. That's the first time and the last instance you'll hear me say words to that effect, so burn it into your memory. Just because I don't bawl doesn't mean I am indifferent. You think you're the only one hurting?"

Skye stepped forward to stop Ashley from throwing another punch in Brett's direction. "Stop it. This isn't helping anything."

"Easy for you to say," Ashley said. "You get your boyfriend back now. What about me? He was one of the few family I had. He loved me more than my own parents did. I don't care if my biological parents die or not, but him..." she stated before her speech was cut off by a fresh surge of tears streaming down her face. "I could have got him out, and I wasn't even given a chance."

"You'd have died too," Brett said. "Before we embarked on this journey, he had a sensor implanted in his back. That monitored his life signs. At the first sign of his heart stopping, that vest went off. He was nearly dead when we heard from him after I got through Charlie's jammer."

"I know it's a bitter pill to swallow," Michael said. "I didn't even know him that well and I'm broken up. There truly was nothing any of us could've done."

"So, he's really gone," Angie said. She took a step backward and rested her palm on the handrail of the stairs to steady herself. "Who did he kill?"

"You'll find out tomorrow anyway," Brett said. "Charles Baskins was the target."

"Holy shit nuggets," Angie swore. "This will impact the political landscape for decades. It could rally more to his cause."

"The media will also run interference for him," Brett said. "They love talking about dead men with flowery words, regardless of who they are. Sorry for making your job harder. You're probably going to be called all manner of words while you're exposing his corrupt side now that he's dead."

"It doesn't matter one bit," Angie said. "The world needs to know everything he's done."

"I'll work with you over the coming months," Brett said. "You will only print what I say, and we'll give you an entire career over Mr. Baskins. You'll be covering the greatest political scandal in the past half century. That should keep him from becoming a martyr. If we show the public the nasty shit he's done, it'll guarantee his party cannot capitalize. How about that?"

"You'd help me with more than just the guy at the rally?" Angie asked.

"I'll help as far as not exposing one of us goes, yes. I have receipts that don't tie back to the coalition that show him in an unflattering light. Namely, his aide's phone records we picked up from his body the other night. I have evidence. His aide was sloppy with security. I've combed through the phone in my off time and noticed quite a few corrupt practices they've been engaged in. You'll have more than enough ammunition without exposing us if you stick with me. You'll claim the phone was left by the attacker that tried to kill you - because that's the truth."

"I'd be honored to help bring the truth to light," Angie said, wiping away a tear. "It's why I became a journalist."

"Fine. That's settled then. Now for more immediate matters." He glanced at Ashley, who sulked as she sat on the first step of the stairs near Angie. "Let's go over details now."

"Right now?"

"Unless you'd rather wait," Brett said. "Come with me." He wheeled himself into a nearby room and motioned for Angie to follow him, leaving Michael, Skye, and Ashley still in the lobby.

"I can't believe it," Ashley was staring down at the immaculate tile flooring. Her voice was numb and distant. "I can't believe he's dead. It's like I'm in a nightmare that I keep hoping I'll wake up from."

"No such luck this time." Skye walked over and sat down beside her. She placed an arm on Ashley's shoulder, only to find her friend leaning into her. "He did what he felt he had to, to keep us safe. We can debate the efficacy later, but for now, realize that he loves you. He loved all of us more than we can possibly understand, except maybe Michael here." She pointed at the young man standing nearby. Her attempt at levity failed, as Ashley didn't even crack a smile.

"I should have gone inside with him against his orders," Ashley said. "If I had, he'd still be alive. It's my fault."

"That isn't a productive area of discussion," Skye said. "You did your job. Striking down some of the best security money can buy allowed him the opportunity to infiltrate the place. You did everything he asked of you."

"I should have done more," was Ashley's only response. "I was supposed to be his bodyguard, and I let him walk inside alone because of orders? Bullshit. I trusted him that he'd be fine. Look where that got him."

"I'm sorry. I don't mean to insert myself into this, considering I didn't know him all that well," Michael said, "but I just have to say my piece and I'll be quiet again. One thing I understood was that he loved you all. It was evident, even to someone as slow emotionally as me. He was selfless - that much was obvious. He did all this to save Mr. Walton, correct?"

"That's right," Skye said.

"No normal soul would consider that," Michael said. "Most would cower and wait for someone else. It takes strength to stand against the world for your friends and family. The fact he considered sacrificing his life to save his friend Mr. Walton is beyond rare. I may not have served with him long, but I am honored to have had the opportunity. That's how I choose to look at it. Am I sad? You're damned fucking right I am. I wish I'd known him better, but I was too shy to speak to him much. It's like meeting your favorite superhero. I don't believe he had any regrets, for what it's worth."

"I know," Ashley said. "He saved me from a pervert my parents sold me to. He could've left me there and let the cops deal with me. It'd have been easier if he had. He couldn't do it, though. He couldn't just leave me scared and alone. That set events into motion that led to this. I know in my heart he never regretted that decision, and that makes this even harder on me."

"You're not the cause of tonight," Skye said. "Do not start thinking like that. He wanted us to overcome his death, not blame it on ourselves."

"That'll take a shitload of time, judging by how I feel currently."

"That's perfectly alright. I'm not looking forward to telling Cynthia, though. Oh, that'll be a barrel of fun."

"Cynthia?" Michael asked.

"Masked Justice's future wife, well widow now I suppose," Ashley said. "She's pregnant too, to boot. He left that baby with no father."

"For me," Skye said. "If anyone should feel responsible for this, it's me and Jason. He made that deal with the president to get him pardoned."

"Blast it all." Ashley got up and kicked the rail at her side. "It's not fair."

"Life never is," Skye said. "We just make the best of the

hand we're dealt. I say we use this anger for something productive."

"Like what?"

"How about we train until we drop from exhaustion? Michael's driving tomorrow."

"I am?" Michael asked.

"Yes, you are," Ashley said.

"I suppose I can tell the higher ups that I had to drive you all back to your homes," Michael said. "They'd understand, probably. They won't even care, since they'll be too busy clinking champagne glasses, I bet."

"Then we'll work off this insufferable anger," Skye said. "It's the only way you'll get any sleep tonight."

"I need to punch something," Ashley said, getting up and following Skye.

"Be sure to get some good shut eye, Mikey," Skye said over her shoulder. "We're counting on you tomorrow morning!"

"I'll get some sleep then, I guess," he called out after the retreating women. He turned and looked up the stairwell. "Damn," he said with a shake of his head.

22

————

Jason sat in the front row of chairs, pointed toward the television. It was showing the latest breaking story in what they called "The story of the century". Every single inmate watching was waiting with bated breath for the commercials to end.

They soon did, and a news anchor appeared. "Ladies and gentlemen, I don't know quite how to explain this development, so I'll be blunt." A picture showed in the screen's corner. It showed the remains of Charles Baskins' home from last night. "Charles Baskins died last night. Officially, police aren't sure if it was a gas leak, or if foul play was involved. There were no bodies found, but his security who were guarding his girlfriend seemed positive he was indeed present when the explosion went off."

"Oh, my word," Jason said, a smile finding its way onto his face inadvertently. "He actually pulled it off," he said under his breath.

"What are you happy about?" Willy asked at his side with his arms crossed. "You not a big fan of Mr. Baskins?"

"I hated that prick," Jason said.

"Given your story, I guess I understand," Willy said, turning back to the television they all shared.

The reporter carried on talking. "Several dead security were found outside the residence, some marred beyond the point of recognition from the blast. Officials believe they died before the blast, meaning whoever got inside killed them to get there. This is hearsay, folks, to be clear. Nobody's sure what happened except whoever perpetrated this heinous act. I doubt they'll be willing to step forward and claim responsibility for killing a House of Representatives member, either. The question is, will the Traditional Representatives movement be stalled by this cowardly act? This reporter suspects sadly that it might. Now we send it back to Sandy with the weather for today, Sandy?"

"I'm heading back to the block," Jason said. "I'm not watching the rest of this."

"I'll accompany you," Willy and Jason got up and headed out of the common room. "You seemed ecstatic about his death. Can you tell me why?"

"He hated Masked Justice and made our lives shit. Do I need more of a reason?"

"There's something you're not telling me."

"That's rule one I learned in here. Over-sharing is a bad idea inside."

"That's too true. There's too damned many snitches trying to ride your case in here."

"Hence why I don't feel like explaining any further. You never know who's listening. I'll give you a little bit, though, since you're helping me out. Baskins was known to hire assassins to do his dirty work. Let's just say one of them succeeded, and this hatred I have for him was born from the fruits of his labor."

"That explains a lot," Willy said. "The front never was interested in politics, so I never paid attention to it."

"Things change when you meet the tech guy of Masked Justice, huh?"

"Is it true he only targets the guilty?"

"In all my time knowing him, I never knew him to harm an innocent. He started out going after child fuckers and kind of branched out inadvertently to human traffickers and wife beaters. That's what drove me to seek him out, that and I was hoping to find my friend."

"Well then, I suppose I don't hate the man. The front traffics in drugs, not people, and that's a line we won't cross. Our child policy you'll find is shared by most of the inmates inside. There are some lines even hardened scumbags won't cross. Besides, that shot of him jumping from building to building while one blew up was as badass as hell."

"Oh, don't remind me of that night. That set off a series of events that led me here." Jason stopped when he noticed two inmates further down the hall turn to face them and stare them down. "Speaking of which, I recognize that man. He was the witness who turned rat and sent me here, the little shit."

"Which one?" Willy asked.

"The taller one on the left." Jason and Willy kept strolling toward the pair, who was approaching as well. "Well, here we go, it looks like. It's not too late for you to leave me for dead, you know?"

"If it became known I left Masked Justice's partner to get his ass beat, I'd be the one in trouble with most of the populace in here. I don't know if you noticed, but the ones who wish you dead are the minority."

"On your head be it, but thank you nonetheless." Jason and Willy stopped ten feet away from the other men.

"There's an ugly mug I could've gone a lifetime without gazing at again. Did all that squealing make your throat dry?" He pointed down to his groin. "I got something for you if so."

"You got some nuts," Fitzgerald's former employee said, taking a step forward. "You know who I am?"

"A mere lackey of a criminal who wanted to kill a kid to cover his ass?" Jason asked. "That's what I remember and why we killed your boss, you waste of human life."

"You run your mouth kind of reckless, don't you? I'm Mack. You betrayed the boss, and I had to watch my friends all die in a hail of arrows or to the infernal fire. It's because of you lunatics I had to live on the run for nearly a month, eating out of dumpsters. Who's the sasquatch here? Let me guess. Your name's Pablo, right? I'll give you two trays today if you just walk away. It's Taco Tuesday after all."

Jason looked up at Willy with a bemused grin.

Willy looked unfazed by the insensitive comment, instead only wearing a smile. "My mother was Honduran, you dolt. My father was American. You know what, just for that I'm going to kick your ass."

"Mack." The shorter man at his side grabbed at Mack's arm. "Maybe we should back off."

"Hell no, Louis. We're doing this. Just use the thing I gave you. I'll get the Poindexter while you get Pablo."

"I ain't fucking with that beast after you pissed him off."

"You will or I'm calling in your debt, and you know what happens if I do. You're dying as soon as I do, since you can't pay. Now do it!"

Jason cracked his knuckles, and both groups were now closing the remaining distance. "You alright with the debtor?"

"I'm fine," Willy said. "If you pull a weapon, little man, I kill you. If you fight bare handed, you live - simple as that."

The four inmates approached within a few feet of each other and split for their respective fights. Jason and Mack squared off as Willy and the terrified partner did the same.

"What about you, Mack?" Jason asked. "Are you packing any weapons?"

"I don't need them to kill you," Mack said as he launched a right hook to Jason's chin.

Jason recoiled from the blow, but the recovery was short-lived as he yelled and charged at his opponent. He raised his elbow and slammed it into the man's chin. He learned from his opponent to not stop so soon, so he launched his other hand as quickly as he could toward his opponent's face.

The blow connected, but Mack wasn't concerned with such novel concepts as fighting dirty or honorable. He quickly slipped a couple of fingers into Jason's eyes, causing the young man to cover his eyes and back off, giving Mack time to recover.

Meanwhile, Willy and Louis started their fight. Louis threw the first punch into Willy's ribs, but the blow didn't seem to affect the towering man much, judging by him not reacting to the force he'd delivered.

Willy retaliated by grabbing Louis by his neck and lifting him off the ground and slamming him into the nearby taupe wall. He lowered him to the floor, allowing Louis to breathe before he pulled his arm back and slammed it forward into Louis' ribcage, the same as he'd received.

The blow carried a bit more weight than the smaller fighter's. Louis forcefully exhaled all the breath in his lungs as the wind was knocked out of him.

Jason finally pulled his hands away from his eyes to see

Mack already close and ready to follow up. He raised his hands up to protect his face.

"You think this is a boxing match, kid? Is this your first fight?" Mack threw his left hand out with a quick snap of a jab. The blow connected with Jason's hands in front of his face. He followed up with his right fist coming from under in a vicious uppercut. It bypassed Jason's defenses and snapped his head back. "The problem with that was I was Fitzgerald's prize fighter, you moron. Go ahead."

Jason backed up to gain a few feet distance from Mack. "Is that right? Thanks for the advice." He gave up all pretense of trading punches with the fighter and opted for a different strategy. He ran at him and forced Mack against the wall behind him. Both groups of men fought on opposite sides of the hallway. Jason used his knee to strike Mack in the groin repeatedly. While his opponent squealed and reeled from the onslaught, he used his right fist productively by giving Mack his own hook. The blow knocked Mack to the ground, but he got to his feet quickly.

"Low blow," Mack said.

"The eye gouge was alright though, right?" Jason asked, already in pursuit, trying to press the advantage he'd created.

The fight between Willy and Louis, however, had long been decided. Willy had been punching the poor inmate the whole while. "I think your boy's already done."

"Don't count me out yet," Louis said. He threw an elbow up at Willy's chin that connected, forcing the behemoth's head to turn to the side. He ducked down and started throwing elbows at Willy's knee cap.

This forced Willy to fall to his knees, and now Louis had the upper hand, literally. "Fucking hell," he said. Willy reached upward and grabbed Louis by the throat again, but this time, instead of merely holding him in place, he squeezed hard. "Go to sleep. I don't want to kill you."

Louis scratched and clawed at the large hand wrapped around his throat. He tried to breathe, but his airway was blocked. He panicked, but he could feel a surge of adrenaline as his body kicked into fight-or-flight mode, if it wasn't already. When he tried to speak, it came out as rasping and wheezing.

Jason, meanwhile, was going toe to toe with Mack. He'd seen more kicks leveled at his head in the past minutes than he had the entirety of his life combined. He ducked, blocked with his forearms, and generally did anything he could to keep his brain un-concussed. His arms were growing numb from the continuous high impact blows they were absorbing, and it was only through sheer will that he didn't cry out from the pain of each blow.

"I knew you were nothing but a pretender," Mack said. "You killed those two with a hammer, but you've got nothing in a straight fist fight." He abandoned the kicking routine and started bombarding Jason with punch after punch in rapid succession. He switched his targets with every punch. Some aimed at Jason's head, while others aimed at his body, intending to tire or knock him out through overwhelming the young man.

Jason did not falter under the storm of blows. He remembered just earlier when he heard Charlie died, and his thoughts focused on one man. *Jim,* he thought. *He killed Charlie to free me, and his fight was nothing compared to this moron. I need to make him proud and beat this guy. I can't die to this jackass after he did all that for me.*

Willy called out over his shoulder to Jason. "I'm almost done with Louis here. He'll be asleep soon."

"Take your time," Jason said, as his head darted to avoid

another blow. He felt the wind from the inaccurate jab Mack delivered, then saw Mack's leg coming up for a high kick again and decided to try something different this time. He caught the leg with both hands, causing Mack to hop in place.

"Let go," Mack said.

"You gave it to me," Jason said, securing his grip on the leg with only one arm now. "Now it's mine." He used his free hand to deliver scathing blows to Mack's hamstring in rapid succession. He ended the series with a heavy blow he put everything into before he finally let go of the leg.

Mack hopped away, placing a hand on his injured hamstring. "You ass."

Jason didn't verbally retort, merely walked toward the retreating Mack. "You don't want to play anymore? What happened to the big bad prize fighter, Mack? Don't tell me you take a few hits, and you crumble?"

"You arrogant little bastard." Mack stopped hopping in place and tried to kick with his other leg. The operative word is "tried". He planted his injured leg onto the ground to anchor himself and lifted his other leg off. The only problem was his injured leg collapsed under the strain he put it under, and he fell to the cold tiled floor below.

He wasn't about to let this stop him. He used his legs to kick at Jason from the floor.

Jason caught one of his legs a second time. This time the desperate blow connected with Jason's stomach so both fighters were in a compromised position of sorts. Jason had the advantage, seeing as he was on his feet though. "You started this for the record. Now I'm going to finish it." He lifted the leg up further after he'd caught his breath again, then went berserk on Mack's knee cap, striking it from the side with reckless abandon. His fists ached and screamed with pain from hitting the sensitive but still sharp part of the human anatomy, but he didn't let that stop him until he heard a loud crack and Mack's tortured screams. He threw the leg down to the tile below. "Have fun with that. You come at me again, and it won't end with your leg being busted up. I'll cripple you for life. Do you understand me, you miserable son of a bitch?"

"Fuck you."

"What the hell?" A male voice called from further down the hall. A burst of static preceded his next sentence. "We've got a fight on block C, corridor 4. I need backup now."

An alarm blared in the men's ears.

Willy finally allowed the now unconscious inmate to slide downward to the cold ground below and turned to look at the correction officer. He yelled to be heard over the blaring alarm system. "It seems the fight's over!"

Jason looked down at Mack writhing on the floor, cradling his knee. "I finally won a fair fight," he said to himself, low enough not to be heard by Willy. He moved closer, within a few feet of Willy, and raised his arms above his head in surrender. "It seems we're wanted in solitary."

Willy watched as the guard was soon flanked by men in riot gear with large opaque shields marching at the pair. He followed Jason's surrendering body language. "It was worth it."

"My thoughts exactly," Jason said as he prepared for the manhandling the pair was about to receive.

23

"I'd be lying if I claimed our meeting was going to be pleasant," Brett said. He looked at Allen and Michael in the office.

"It's going to be one of those meetings, huh?" Allen asked. "Perfect. Who all are we waiting on?"

"Cynthia, Skye, and Ashley," Brett said. "Don't worry so much, it's after hours. It's not like you're going to miss business for this meeting."

"It's not business I'm worried about; I'm worried about this bad news you have planned to deliver, apparently. I hazard I might know what it is, judging by the names you rattled off and the one missing."

"Quite so," Brett said. "You always were quick, detective. It serves you in your occupation. I don't guess you want to be the one to tell the grieving widow and spare me the pain in my ass?"

"You couldn't dump this shit on me if you tried," Allen said. "You were involved, you do it. I'm just providing the venue for this shit sandwich to be eaten."

"For what it's worth, I feel honored to have known him for as long as I did," Michael spoke up.

"We all are, kid," Brett said. He turned the wheelchair to face the large windows behind Allen's desk. "Someone's got to tell his girlfriend the bad news. She's probably already put it together."

"You think so?" Michael asked.

"She knows we've returned, and her man wasn't there. She's not stupid, kid - she's a lawyer. This meeting is to make it real to her. She's probably still harboring false hope that Jim got caught in traffic or something silly. We're here to break those delusions and help her start the grieving process, not to mention…" He reached into his jacket pocket and produced the large envelope Jim had given him before. "I have something to deliver to her from the late Masked Justice."

"What's inside?" Allen asked.

"Hell if I know," Brett said. "He made me promise not to look until I gave it to her. I may be a horse's ass, but even I'm not low enough to spy into his personal correspondence with his girlfriend after he died."

The door flung open without warning, halting the men's conversation in its tracks. Brett turned to see Ashley, Skye, and a crying Cynthia walk into the room.

Allen cleared his throat. "I think everybody's here now if you want to start."

"He's dead," Cynthia said. The room descended into awkward silence at her statement. She waited a few seconds for an answer, but none came. "Isn't he dead? That's why we're here, I assume." She took out a tissue from her purse and wiped her puffy eyes.

Brett wheeled up to Cynthia and looked her in her crying eyes with a stone faced glare. "Yes, he is; but before we start the waterworks, he had something for you." He reached up and handed the envelope to the grieving lawyer.

"What's this?"

"For all I know, it's a will. I don't know," Brett said. "He told me to give it to you without peeking, and that's what I did. It's yours to read at your leisure now."

Ashley lashed out and kicked Brett in his legs, causing his wheelchair to roll backward toward Allen's desk. "You're an insensitive ass. At least be nicer."

Cynthia opened the envelope immediately while Ashley pushed Brett away. She reached inside and found two folded up pieces of paper and a solitary USB drive. She pocketed the drive, unfolded one paper, and read it to herself for a few moments before speaking up. "I'll read this one out loud, since it involves more than just me. It looks like it is indeed a will." She stopped to wipe away a few more tears that she just couldn't stop after Skye and Ashley broke the news just a mere half hour ago.

Skye leaned over, trying to get a look at the paper herself while Cynthia collected herself.

"Hello, love," Cynthia started reading. Her voice cracked at the word love, and she had to collect herself again before she could continue reading. "If you're reading this, I'm sorry to say, I either lost or came to a draw with Charles. The other letter in this is my personal message to you and the group. This one is my last will for my child or children and the family. Yes, I said family. That includes Skye, Ashley, and even Brett."

"Nice to feel appreciated," Brett said. That earned him a slap to the rear of his head from Allen sitting behind him.

"Shush," Allen said.

"My weapons and armor are to be kept and stored away. Please pay attention to these words when I write them.

Please discourage my children from taking the same path I did. I don't wish them to die in a similar manner as their foolish father. I cannot stress that enough. Having said that," Cynthia read, "if they're as impulsive and sometimes stupid as their father, I want them trained to be far better than me. If the worst happens and they follow the same path, Cyn, I want you to give them my old mask and gear. Brett, I will expect you to make sure they don't die like me."

"Training Masked Justice's kids too?" Brett asked. "Man, just saddle me with a multi-decade hassle, won't you? Though the results I could get training them from a young age would dwarf their father, and they'd be legends in their own rights - maybe even surpassing their father." He rubbed his chin, imagining the possibilities while everyone else either rolled their eyes or shook their head.

"He himself said he hopes they never need it," Ashley said. "Try to not have selective hearing when it suits your purposes, you insensitive jerk."

"I pray he never follows this idiotic path that led us here," Cynthia said. She had mostly stopped crying, but still shook from the sheer exhaustion of her intense crying she had experienced in the last half hour. She gripped the papers and cleared her throat. "May I continue?"

"Go ahead," Skye said. "I want to hear the rest."

"I wish for the money on my paper wallet to be distributed evenly between Ashley, Skye, Cynthia, and a share for my children. They need to understand their old man was thinking of them. As far as my apartment is concerned, I'd love for Ashley to live there. I imagine Skye and Jason are going to get married as soon as he's free from jail. Congratulations on that now if you're present when she's reading this. You'll be a great mother, both you, Skye, and my love, Cynthia." Cynthia quickly gave the papers to

Skye and left the group. "Keep reading. I'll read it later. I can't do this anymore now." She went into the lobby of Allen's office and cried audibly.

"I guess I'll continue where she left off since she said to," Skye said. "I implore all of you to give up this lifestyle I guided you into. It doesn't lead anywhere good. I don't want you to die in combat. Grow old and die in bed surrounded by loved ones. Learn from my mistakes. I hope every one of you leads a fulfilling life. Thinking of you all enjoying life and taking it easy gives me courage for tomorrow night. I know I can count on you to support each other and help. Farewell and live a happy life. Love, Jim Benning." Skye flipped the page to see if he'd written on the paper's back. "That's all of that one."

Cynthia had quieted down halfway through Skye's reading. She slowly opened the door and stepped back inside. "Sorry about that."

"No worries at all," Allen said.

"How far did you get?" Cynthia asked.

"We finished what you started," Skye said. She swapped to the second page. "You want to read it?"

"Go ahead," was all Cynthia said.

"Alright," Skye said. "You probably noticed the USB drive I left. Cynthia, my love, I want you to give this to our children and have them watch it when they turn eighteen. You can watch it too if you like, but no one else. You'll know why when you watch it. I love every one of you like my family. Though I wish circumstances hadn't resulted in this, it was always a path of my own choosing. I blame no one else. Cynthia, my love, you were always right when you called me an idiot for this crusade. I'm sorry about everything. The back of this letter is for your eyes only. I pour my love from our childhood memories to our teenager hijinks, to right this moment onto the page. I love you and hope, from the bottom of my heart, that you find happiness again." She lowered the page and folded it again before stuffing it in the envelope and handing it to Cynthia.

"That's that then," Brett said. His phone rang in his pocket. "Oh, that's me." He fished out the device and raised it to his ear after a press of a button. "Yeah, it's me. It's not a great time. Oh? Alright, tell me then." He waited a few moments, listening to the caller, and nodded. "I see. I'll be sure to inform them. Thanks for telling us. I'll be in touch. Bye." He hung up and jammed the phone in his pocket. "Okay, I have news I guarantee you all want to hear, especially the detective here."

"Me?" Allen pointed to himself.

Brett pointed at Skye. "I guess she might want to know, too. That was my contact at the Coalition. They wanted to thank us for our service, but there was a slight complication with Jason's pardon."

"Oh, don't even tell me they're backing out now," Skye said.

"Just like a slimy politician to promise one reward and deliver another," Cynthia said with a mocking scoff.

"Let's at least hear what they said," Ashley said. "What did they say specifically?"

Brett kept a straight face as he spoke to the group. "The president figured you guys wouldn't want to wait for a conviction, so he changed the deal a bit. He talked to the attorney general and got him to pressure the local DA to drop the charges. The president used his influence to squash the trouble young Jason had delved into. Jason's being released tonight! To be exact, in about forty-five minutes."

"You son of a bitch." Ashley walked up to Brett and kicked him in the shins. "You had to bury the lead?"

"You mean right now?" Skye was suddenly nearly breathless. She licked her lips and marched up to Brett, pushing Ashley out of the way. She leaned down and planted both hands on Brett's shoulders. "You're not fucking with us, are you?"

"As God is my witness," Brett said. "If you head there, he should be ready when you arrive. He's been told to expect you to pick him up."

"Congratulations," Cynthia said, her voice not conveying the sentiment. "I'm going to go home and grieve. Give Jason my best wishes, would you? I'm positive Jim would've been ecstatic hearing this news." She headed for the door and gazed over her shoulder toward the group. "I need to be alone now." She left without further words.

"If we're headed over there, I'm heading with you to pick him up. Maggie will understand," Allen said. He stood up out of his chair behind the desk. "Who all's coming with me?"

"Skye and I are," Ashley said. She turned and looked at Michael. "What about you, big guy?"

"I'd love to go if you don't mind," Michael said.

"Of course not," Ashley said. "Let's go fetch our partner."

24

———

"It's your host, Josie Bradley, here on VIP Guests again. We're back today with Ms. Summers, who's taking quite a bit of flak considering recent events. Ms. Summers, some say you're tarnishing the legacy of a great man. Defecating on his grave essentially, forgive my vulgarity. What do you say in your defense?"

"I'd say I have irrefutable proof that he was involved in a sinister cover up that will rock this nation. Charles Baskins was no great man. He was a manipulator, a wicked man, and a horrible leader."

"Those are some big words, Ms. Summers," Josie said with wide eyes. "Luckily, we're a neutral show, so present your argument."

"If you'd show slide one," Angie said.

The large screen behind them showed two phone numbers.

"See those?" Angie asked. "One of them one Mr. Baskin's aide's phone number. I'll corroborate this in a moment for the booing skeptics. This other phone number was Erin Jules.

You can look that up on social media if they haven't already scrubbed it yet. It's where I found it anyway. You'll notice the date of the phone calls. It was a week before the protest."

The studio crowd murmured at the evidence.

"Please switch to slide two," Angie said.

The screen switched to the bank accounts Brett had discovered earlier.

"What is this?" Josie asked.

"The bank accounts of Mr. Baskins and Mr. Jules. Again, notice the highlighted parts." Angie pointed toward the screen. "This was mere days before the so-called protest. Notice the matching amounts. It was taken out of Mr. Baskins' account and funneled directly into Mr. Jules'. Not to mention, I have the phone records of Mr. Baskins' aide. I found this the night an assassin tried to kill me. The implication being his aide was the perpetrator here. Angie pulled out the phone that Henry had left when he died, and showed the screen to the camera, which zoomed in. She navigated to the settings page. The phone numbers did indeed match up. She pressed a button, and the audio started playing.

"Mr. Jules, we have forwarded the money to the account. Are you ready to do your duty now?"

"I am more than ready, sir," Erin Jules said. "How do you want me to execute it?"

"Just get to the front of the crowd and shoot one of the security guards near Mr. Baskins. Do not hit him, that's vital."

"I'd never harm Representative Baskins, sir," Erin said. "He's the only hope for this country. It'll be done. Don't you worry."

"Good. With your help we'll get these rubes to vote for

him for president next go around. You're doing a service to your country. Godspeed, sir."

"Goodbye."

Angie hung up the phone with a smile. "Any other questions?"

The studio audience remained in shocked silence until they suddenly exploded in discussion amongst themselves.

"Please, folks, let's remain orderly here." Josie tried to quiet the crowd and eventually succeeded. "That is some evidence you have, Ms. Summers."

"I wouldn't be showing all this if I wasn't convinced. Charlie Baskins was a lowlife. He hired other men to do his dirty work, emphasis on dirty. It's my opinion he hired that man to kill the guard and himself in order to drum up support for his party and to prepare for a presidential run as you yourselves just heard. A grieving father is dead because of his ambition. Probably more than one, if the truth was known. I'm not stopping on this one. I'll dig until I reveal every single wicked deed he's done or I'm thrown in prison."

"You're a brave woman," Josie said. "For what it's worth, you have my respect for your bravery and determination. Just know not everyone will believe you."

"If they don't believe evidence, what will they believe?" Angie asked.

"Quite so," Josie said, turning to the camera. "Remember what you've seen and heard here today, folks. There's a high chance that it'll be erased by those that wish it. Make a copy of this broadcast, show it to everyone you know. Please, let the truth be free from its cage."

"Monsters who sacrifice the common citizen for further power have no business owning said power," Angie said. "Never forget that, folks. What do you think he'd have done if he'd received it? Nothing good, I assure you."

"Quite so," Josie said. "I'm receiving a verbal lashing in my ear for this, and they're telling me we're breaking to commercial." She slammed her palms on the desk. "Remember what I said. Make a copy of this. Show it to everybody. They're already trying to censor this information. We can't allow them to succeed. The truth shall prevail!"

The broadcast was cut off to a commercial immediately after those words...

25

———

J ason had been dragged out of his solitary cell without explanation from the guards. The only explanation he'd received was when they gave him a package containing the clothes he'd entered the jail in and told to change. It was evident then what was happening. He hadn't even had time to say goodbye to Willy, Eustace, Ralph, or Benny. It all happened so fast. When he'd asked why, all his wardens explained was that someone pulled strings, his charges had been dropped, and he was extraordinarily lucky to have friends in high places.

He finished lacing up his shoes and stood up. "It feels refreshing to be in my street clothes again." He stretched, getting used to being out of a jail jumpsuit.

A guard knocked on the nearby door. "Walton, you done yet?"

"Yes, sir," Jason called back.

The door opened, and a guard entered. "Come on. Let's get you out of here."

Jason fell in behind the guard as they moved toward what he recognized as the front of the jail.

"You're one lucky bastard; especially given your trouble-making in here. I don't know how you did it, but someone high up likes you, for them to swing their dick around for you."

"It wasn't luck," Jason said with a little smirk.

"Whatever, vigilante." The guard opened a door and stepped through. The line of glass doors where he'd entered the jail were visible and with it, the outside world.

There were no barbed wire fences or anything of a stereotypical prison, since it was merely a city jail. It was simply a city street and a parking lot.

"This country's going to shit, and this bullshit's hard evidence," the guard said, clearly sour with the turn of events.

"You think so?" Jason stepped through the doors.

"Yeah. People started rioting outside the Attorney General's office when they heard of your release. You want actual advice? Go into hiding. Many are not happy with you gaining your freedom after helping that murderer Masked Justice."

"Allegedly," Jason said.

"Whatever, smartass." The guard grabbed him by the arm and pushed him toward the glass doors. "Get out of here. I hope to see you again soon."

"Not on your life," Jason said over his shoulder. Turning, he reached his hand out toward the approaching glass door and pushed it open. The first action he did outside was close his eyes and inhale a deep breath. When he opened them, he gazed at the parking lot to see a familiar couple of vehicles with a small crowd nearby. He recognized those faces, so he rushed over at a jog.

He was greeted by waves and smiles as he approached. Skye met him in the middle and embraced him before the two shared a passionate kiss. They walked hand in hand toward the rest of the group.

Jason took stock of who showed up. "Is this everybody?" He noticed Michael. "Who's this?"

Michael stepped forward from the group and gave a formal bow. "I am Michael Miller. I assisted in the mission to rescue you. It's an honor to meet you." He extended a hand toward Jason and shook it before returning to the rear of the group.

"Assisted, huh?" Jason asked. "Jim couldn't meet me here?"

Ashley looked away. "Yeah. Jim couldn't make it, but he wanted to."

Jason took a moment to process what her news meant, and he felt a stab of guilt in his heart. "You mean he's...?"

"Dead." Ashley clenched her teeth, willing herself not to cry again. Not now, not in the jail's parking lot.

"Oh, man," Jason said, pulling Skye tighter against him. "I was hoping when I saw that no bodies were found that it meant he'd escaped. What about his mother?"

"That's Cynthia's domain. Maybe she's explained the truth. Sadly, no such luck on Jim's escape," Ashley said, turning to Jason. "We'll go over the specifics later. This is a bloody celebration. Let's not frown or cry. You appear like you've had time to exercise. That's at least one positive about jail, apparently."

"Yeah. Workout, fight with shanks, fight a former prize fighter for the Fitzgeralds - you know how jail works. It's a regular party that smells musty and like old ass." Jason turned back to Skye and pulled her head close. He took a deep breath of her shampoo cleaned hair. "That's better."

"You know, young man, they dropped all charges," Allen said. "Do you realize what that means?"

"That I have a job?"

"You are quite the optimist, aren't you?" Allen asked. "Who's to say I haven't replaced you since I figured you might not be released?"

"It's not like you have a secretary anyway," Skye said. "If you do, you should fire them for the mess in that office."

"Yeah, fine. So, I still have that job opening. Sue me."

"I didn't necessarily mean with you, but I imagine with a criminal record, it's hard to find gainful employment. Though I would prefer the old job I had, but I'd understand if you don't wish to be associated with me. I'm controversial now they tell me. Is it true there was a riot outside the Attorney General's office today?"

"It's true alright," Allen said. "It's mostly the anti-vigilante crowd. They're pissed at evidence turning up today that their idol, Mr. Baskins, wasn't as virtuous as they thought."

"Thanks to Ms. Summers," Skye said. She leaned her head into Jason's shoulder with a warm smile. "She's doing a fine job tossing all the dirt onto Charlie's gravestone, and I, for one, applaud her efforts."

"It couldn't happen to a shittier person," Ashley said.

"I can't wait to return home," Jason said.

"I bet so," Allen said. "Was the three hots and a cot not to your liking, Mr. Walton?" He released a raucous laugh.

"You call that slop a hot meal?" Jason gagged in remembrance of the food they'd served him. "That was cruel and unusual punishment."

"Come on, kid. We'll escort you to my place for a little welcome home party. Maggie can't wait to see you again. She wasn't happy I didn't grab her for this little reunion, but it was a spur-of-the-moment affair."

"That sounds wonderful," Jason said.

"You're with me, stud," Skye pulled him toward the car she'd drove in.

"Follow me. I'll guide you there," Allen said. "Come on, Ashley and Mr. Miller."

"Me?" Ashley asked.

"Let's give the lovebirds some privacy. I'll drop you back home afterward."

"Alright then," Ashley climbed into the detective's car with Michael while Jason and Skye got into hers.

Skye started the engine and started talking. "I've been giving this a lot of thought the past week."

"Given what a lot of thought?"

"Let me finish," Skye said. "You heard of the saying, 'You don't know what you have until you lose it'? I now understand what it means." She faced Jason and grabbed both his hands and stared straight into his eyes. "Will you marry me?"

Jason was taken aback. "Yes," It was the only word which entered his mind and so it exited his lips.

They leaned closer and embraced before they shared another kiss on the lips. They were interrupted by a horn honking beside them. When they looked over, they saw Allen giving them a thumbs up before backing out.

"That ass always enjoys being annoying at the worst times," Jason said, turning back to Skye. "Come on." He grabbed her hand. "Let's return to the rest of our lives together."

Skye pulled out and got onto the road behind Allen.

Jason looked out the window. Memories of Jim flooded his mind. He found tears falling down his face without even realizing it. "It's because of Jim I received this opportunity. I'm not about to squander this precious gift."

"You should see his last will. We'll need your help with

executing part of it," Skye said. "He wants us all to stop this vigilante gig now that he's gone. He said he doesn't want us to die like him."

"I agree with him," Jason said. "I've been to jail. It's not a paradise. I don't want that for you or Ashley."

"Jail makes a man question his life decisions, huh?"

"You bet your sweet ass it does," Jason said, looking over with a warm smile. "I don't wish the mother of my child to be locked up with those animals. I want you safe to live a happy life. We've done our part for the world."

"Maybe you're right."

"Let's just hope you're a better father than mine was," Skye said.

"I aim to be. I'll never abandon either of you again. Not even honor is worth it, I learned. I love you," Jason said.

"I love you too," Skye said. "Now let's go. We've got a party to attend."

THANK YOU FOR READING!

The Justice saga continues in Justice Born Anew coming out next year. If you'd like to support this work, please consider leaving an honest review on Amazon. Thank you and have a great day!

ABOUT THE AUTHOR

Alex J Fischer has been writing for close to a decade, published over a dozen action/adventure novels, and won six National Novel Writing Month challenges in a row.

Alex grew up in a small town in Ohio and still resides there. Hobbies include writing, video games, and watching crime shows.

ALSO BY ALEX J. FISCHER

The Morris Family:

Welcome to the Family

The Silver Lining

Any Means Necessary

The Fourth Bullet

A New Generation

Full Circle

Sons of the Syndicate

Fractured Legacy

Order of Vengeance Motorcycle Club

The Order of Vengeance

Vengeance Above All

The Collector:

The Debt Collector

Pawns on the Hunt

Queen's Gambit

Masked Justice:

The End of Innocence

Masked Justice

Blind Justice

Silent Justice

True Justice

Justice Before Dishonor

Justice for All